Praise for the Elliott Lisbon Mystery Series

SWAN DIVE (#3)

"*Swan Dive* reunites us with Elli, a delightful amateur sleuth with an aversion to germs, who's always willing to right a wrong. Using her uncanny cleverness and deep-seated loyalty, she deftly handles whatever comes her way—eventually...in this perfectly delightful cozy mystery series."

– Fresh Fiction

"Elli conducts her detecting with confidence and an occasional lack of foresight, but she has the skills and intelligence to pull it off. The enjoyable worlds of professional dance and cooking elevate this mystery, and Elli is an admirable and engaging heroine. Deft writing and clever dialogue further ensure that readers will be looking forward to the next installment in Elli's adventures."

– Kings River Life Magazine

"The book flowed smoothly along, giving me a chance to sit down and dig deep into the mystery right along with Elliott. All in all, an enjoyable mystery that is highly recommended."

– Any Good Book

"I loved this book! The location, off the Atlantic coast and typically warm, and the quirky characters that keep showing up really help to make this a delightful and entertaining read."

– BookLikes

WHACK JOB (#2)

"The irrepressible heroine is delightful and her ongoing banter is nonstop fun."

– Ellery Queen Mystery Magazine

"A cross between an educated, upper class Stephanie Plum and a less neurotic Monk. Put this on your list for a great vacation read."

– Lynn Farris,
National Mystery Review Examiner at Examiner.com

"Packed with humor, romance, danger and adventure, this is a good mystery full of plot twists and turns, with red herrings a plenty and an ending that I found both surprising and satisfying."

– *Cozy Mystery Book Reviews*

OTHER PEOPLE'S BAGGAGE (prequel novella)

"A cozy triple-scoop that tastes divine...the pleasantly contrasting novellas make it easy to finish off a story in one sitting."

– *Library Journal*

"Lost luggage has never been this fun! With well-drawn characters, *Other People's Baggage* is your first class ticket to three fast-paced adventures full of mystery, murder, and magic."

– Elizabeth Craig,
Author of the Southern Quilting Series

"Kendel Lynn's *Switch Back* is a clever, entertaining mystery with small town flavor and Texas flair!"

– Debra Webb,
USA Today Bestselling Author

"The mix-ups are a creative theme for tying the stories together, and I loved seeing how each sleuth dealt with the problem. A very fun collection!"

– Beth Groundwater,
Author of the RM Outdoor Adventures Mystery Series

SWAN DIVE

**The Elliott Lisbon Mystery Series
by Kendel Lynn**

Novels

BOARD STIFF (#1)
WHACK JOB (#2)
SWAN DIVE (#3)

Novellas

SWITCH BACK
(in OTHER PEOPLE'S BAGGAGE)

AN ELLIOTT LISBON MYSTERY

SWAN DIVE

Kendel Lynn

HENERY PRESS

SWAN DIVE
An Elliott Lisbon Mystery
Part of the Henery Press Mystery Collection

First Edition
Trade paperback edition | March 2015

Henery Press
www.henerypress.com

ISBN-13: 978-1-941962-51-0

Printed in the United States of America

For Georgie

ACKNOWLEDGMENTS

I've received many blessings and much love and more support than I could've imagined, and I'm most grateful.

Thank you to Hank Phillippi Ryan, Ruth Smith, Barney Lipscomb (Botanical Research Institute of Texas), Pete Radovic (Los Angeles County Sheriff's Department), Sisters in Crime (National, Guppies, and North Dallas), and as always, extra love to my mom, Suzanne Atkins.

Thank you to the authors and staff members in the Hen House, with a special round of chicken hugs to my incredible editorial team: Erin George, Rachel Jackson, and Anna Davis. This coop is stronger because you're all in it.

Thank you to Art Molinares for keeping the dream close, and to Diane Vallere, the truest friend a girl could want.

ONE

(Day #1: Thursday Evening)

I was sitting front row center of the Sea Pine Island Community Theatre waiting for Act II of *The Nutcracker* when I received a short text: *Emergency. Sugar Plum Fairy dead. Dressing rooms. Now.* It was from the artistic director. A drama queen if ever there was one. This was the fifth "emergency" in the last two hours. The fourth text included the words "catastrophe" and "maimed." One of the nutcracker soldier's tassels had popped off.

"Another crisis backstage," I said to Matty Gannon, my second best friend, though we'd recently upped it to dating status. "Be right back."

I hated leaving my perfectly-placed seat, a perk of being Director of the Ballantyne Foundation. Of course, it's not that perfect when you have to depart while everyone else is still seated. I tucked my program into one of the deep pockets of my long skirt, carefully lifted it above my ankles, and made my way to the center aisle. It wasn't without casualties. I stepped on three feet, kicked two shins, and I'm pretty sure I felt up Zibby Archibald, the oldest member of the Ballantyne Board.

A minute later I passed through the backstage door and into a world of harmonious chaos. A juxtaposition of beauty and industry: massive can spotlights, dangling ropes, and dancers swishing by in gossamer costumes with fanciful feathers.

A girl dressed in a fluffy blue tutu and twinkly tiara grabbed my arm and pulled me to the side. "Is my crown straight?" she asked. "One of the mothers jammed it on my head and I'm locked out of the dressing room."

"It looks lovely," I said.

"Courtney! Places. Places now! Stop dillydallying," Inga Dalrymple said. The artistic director was a thick but tall woman, a mashup between a football linebacker and a basketball forward, and all dolled up for opening night. Black sequined long-sleeve top, matching sequined tuxedo pants and black ballet flats. The store bought kind, not the actual dancer kind. She smacked the foot of a carved wood walking stick onto the hard floor. "Go!"

Courtney skittered away as Inga approached me. "Over here," she said and turned without waiting to see if I followed.

We walked down a long corridor, past child dancers and their mothers, around rolling trunks and a tangle of cables to a plain brown door. The names "Lexie Allen" and "Courtney Cattanach" were typed on a sheet of paper and taped to the front.

I peeked inside, glanced around the room. A large lighted mirror with big Hollywood movie star lights dominated the center with an assortment of makeup brushes in shapes I'd never seen before. A vase of pink roses sat on top near a tidy basket of fresh fruit and a platter of cupcakes. Costumes and shoes were scattered willy-nilly around the room, buried by clothes upon clothes, as if a closet exploded, coughing up garments and spitting out hangers. And there, dressed in sweats, nearly blended into the background, was Lexie Allen. Half on the sofa, half on the floor. Clearly dead. Her face twisted in agony, a light ring of foam on her top lip.

I gasped and my hand flew to my mouth. "Oh my God...Oh my God." The Sugar Plum Fairy was dead. Actually dead.

Inga pulled me back into the hall and snapped the door closed. "The Mouse King found her about ten minutes ago," Inga said. "I checked, and she's not breathing."

"Oh my God. Are you sure? What happened?" I leaned against the closed door with my hand on the knob.

"I don't know what happened, and yes, I'm sure. She wasn't feeling well before the show, so Courtney took over as Sugar Plum Fairy. Maybe something Lexie ate? A seizure? Her mouth is foamy and she's hunched over. She's not bleeding. I called 9-1-1 already. Said they'd be here..." She glanced at her watch. "Right now. Any minute. I don't know what's taking so long. What is taking so long?"

"I'm sure they're on their way," I said, slowly nodding as I tried to absorb the situation.

Sweet, vibrant Lexie Allen, college student and Sugar Plum Fairy, lay dead ten feet away. She was the only daughter of Mr. and Mrs. Allen, who were dear friends of Mr. and Mrs. Ballantyne, of the aforementioned Ballantyne Foundation, where I worked. To make matters more emotional, the Ballantynes were the closest thing I had to family. To make matters more complicated, the Ballantyne Foundation had sponsored this production of *The Nutcracker*.

The orchestra played the first bars of the second act and Inga smacked her stick on the floor.

I stopped nodding. "We need to cancel the performance," I said.

"Impossible. The second act just started, the dancers are on the stage," she said. "We can't stop. We already went on without her." Her face paled to the color of milk and she looked visibly shaken. "You need to handle the police. You're one of them, right? Some kind of volunteer? I'll handle the dancers until it's over."

People would be mortified when they found out we carried on as if we didn't care. But what could we do? Run on stage and broadcast the news to a theatre filled with families?

I thought about all the children in the audience. Every third patron had a grandchild with them. It was opening night, not a seat empty. I didn't want to traumatize them by announcing the Sugar Plum Fairy was dead. She held a special place in their hearts this time of year, only two or three notches down from Santa and the Elf on the Shelf.

I put my palm out in the stop position. "Let me think." There were hundreds of people in the theatre. The police would need statements. At least I thought so. I wasn't actually one of the police and I wasn't a volunteer. I was a PI-in-training and my training had yet to involve a dead ballerina on opening night. "Okay, let's do this," I said. "Keep the show going. I'll work with the police to coordinate interviews once they arrive."

"Coordinate interviews with whom? You can't mean the entire theatre? Over food poisoning?" She clutched her throat. "Of course. If she ate something spoiled, others might, too. Like bad sushi? She always eats sushi from that market on the corner."

"I don't know." I pictured the look of agony on Lexie's face. Her foamy lips and crumpled body. I doubted a box of gas station sushi did that.

The oversized exit door in the very back swung open. A burst of evening breeze blew in ahead of two Sea Pine police officers. I recognized one of them, Corporal Lily Parker. She was tall, leggy, and if she switched her uniform for a tutu, one might mistake her for a principal dancer in the company. Parker held the door as two paramedics hurried in pushing a gurney.

"Over here," Inga said. She led them to Lexie's dressing room and they rushed inside.

I pulled out my cell as Matty Gannon walked up. "Everything okay?"

"One of the dancers died," I said softly.

"One of the dancers died?" Matty asked.

I held up a finger. "Give me two seconds." I dialed Carla Otto, head chef for the Ballantyne. "Bring hot chocolate and cake to the Sea Pine Community Theatre. We're hosting an after-party for three hundred people in less than one hour."

"What are you talking about? The benefactor's benefit party isn't until next week."

"Lexie Allen passed away in her dressing room and the police just arrived and we can't let anyone leave until the police interview each of them," I said. "Unlimited funds for whatever you need. Just get here."

"On my way," she said.

I wasn't worried about what she could produce in thirty minutes. I once watched her turn out a gourmet spread with only a jar of pickles and can of spam in ten minutes flat.

"It's awful," I said to Matty after I hung up. "Lexie Allen. A friend of the Ballantyne family. I knew her. I just talked to her like two days ago."

"What can I do?" Matty wrapped his warm hand around mine.

"Help Carla when she gets here. I'll try to keep the backstage chaos from spilling into the theatre. Perhaps one of the crew can get tables for the lobby?"

The back door opened. Another cool breeze swept in, this time bringing the spicy scents of sandalwood and Cuban tobacco. Nick Ransom. The ex-love of my life and the current lieutenant of the Sea Pine Police.

Matty squeezed my hand and nodded at Ransom, who nodded back. Matty walked up the long side corridor toward the front of the building and Ransom walked straight to the dressing room and spoke with Corporal Parker.

I walked over, my long dress swishing with each step.

"...not breathing when she found her," Parker said and checked her notebook. "Inga Dalrymple. With a y. Says she called 9-1-1 right away. Then spoke to Elliott about finishing the show."

"The show must go on?" Ransom said.

"Until you absolutely need to speak to the audience," I said. "Carla's on her way with cake and coffee to serve after the performance. This theatre seats three hundred. That's a lot of interviews. Going to take some time, and that's after you finish working back here and talk to the crew and dancers. I'm assuming since she died alone, and not accidentally, there will be a full-scale investigation."

The door to the dressing room next to Lexie's opened and a young dancer came out, tears streaming down her face, streaking her glittery makeup. "Is Lex, um, is she really? Were the ambulance people able to help her?"

Behind her in the open room sat two more dancers. A little girl in a white snowflake costume and a guy in gray velvet pants and royal purple vest. A mouse head with a severely long nose and enormous crown sat on his lap. He stared at Ransom and me, his face drawn in sorrow.

Corporal Parker led the girl back into the room. "I'm sorry, she's gone," she said. "Did you know her well?"

Before I could hear the answer, Ransom turned to me. "How about you? Did you know her? Isn't this a Ballantyne production?"

"Yes and yes. Though I didn't know her well. Her parents are friends of the Ballantynes. I've seen Lexie a few times over the years. Kind, sweet girl. We just held a luncheon last week. She's a student at UNC Charlotte, I think. She used to dance here on the island at a local studio. Inga Dalrymple's Dance Company, next to the Bi-Lo on Cabana Boulevard. Lexie and her friends have done this production three years running now."

A group of dancers rushed by and a crewman with a headset barked orders into his mic. I stepped over two long cables to get out of the way.

Inga marched down the long side corridor from the lobby. A woman with highlights to the point of actual multi-colored blond stripes marched behind her.

"Unacceptable," Inga said to the woman. "It's opening night."

"I want to know why my daughter isn't dancing in the Land of Sweets," the lady said and blocked Inga's path. "She should've been promoted from a gingerbread soldier last year. She's better than that other girl."

"Now is not the time," Inga said.

"It's the perfect time because I need an answer." She raised her voice to be heard over the applause. Music once again drifted from behind the thin wall.

Two crime scene techs carrying blocky cases excused themselves between the two women. Inga pointed them toward Lexie's dressing room. "They came in through the lobby," she said to me. "Wouldn't be so bad if they didn't have SPPD slapped all over their jackets." Inga was a yell-talker, her volume two notches higher than suitable social standards. In a cartoon, the imaginary power of her voice would've blown back my hair.

"Did someone notice?" I asked.

"Everyone noticed. At least the front house personnel and four patrons using the ladies room." She put her hand to her forehead. "Doesn't matter, I suppose. The performance is nearly over. Courtney just started the Sugar Plum Fairy dance."

"Wait," the mom said. "What's going on?"

"How many people are allowed backstage before the show?" Ransom asked.

"Dancers, choreographers, crew, lighting, orchestra, staffers, and well, just about anyone," Inga said, then pointedly glared at the mom. "And the parents. They're everywhere."

"Oh my God, her parents. Are they here?" I asked.

"Whose parents?" the mom asked.

Inga leaned on her stick. "They're second row. I spoke to them before the curtain went up. Told them she wasn't feeling well. They said she's been working too hard with this production and school and got up to speak to her. I don't think they stayed."

"Lexie Allen," the mom said. "You're talking about Lexie. I saw the Allens leave right before curtain. Everyone was already seated. Quite rude. Who leaves before the production starts? They walked straight out the front door."

The music from the pit swiftly changed and Inga blanched. "The last dance. The curtain is going to fall in minutes."

"I'm going to need everyone to stay in the theatre," Ransom said to Inga.

She pointed her stick at me. "That's your job." To the mom, she said, "Come with me. We'll talk out of the way. It's about Lexie..."

My phone buzzed and I read the message. Carla had arrived. "I'll be in the lobby," I said and hurried to the front of the theatre.

Carla was in a flurry. Her wild black curly hair was held back by a scarf and her chef's coat was misbuttoned. She and a half dozen helpers hustled around several long tables that spanned the entire length of the lobby. They were laying out a dream spread straight out of *The Nutcracker* playbook: sugared plums, bon bons, candy canes, decorated cakes, colorful tarts, large coffee urns, and hot cocoa with marshmallows and shaved chocolate bits. Down at the far end of the lobby, Matty and two crewmen were setting up a high bar and rows of folding chairs.

"Carla, how did you ever do this?" I said.

"Unlimited funds and no less than five favors."

"It's perfect. And now we need to hold hundreds of patrons hostage for the next two hours." I figured I'd better grab the keys before anyone snuck out early. I hurried down the carpeted corridor in time to see the medical examiner, Dr. Harry Fleet, drag in the back door. He had dark skin, baggy eyes, and his clothes were rumpled as if he slept in a hamper. One might think he had been summoned to the theatre from a deep slumber, but I've seen him during the day. He looked the same.

He grunted hello and went straight to Lexie's dressing room. I got the keys from the theatre manager and went back to the lobby. I locked the entry doors, stuck the keys in my pocket, and rushed backstage. A warm flush crept up my neck and I started to pant. My full-length gown was heavy brocade and the running around was way more exercise than I was used to. Plus, the pins in my hair had abandoned their post and chunks of auburn tresses now flopped against my cheeks.

I found Ransom in the doorway to Lexie's dressing room, talking to a crime scene tech wearing protective clothing. "You have any idea how long you'll be?" I asked.

He glanced at the tech who looked over at Harry. "Take her out in about thirty minutes," he grunted.

"We'll need about another two hours to process the room," the tech said. "Who knows how long for the entire theatre."

"I'll ask Parker to put some officers in the lobby," Ransom said. "We'll get everyone's name and number, arrange interviews for tomorrow and this weekend if we need to."

I squeezed his arm. "Bless you. That's perfect."

Matty approached from the long hallway. "Elli, Carla's all set up front. Orchestra's about done."

I dropped my hand from Ransom's arm.

"Gannon," Ransom said.

"Lieutenant."

They stared at one another and I looked at them in turn. Repeatedly. Another hot flash hit me. The room was crowded and I was uncomfortable around both men and my heavy dress was suffocating. I pulled the program from my pocket and started fanning myself.

Inga Dalrymple rushed to us. She stepped on my dress and I pitched forward into Ransom. "The dancers left the stage and the orchestra is still playing. Patrons are beginning to leave."

Ransom gently steadied me. "You're on."

I tucked away the program, squared my shoulders, and took a deep breath. Thirty seconds later I stood center stage beneath the dazzling lights. They were as hot as they were bright. A crew member handed me a microphone as sweat rolled down the nape of my neck.

"Ladies and gentlemen, may I have your attention," I said. "There's been an accident backstage." People turned toward me. Some sat, others slowly retraced their steps down the aisle.

"Lexie Allen, our dear friend, and one of the loveliest dancers to grace this stage, passed away earlier this evening."

Gasps and exclamations filled the room. Shocked utterances followed soft questions. "What happened?" "When?" "You're sure?"

"I'm afraid I can't answer your questions. I simply don't have any answers. But the police would like to speak with you, especially if you saw Lexie Allen immediately before tonight's performance." After I gently explained the ongoing investigation, I invited them to stay for coffee while the police took down their information.

As they filed up the carpeted aisles toward the exit, I returned backstage. Courtney sat in the Mouse King's dressing room. She was crying on the small sofa, seated between the Mouse King and the Cavalier. I recognized him and his costume from the year before. Dancers hovered around them. All crying.

"What happened?" a girl in a pink nightgown asked. "Lexie was fine when she got here."

"She said she wasn't feeling well, so she asked me to take the Sugar Plum Fairy," Courtney said. She plucked at the appliques on her fluffy tulle skirt. "She didn't look that bad."

"I checked on her," the Mouse King said. "She didn't move."

"We'll get their statements later," Ransom said from behind me. "Right now, we need to clear this area."

I left the group to their sorrow. "I'll check with Carla, head to the front," I said, just as Matty walked up.

"Thank you for helping with the food and drinks and setup in the lobby," I said. "And for staying so late."

"Of course," Matty said. "You're my date. I'll take you home however late it is."

"If you need to get going, Gannon, I can take her home," Ransom said.

Matty stiffened, but didn't reply. With words. He simply put his arm around my waist.

I stood between them. Matty Gannon and Nick Ransom. The former, one of my best friends, and the latter, my first love. Matty's boyish good looks and casual demeanor in contrast to Ransom's handsome sharp features and polished appearance. One the headmaster at Seabrook Preparatory, the other a lieutenant with the Sea Pine Police. I'd sort of been dating them both for about two months. They made me nervous.

"I'll be here very late, Matty. You really should go." I walked three feet away from Ransom, putting distance between the two. "You have morning classes tomorrow, and this will go on for hours. Carla can drop me at home."

He hesitated, but then leaned down to kiss my cheek. "Okay. But call if you need me. I'll see you tomorrow."

"Tomorrow? We don't have a date tomorrow," I said and glanced at Ransom.

He, too, looked at Ransom, then back at me. "The tree lighting at the Ballantyne," he said and walked away.

"Oh, right, sure, tomorrow, then," I said smoothly and half-waved at his retreating back. I put my hands on my cheeks and sighed. Two officers cut in front of me while three more dancers fluttered by. The soft orchestra playing in the background had been replaced by the industrial racket of clanging equipment.

Ransom took my arm and led me to a quiet corner. We stood barely six inches apart, and he spoke softly. "Sorry this evening ended the way it did. It's difficult when you know the deceased."

"Did you find her parents?"

"At home. The captain spoke to them about a half hour ago."

"I'll call Mr. Ballantyne as soon as I leave." I sighed deep, from the bottom of my soul. To lose a loved one was tragic. To lose a child at Christmas was cruel.

I left Ransom backstage and walked through the theatre. It was vacant. A heavy velvet curtain covered the stage, its bottom puddled on the floor. *The Nutcracker* was over, the patrons were leaving, and Lexie Allen would dance no more.

TWO

(Day #2: Friday Morning)

I woke the next day from a troubled sleep. The skylight over my bed showed a clear Carolina blue sky. Not a reflection of my mood. I replayed the night before in my mind. The sight of Lexie on the sofa. Her parents getting a knock on their door from the captain of the Sea Pine Police. The crying dancers. Nick Ransom and Matty Gannon.

Staring up at the bright sky, I organized the day in my mind. Today was the annual Christmas tree decorating at the Big House. Every year we chose a theme, then commissioned custom ornaments from artists around the country. The first grade class from Seabrook Prep would trim the tree. As headmaster, Matty Gannon would supervise (and hang most of the ornaments). We almost postponed decorating a week because of a flu outbreak, and I was nervous not enough time had passed for the germs to have lost their potency. There's only so much I can do with hand-sanitizer. But everyone from Matty to the teachers to the school nurse assured me the children were well, and I couldn't just lie around my cottage all morning and be mopey and blue. A luxury for another day.

I showered and dressed in white capris and a red linen tunic, a privilege of a warm-climate December, then walked down the stairs of my beach cottage. It had whitewashed walls, rag rugs on the floor, and a compact kitchen. I ate my cereal over the sink and watched the lights twinkle on my tiny Christmas tree. Beyond the tree were several vintage Santa carvings, each dolled up in a beach theme. One with a surfboard, one in sunglasses, one on a bike. Beyond that was the sliding glass door that led to the deck that led to the sand that led to the ocean. After a brief internal pep talk, I rinsed my bowl, grabbed my hipster handbag, and went out the door to the garage.

Normally I would ride my bike the two miles to work, but it was already after nine. And morning exercise would not improve my mood. I put the top down on my Mini Coop and tucked my hair beneath a colorful canvas hat so the stray red curls wouldn't blind me while I drove.

The Ballantyne Foundation's Big House was exactly that: a big house. It sat on a hill overlooking all of Oyster Cove Plantation, situated squarely between the ocean, the golf club, and the heavy iron entrance gates. The Ballantynes had owned their South Carolina land since the sea mountains formed Sea Pine Island however many million years ago. Of course, I've only worked there for the last fifteen. I'm not that old.

I parked in the circular drive and entered the grand foyer. A custom silk beauty of a spruce rose eighteen feet between two curved staircases. The perfect size for the two-story entry. The Big House was almost fifteen-thousand square feet—and that didn't include the Ballantynes' private residence on the third floor, only the public spaces, offices, ballroom, kitchen, library...

We put up the tree two weeks before Christmas Day and took it down one week after. No eight-week-Thanksgiving-until-January endless holiday season. This wasn't Disneyland. But our dedication to splendor and fantasy rivaled those Imagineers. The annual Ballantyne Christmas tree always bore fresh ornaments, never the same theme as another year. We'd commissioned everything from porcelain partridges and pears (along with the other eleven days of Christmas) to hand-forged silver bells. That's not to say every idea was successful. The year we did snowflakes (no two alike), it took six months to rid the Big House of all the glitter. Those little sparkles were everywhere.

Enormous boxes sat in front of the spruce, their lids stacked in the far corner. Each box was divided into four inch squares with a single ornament tucked in each one.

"Last night sucked," Tod Hayes said as he walked up beside me. He was the Ballantyne administrator. He wore his hair trimmed, his clothes neat, and his expression droll.

"Your night sucked? Dude, it was nothing compared to mine," I said.

"I went with the captain to see the Allens."

"You did?"

"It was agreed someone from the Foundation should be there and Lieutenant Handsome felt you were indispensable at the theatre."

"Oh, Tod, I'm so sorry," I said. "Must have been awful."

"Awful, awful, awful," Zibby Archibald said as she slowly entered the foyer. At eighty-seven, she may have been the most senior member of the Ballantyne board, but probably had the youngest spirit. She wore a wide brim straw hat with gigantic hot pink poinsettias pinned to every visible surface. She'd dyed her hair to match the flowers. She took one look at the ornaments and shook her head. "Dearie me."

Tod glanced down. "You said it, sister. The children will be here at two sharp."

"We better get the rug," Zibby said. She walked across the foyer and grabbed a corner of the twenty-foot hand-loomed wool rug that covered the floor, then hauled it toward the ornaments. She moved faster than I would've thought possible. That sucker was heavy.

"Whatcha doing, Zibs?" I asked.

"These *Nutcracker* sugar princess ornaments are little Lexie lookalikes," she said and heaved the rug over the boxes. "The ballet chief was parking in the lot when I came in. Wouldn't be decent for her to see these."

"The boxes have lids," I said.

Zibby patted my arm. "Well, if we didn't have the rug."

The foyer door opened and Inga Dalrymple walked in. "Elliott, I was hoping to talk to you." She paused, looked at Zibby's hat and hair, then cleared her throat. She raised her voice as if speaking to a large crowd instead of three people standing seven feet away. "We all know losing Lexie was tragic and terrible and I can't even think about it. But I'm here to assure you, our main sponsor, the performances will continue."

I started to speak, but she tapped her stick on the bare hardwood floor and continued. "It was a hard decision, but it's done. It's a distressing situation, but I've got a distraught troupe, frantic parents, and hundreds upon hundreds of ticketholders all calling to find out what's going on. So this is what's going on. The show."

"Even tonight's?" I asked.

"Especially tonight's," she said. "Which brings me to the second reason I'm here. We need to dedicate this evening's performance to Lexie. And let the audience know a scholarship, sponsored by the Ballantyne, will be named in her honor. Is that possible?"

"To do, yes, but not for tonight's performance," I said. "I'll need to present it to the board—"

"It has to be today." She lowered her booming voice to a normal octave. "Please. I can't stop to think about Lexie. Or what happened. Or the show going on without her. I need to get this settled and move on to the next thing. And the next and the next."

Zibby ambled over and pattered her hand. "A lovely gesture, Inga. I'm sure the scholarship will get undisputed approval."

She was right. Who would turn it down? "We can make the announcement and say it's in the works," I said.

Inga nodded once, then cleared her throat again. "Thank you for your support." She turned on a heel and walked out.

"I'm not sure keeping the performance schedule is such a good idea, but the scholarship is," I said.

"You have bigger fish to fry." Tod gestured toward the rug-covered ornament boxes.

"Right, the ornaments." This year's theme: *The Nutcracker*, featuring replicas of the Sea Pine Community Theatre's production costumes. Including the star of the show, Lexie Allen as the Sugar Plum Fairy. "These hand-painted ornaments took weeks to commission, craft, and ship. We need a Plan B for the decorations before the children arrive at two this afternoon."

"Yes, I do believe that's the situation," Tod said. "It's almost ten now. In case you need a recap."

"What are we recapping?" Carla said. Light patches of flour speckled her white chef's coat and she held a large stainless mixing bowl filled with cookie dough.

"I have an idea," I said.

Three hours later, I emerged from the kitchen frazzled, but triumphant. I don't usually spend so much time in the Ballantyne's kitchen. Or any time in any kitchen, including my own. But an emergency calls for all hands on deck. Even my perfectly sanitized ones.

I carried a tray of cookie dough ornaments through the sunroom and out the double doors to the terrace. The sun was high and the sky was clear and the lap pool sparkled in the most delightful way. My childhood holiday vacations were spent peering out the window at snow-covered streets. Freezing, frigid, ridiculously cold wish-I-could-go-play-outside holidays. White Christmases were totally overrated. I'll take sun and sand, thank you very much.

I set the tray on a patio table and cranked open the large market umbrella. Two dozen children chased each other around the back lawn, dodging around the oak trees and towering magnolias.

Zibby spread out ornaments on two other tables while Tod set out paints.

"How clever you are," Deidre Burch said as she walked down

the steps to the deck. Another longtime board member, Deidre wore her gray hair in a swingy bob held back by orange readers on a beaded chain. "I worried about those ballerina ornaments. Horrifying to see hundreds of little Lexies on that tree."

The kids scurried up to the tables on the deck. A young boy coughed and I moved two steps to my left. Away from the kid. "Not sure how long it will take to both paint and hang, but probably more entertaining for the children," I said.

Matty came out from the house carrying a five foot bag of popcorn. "Who wants popcorn?" As the kids screamed they all wanted popcorn, Matty directed one to grab the box of thread and another to set up an assembly line.

"You pop all that?" Deidre asked.

"Are you nuts? We called the movie house and Matty picked up a bag of pre-popped."

I watched Matty with the children. Kind and patient, easygoing and good-natured. Throw in tan and athletic with soft brown hair and warm brown eyes, and there wasn't a reason that boy was still single.

Once he had a handful of kids stringing buttery garland, he came over. "Hey Elli," he said and leaned over to kiss my cheek. "Do you need anything?"

"No, I'm okay. A long night and all that, but this decorating should keep me busy."

"This is just phase one," Tod said. He carried another tray of cookie ornaments. "We still need to get them on the tree."

"Let me just say that I got this dilemma fixed in less than three hours," I said. "I'm on my game, people."

"And what a dilemma," Deidre said. "So sad. So much wrong. Those poor dancers. You know Lexie was staying at my rental in Sugar Hill? Her and her three friends. Breaks my heart."

"By the way," Tod said to me. "Lieutenant Handsome is in your office."

"Right now?"

"Yes, that would be why I'm telling you. Right now."

That was unusual. Ransom didn't normally visit me at the Big House. I brushed my clothes with my hands in case random kitchen dust had landed on me and my glance caught Matty's. "Be right back," I said with a tentative smile.

Mr. Ballantyne had converted the music room into my office when I officially became director nearly nine years earlier. Tall windows dressed in wide plantation shutters ran along the entire side wall, leaving sunshine stripes on the dark wood floors.

Nick Ransom sat in a side chair in front of my desk, one leg of his tailored suit casually crossed over the other. He was the first boy—man—guy?—I ever loved. We met in college and he broke my heart when he left without a word. Actually, he left seven words on my answering machine. He went on to the FBI and I went on without him.

I breathed in his familiar cologne. Some days I just wanted to reach out and touch his face. Make sure he was really here.

"Hey, Nick. What a surprise." I took two quick squirts from the hand-sani pump on my desk and plopped into my chair. "It's nice to see you."

"You, too. But this is a business visit, not a personal one. To fill you in on the Lexie Allen case. As a courtesy." He took out a small notebook and leafed through the pages as if checking his notes. "It looks like an accidental poisoning."

"Accidental?"

"Could be suspicious, but likely Lexie accidentally poisoned herself. Turns out she was quite the cook. She was into baking recently, especially exotic ingredients. She used toxic berries in a batch of frosted cupcakes. Ate one before the performance and it killed her."

"Toxic cupcakes?"

"Looks that way. She had several similar-looking berries in jars on the kitchen countertop. Mixed up one nightshade with another. Ended up with belladonna. We checked fingerprints on all the containers. Only Lexie's. Her roommates confirmed she'd been baking lately, nearly every single day. Two of them got sick from something she made two days ago. Wouldn't eat anything after that. Too risky."

"Belladonna jars?" I shook myself. Accidental poisoning? That made no sense. He was throwing information at me rapid-fire and I barely kept up. Though I wasn't actually asking smart questions. "Why would she have toxic berries? Why would she make such a thing? Why would she eat cake?" I assumed dancers had some sort of health ritual that did not involve berry-filled frosted cupcakes.

"Another possibility we're exploring, though not publicly, is suicide," he said without answering my questions and closed his notebook.

"Suicide?"

"Made for a very dramatic scene, which is not unusual for a young adult. Especially an artistic one. She bakes the cupcakes, gets dressed for the performance, dies right before going onstage in front of all her friends."

"She was wearing sweat pants, not a tutu," I said.

He shrugged. "The poison probably hit her more quickly than she expected."

"Sure, sure." I heard a hoard of kids rush down the hall and into the foyer. All giggles and shouts and footfalls and coughs. I took another squirt from the pump. "Just so I've got it," I said slowly. "You're saying Lexie Allen kept poison berries in her kitchen, and either she grabbed them by mistake, or deliberately to kill herself?"

"The evidence is stacking up that way," he said and stood. "I'm sorry, Red. I know this one hit close to home. We'll get it wrapped up quickly."

He looked sympathetic. Genuine, sincere, kind. And full of shit. I'd known Nick Ransom since our first evidence class in college more than twenty years earlier. He was sharp, intense, and extremely thorough. He didn't keep his cards close to his chest, he kept them face down on the table. Like Harvey Specter negotiating a settlement with an unwitting adversary about to sign away the rights to his own company.

"No foul play?" I asked.

"It doesn't seem so."

"And all the crime scene techs, police personnel, interviews, and investigating at the theatre? You were there most of the night."

"Standard procedure," he said, looking me straight in the eye.

I waited two full blinks and then thanked him. "I appreciate the heads-up. Nice of you to keep me in the loop."

"Just making sure you're up to speed, so you don't feel the need to get involved." And there it was. In case I'd missed the point of his "update." We walked down the hall and into the busy foyer. "I know you've got your hands full this time of year," he added.

Matty lifted a tiny girl up close to his shoulder so she could loop a string of popcorn around the tree. A boy hung a colorful ornament on the lowest branch, keeping his other hand pressed into Matty's leg for balance, and a third promptly dropped her ornament on the floor. It splintered. Crying ensued.

"Indeed," I said.

"I'll leave you to it," he said and left.

Leave me to it is right, I said to myself as I stalked straight back to my office. The phone rang as I grabbed my hipster handbag from the bottom drawer.

"Elliott! Hello!" Mr. Ballantyne shouted into the phone. The line crackled, though I could hear him clear as the sky outside. "This is a terrible day for us, my dear Elli. Terrible! Vivi is devastated."

"It's awful, sir," I shouted back. I lowered my voice. He was in Guatemala, not on the moon. I'd only spoken to him briefly the night before, and he sounded the same. And I couldn't imagine how sad Vivi, his wife, was. She was as gentle as a kitten on a stack of down pillows. Together they'd run the billion-dollar Ballantyne Foundation since the day Edward Ballantyne inherited it from his father over fifty years ago. "Again, I'm sorry for your loss, sir. I stayed at the theatre, but Tod spent time with the family last night."

"He's a good boy, our Tod," Mr. Ballantyne said. "I'm not sure what happened to that lovely young lady. Poisoned, of all things.

Certainly a strange state of affairs. We must do something."

"I'm already on it," I said.

"Good to hear! I spoke to the captain this morning. Let him know we'd want to poke around a bit. I don't mean to contradict their good judgment, but it can't hurt to make sure. He said he'd send over the lieutenant."

"He just left, sir," I said. "I'll put all my attention on the case."

"I expect nothing less, Elli, dear," he said. "We're off to another refugee camp outside the city. The trains are running today. Stay on top!" And with that, he clicked off.

I wasn't sure if he meant me or the refugees riding the rails north to freedom. But I definitely planned to stay right on top of things here.

Two minutes later, I tracked down Carla in the foyer organizing ornaments while Matty and the kids painted another batch out on the terrace. "Aren't you popular, chicken? Two suitors in one day. I hope you know what you're doing."

"One suitor and one suit," I said. "Nick Ransom just gave me a soup sandwich. Accidental. Suicide. Stops by as a courtesy. Ha. Someone hurt that girl on purpose and he knows it."

"He said it was accidental?"

"Yep. He crammed a twenty-minute briefing into a five-minute conversation. Hoping I'd ignore the obvious and he'd keep me off the case." My director duties at the prestigious Ballantyne charity sometimes stretched beyond board meetings and charity balls. I'm also the real world counterpart to Archibald McNally, performing discreet inquiries for the Foundation's faithful donors and closest friends. Getting my PI license and working with the police enhanced my skill set. Ransom wasn't impressed.

"How did she accidentally kill herself?" Carla asked.

"Poisoned berries, he said. Apparently she liked to cook with exotic ingredients and mixed up her nightshades. One called belladonna. You ever hear of such things?"

"Sure. Deadly nightshade. Not sure they're poisonous after you cook them, though."

"Mamacita, don't mess with Santa Claus," Zibby sang as she wobbled up to the tree. She'd hung an ornament from her left earring and wore a popcorn strand around her neck. "Mamacita...she's the one to see."

Carla snapped her fingers. "You said it. Mamacita has the most exotic botanicals in the South and she's right here on the island. Now that's cooking with some love. If anyone has nightshade, it's Mamacita."

"I've never heard of her," I said.

"Recommendations, that's how she rolls," Zibby said.

"Behind the Gullah Catfish Café off Marsh Grass Road," Carla said. "Sublime garden and greenhouse."

"If you say so, then I'm headed out," I said. "Probably be gone most of the day."

"Knock twice and take a gift," Zibby said. She turned to Carla. "You ever buy her alligator butter? Dab it on a slice of green olive and eat it on a saucer..."

Their conversation faded as I went to the terrace to find Deidre. She was finishing up the last ornaments, carefully placing them on a large steel tray. She'd put her reading glasses on her nose to inspect the paint jobs. The cookie ornaments were shaped like various candies: canes, bon bons, the ones with the twisty wrapper ends. The paint was bright and cheery and sloppy, as if painted by schoolchildren.

"Deidre, sorry to interrupt," I said in a low voice so the kids wouldn't hear us. "I was thinking about those poor dancers at your condo. Were they close to Lexie?"

"Two were her best friends, the other her boyfriend," she whispered. "Could it be more tragic? They took their college break early to dance *The Nutcracker* at Sea Pine one last time. The Sugar Plum Fairy, the Mouse King, the Dew Drop Fairy and the Cavalier. All the lead roles. Is that why the lieutenant wanted to talk to you?"

"He was filling me in, as a courtesy," I whispered. "Actually, I was thinking it would be a good idea if I took a look around the condo."

"You think it's more than an accidental poisoning?"

"Who said it was an accidental poisoning?"

"Sugar, the whole island knows that poor girl got sick eating her own cupcakes," she said and leaned in close. "Rumor is it was an accident. Unless you're saying otherwise."

"I'm not saying otherwise." Not out loud, anyway. "I only want to take a quick look. Dot an i, maybe cross a t."

She looked at me over the top of her bright readers. "Uh-huh. Someone from the ballet company is there now, cleaning things up while the kids are at rehearsal. You're welcome to stop over. I'm sure she wouldn't mind the company."

"Let me think about that, Deidre. I appreciate the offer."

Keeping someone company wasn't what I had in mind. I needed to see what the police saw and see what was missing. Ransom clearly wasn't considering this a joint investigation. He wouldn't be sharing information and he had a head start. It was just too hard to swallow that Lexie baked poison berries into her own cupcakes. Accidentally or otherwise.

THREE

(Day #2: Friday Afternoon)

Sea Pine Island was shaped like a shoe or a foot or a boot or some kind of podiatrist drawing. The heel part of the island faced north toward Beaufort, South Carolina, while the toes pointed south, straight at Tybee Island, Georgia. Cabana Boulevard ran the length from the toes, across the arch, up the ankle, and over the bridge to Summerton.

With the top down on the Mini and a hat on my head, I zipped out of the Oyster Cove Plantation gates and onto Cabana. I was headed to a quaint shopping area nestled somewhere at the topside of the foot. Zibby mentioned taking a gift to Mamacita and I had no idea what to take an herbalist who made alligator butter.

From Cabana, I made a right onto Marsh Grass Road and followed the two-lane road as it wound around the marshlands, the briny salt air mixing with the scent of fresh cut grass. About two miles later, I turned into an old weathered center of four shops. A dog grooming parlor, a bicycle repair shop, a boot camp gym, and my destination: an artisan boutique. A little bell jingled when I entered and a wall of heavy patchouli air greeted me.

The shop contained handmade everything from hemp clothes to wire lawn chairs. A round wood table was placed in the front window with a feather tree on top. Delicate glass ornaments hung by the dozens on every branch.

"May I help you?" a woman said with a bright smile. She wore a palm tree print caftan with a matching scarf on her head.

"I hope so. I'm in need of a gift and it's last minute," I said. "She likes gardening. And alligators, if that helps."

"I'm sure we have the perfect objet d'art," she said and roamed around the room. "I have something in mind..."

She picked up a metal lawn sign. It was hammered into the shape of an alligator in flip-flops with a sharp stake running through its center.

"Well, that's adorable," I said. "Though perhaps a bit literal." That was for a certain type of customer and I had no idea what type of customer Mamacita was.

We went through three rounds of assorted craftsman gifts: a delicate wind chime made with seaglass, a set of clay mugs from a local potter, and an oversized sweetgrass basket. In the end, I decided to stick with my rule for gift-giving: when in doubt, pick out something I'd like. She wrapped up the wind chime for Mamacita and a similar one for me. If you can't give gifts to yourself, where's the Merry Christmas in that?

I zipped onto Marsh Grass Road and drove another mile inland, looking for the Gullah Catfish Café. As one who never eats seafood of any kind, fresh or not, I hadn't ever been there. I slowed to a crawl, putt-putting on the rock shoulder until I spotted it. A ramshackle of a structure with a driftwood sign nailed to the front. Two mismatched plastic patio sets flanked a screen door. A tabby cat cleaned his front paws under one of the tables. Cars parked haphazardly in front, on the side, and out by the shoulder. The strong smell of cooked catfish sank into the convertible and I kept my foot on the gas.

The dirt drive wound around the back. I followed it deep into the South Carolina wild, where trees towered thirty feet, a mix of pines and oaks and Spanish moss. I felt as if I were traveling back in time. The rocky road bounced the Mini. Hard not to since it rode close to the ground, and it took another minute before I reached a clearing. Tucked in the brush off to the side sat a single wide propped up on wood blocks. I circled around until I faced the road and parked.

The trailer may have looked tired and rundown, but the surrounding landscape shone proudly. A paradise garden befitting Eve herself. Gorgeous flowering shrubs, ornamental trees, and bunches of flowers and greenery. All lively and blooming, even though it was the end of December.

With gift in hand, I climbed the rickety steps and knocked. Twice, as per Zibby's instructions.

The sound of barking dogs was so loud, I feared an entire wild pack was jostling for position inside. Their nails scratched on the door. Combined with their fierce tone, I was sure it'd be enough to ram through the flimsy wood. I quickly scrambled down the steps and away from the trailer.

"¡Hola!" a voice called from around back. "Estoy en el jardín."

A rocky path cut through the heavily manicured parkland and I emerged to find a master gardener's utopia. A half-acre of cultivated foliage lay before me, all contained behind a chain link fence. A really tall one.

A round woman in a floppy hat walked through the gate. She wore a floral apron and carried a spade covered in dirt.

"¡Hola!" I said. "Me llamo Elliott...Soy amiga Zibby and Carla."

"Si, si," she said. "Encantado de conocerte. Bienvenido a mi jardín."

"Lo siento," I said, apologizing. "Mi Español es...pequeño? Little? Small? As in, that's pretty much all I know. You lost me at conocerte."

She laughed. "It's nice to meet you," she said in accented English. "Welcome to my garden."

"Thank you. Gracias," I added. My biggest regret in school was not taking Spanish classes. Such a beautiful language, and so often spoken, it frustrated me to be on the outside of conversations. I bought the Rosetta Stone, but it was slow going.

"What may I help you?"

I handed her the gift bag. "This is for you."

She unwrapped the wind chime from the tissue and held it up. The blue and green seaglass gently tapped against the delicate chrome centerpiece in the light breeze.

She wrapped me in a hug. "Gracias, gracias. Que hermoso."

I thought hermoso meant brother, but she probably knew more Spanish than I did. "Do you have a few minutes to talk? I'm looking into Lexie Allen's death, and Zibby Archibald suggested you might be able to help me."

"¡Dios mio! That poor girl," she said and crossed herself. "Poison, si?"

"Si. Something called deadly nightshade," I said. "Baked into cupcakes."

She tsked and opened the chain link gate, then gestured for me to enter. "I have many plantas, botanicas, all types I grow."

The garden was organized in rows, but not in any particular order my OCD could make sense of. Most of the rows crisscrossed one another or curved around large oaks and pines. Little stakes stuck out of the ground in random places, written in Spanish, mostly illegible to me.

We stopped at a rusted metal bistro set near the center of the garden. She reached for a pitcher of iced tea on the table and a plastic cup, pouring the tea to the top before I could protest. "My own recipe. Fine plantas and herbs to improve your health."

I thanked her then took the smallest sip possible. I never acquired the taste for iced tea, especially Southern sweet teas. And definitely not a special plantas and herb recipe that tasted faintly of black licorice and boiled eggs.

She hung the wind chime from a plant hook bordering the path, then took me to a shrub patch in the far corner. A picket fence no taller than my shins bordered it. She pointed at a tall plant. "*Atropa belladonna*. Beautiful, but deadly. It grows wild, but I keep mine contained."

"Why grow it at all?"

"Like many danger plantas, it has health benefits." She pointed out other plants. "Hemlock, foxgloves, oleander. That one makes gorgeous flowers, big as your hand. All good for teas, remedies. But not for, how do you say, aficionada? Amateur?"

An amateur cook experimenting with wild ingredients. What was Lexie thinking? Why would she even have them? "Did you know Lexie?"

"Oh si, si. Of course. She was lovely girl. And very interested in my plantas. Vegetables, mostly, but also flowers. The edible ones. A chef, she was." She bent down and pulled stray weeds from around the wood fence stakes. "I gave her many samples, but never from these."

"How would she—"

"¡Oh, dios mío, los venados nuevo," she exclaimed and went to the chain link fence behind the poison garden.

"The deer," she said by way of explanation. "They trample, trying to get my leaves." The vegetation outside the fence was flat and the fence bowed. "But not even they will touch these."

"The police suspect Lexie mixed up the deadly nightshade berries with other berries. How is that possible?"

We walked down a different row, stopping near what looked like wildflowers. "Black nightshade. See the berries?" She plucked two, popped one into her mouth and held out the other for me.

I smiled, but declined.

She shrugged and ate that one, too. "Sweet, dark berries, very close to the belladonna. Delicioso."

She pruned the plants, picking off yellowed parts and shriveled berries, sticking the remnants into the front pocket of her apron.

I still didn't understand how Lexie ended up with the wrong nightshade. Or why she would use these ingredients when the supermarket certainly held all kinds of berries perfectly appropriate for cupcake baking.

"So Lexie wanted the black nightshade, but ended up with deadly nightshade? Did she pick the wrong ones?"

"No. I give her black nightshade, but never the other. And she only came inside my garden with me. She was a smart girl. She knew the difference."

"Can anyone grow belladonna? Maybe she decided to grow it herself."

"Like I say, it grows wild. On the roads. But why? She didn't want poison, she wanted especial, like her." She crossed herself again and resumed pruning.

"One last question. Are they poisonous after you cook them?"

She nodded slowly. "Si. Muy mortal."

"Thank you, Mamacita. For the tour and information. I appreciate it."

"Si, si. Come back anytime. I have wonderful recipes. Not only the poison plants, but plenty of organic floras and medicinal herbs."

"You mean like the ones that are legal with a prescription, but not in this state?"

She laughed and squeezed my arm. "Oh, Chiquita."

I said goodbye and followed the path to the Mini. The dogs commenced their barking as I passed the trailer. Once tucked safely into my seat with my seatbelt securely fastened, I jotted notes in my small book. The nightshade berries definitely looked similar, enough for an amateur, as Mamacita called her, to confuse. But Mamacita insisted she didn't get them from her. If not here, then where? Maybe Mamacita was lying? Or most likely, someone else got them, switched them, and Lexie hadn't a clue. Because if she didn't accidentally poison herself, someone else sure as shit did.

FOUR

(Day #2 – Friday Afternoon)

The sun was beginning to set. The sky's blue deepened with every minute. I needed to stop at the cottage for a wardrobe change before Lexie's dedication at *The Nutcracker*. And to hopefully get a moment with her dancer friends, perhaps take a look at her dressing room.

Wearing a black maxi skirt and a crisp white blouse, I drove to the Sea Pine Community Theatre. Located mid-island, it fronted Locke Harbor, a center with boutique shops, nautical restaurants, and a one-hundred slip marina on the Intracoastal Waterway.

I parked around back near the exit door and slipped inside just after six. The performance started at seven, so I had no more than thirty minutes before the frantic pace turned chaotic. Even though two of Lexie's friends, the newly-promoted Sugar Plum Fairy and the Cavalier, didn't take the stage until the second act, the Mouse King showed up in the first.

Every dressing room door stood open. The closest one to the exit, and farthest from the stage, was the largest. Ten portable lighted mirrors circled the room. Children, the oldest no more than a pre-teen, sat in front of each vanity, applying makeup like professional models before a photo shoot. False eyelashes, heavy liners, glossy lipsticks. Their mothers (presumably) stood behind them, creating intricate hairdos with rhinestone clips and industrial cans of spray.

Yellow crime scene tape crossed the threshold of Lexie's dressing room in a large X. The construction paper nameplate was still taped to the door. Interesting to note that Lexie shared with Courtney, who was dressed in Lexie's costume right before the police arrived, yet somebody else found Lexie inside.

The door was unlocked, so I eased under the tape and slid into the room. I dialed Parker at the station.

"The dressing room's cleared, right?" I asked once she answered.

"Yep. You're legal. Since I'm sure you're standing inside the room."

"Me? No, but I'll go ahead inside, now that I have your permission."

The place was still as messy as I remembered. I tiptoed around and stepped on the end of an iPhone charger. Still plugged in, no phone attached.

"Did you find her phone?" I asked.

"Yep," Parker said. "And other evidence, too. We're pretty good at this."

"Evidence, huh? As in evidence of a homicide, not an accident, right?"

Silence.

"If you won't confirm homicide, at least tell me what other evidence," I said. "Although I don't need you to confirm because I did not buy Ransom's whole it's an accident so I don't need to be involved story."

"Talk to the lieutenant."

"You're no fun."

"So I've been told," she said. "Happy detecting."

I carefully looked around. Though it probably wasn't necessary to be careful. I couldn't make it look worse, and there was nothing to damage. Nearly everything was made of fabric, and I didn't find much after five minutes of solid digging. No phone (the police took it), no poison cupcakes (also took those), no suicide note (probably did not exist).

I picked up a discarded program for *The Nutcracker*. I thumbed through until I got to the cast. Courtney Cattanach, Dew Drop Fairy. Bergin Guthrie, Mouse King. Vigo Ortiz, Cavalier. I circled their names and tucked it into my hipster.

The lighted mirror was lined in photos. All Lexie and Vigo, her boyfriend, the Cavalier, save one tucked into the corner. I plucked it from its spot. Three children in leotards, two girls and one boy, at a dance studio, sitting up against a mirror, a long bar above their heads. I flipped it over: *Lexie, Courtney, and Berg, Our Three Musketeers* written in a sophisticated hand. Courtney sat on the left, Berg on the right, and Lexie in the middle. All were laughing, and Berg was handing Lexie something. Maybe a flower?

I slipped it back into the mirror frame. Why did that happy girl eat those damn cupcakes, and why would someone poison them?

A woman with a more-salt-than-pepper bun on her head came into the room and gently closed the door behind her. She jumped when she saw me. "Oh! I didn't know anyone was in here." She put her hand on her chest and backed up a step.

"Johnnie Mae Tidwell," I said. "We met at the volunteer luncheon last week for the theatre." Johnnie Mae was new to Inga's studio and to the island. And she probably thought I was pilfering through Lexie's belongings. "I'm Elliott Lisbon with the Ballantyne Foundation, one of the sponsors of the ballet."

"Yes, of course. Nice to see you again," she said. "Well, not nice. I mean, under the circumstances." Her face was drawn, her eyes red, not a dab of makeup.

"Did you need something in here?" I'd left the crime scene tape on the door. Interesting she slipped beneath it, too.

"Deidre asked me to clean her condo. The kids are staying there and they left such a mess. Teenagers, you know? She mentioned Lexie's dressing room. I thought I'd clean in here, too." She stood close to the entry, barely a foot inside the room.

"Did you know Lexie well?"

"Well..." She looked past me, into the makeup mirror and beyond, far, far away. Her reflection looked pale and fragile, with tiny opal earrings and a delicate knit sweater. She shook her head as if to bring herself back. "I did. And I didn't." Tears pooled in her eyes, then dripped down her cheeks. "It's the most awful thing in the world."

"I'm so sorry," I said and crossed the room to hug her.

She hugged me as if she never wanted to let go. After a full ten seconds, she pulled back. "I'm sorry. I don't know why this hit me so hard. I only knew her a week." Johnnie Mae took a crumpled tissue from her pocket, then looked at its tattered state. It seemed to sadden her more.

A paper box of tissues sat on the vanity. I grabbed the box and held it out to her.

"Thank you," she said. "This probably wasn't a good idea. To come in here. I keep thinking about Lexie's mother. I lost my only child, too, and it broke me." She blew her nose and took another tissue. "I'm sorry. I don't know why I'm telling you this. I don't even know you," she said with a half laugh.

"Please don't apologize. I lost my parents twenty years ago and I still miss them," I said. "The loss never fully goes away."

"Or the loneliness," she said softly.

Though I missed my parents, I probably missed the idea of them more. I never experienced profound loneliness after they were gone. They loved me, but I arrived later in their lives, and they were inseparable, even to make room for me.

The door flew open and Berg Guthrie burst in, nearly knocking Johnnie Mae to the floor. "What are you doing in here?" He was in his full Mouse King costume and carried the head in his hands.

Courtney and Vigo came in behind him. Both in tees and tights, but Courtney wore her hair in a tight shellacked bun.

"You can't be in here," Berg said. "None of us can. This is private."

"I know it's upsetting," I said. "But I'm assisting the police." The room felt overcrowded and stifling. But more, it felt inappropriate. "Let's go outside." I held the door while everyone shuffled into the hall backstage. "Courtney, I noticed you and Lexie shared that dressing room, but Berg, you're the one who found her?"

"Lexie wanted to lie down, so I left her alone," Courtney said. "Took my stuff down to the kids' room." Courtney led us to Berg and Vigo's dressing room and sat at the lighted table in the center of the room. She opened a makeup bag larger than a carry-on. "I won't do that again. Those dance moms are nasty to be around. Really bad vibe. Even worse than the volunteers."

I winced on Johnnie Mae's behalf, one of Inga's volunteers, but she hadn't followed us into the room.

"Lexie's dressing room should open up soon, right?" Vigo asked me. He sat on the loveseat and rested his feet on a black trunk. "You were in there, and the tape's been torn down. It must mean they're done."

"I'm not sure, but I'll talk to the investigative team," I said.

"You can't go in there," Berg said. "No one can. Leave her be. All of you, just leave her be."

"She's not in there," Vigo said.

"Her spirit is," Berg said. "Her life ended in there. It's not right for someone to sit in her chair and slap on makeup like nothing happened."

"It's just a room. Chill out," Vigo said.

"Show some respect," Berg said. He towered over the seated Vigo, his face red and his fists bunched.

"Stop it," Courtney said and threw a blush brush at the mirror. "Just stop! You two fighting every minute makes everything worse."

Berg backed down, ran a hand through his hair. "It's not the same without her here."

"She wouldn't be here anyway," Vigo said. "She was always late."

Courtney kicked him in the shin.

"What? I'm being honest," Vigo said. "She liked that about me."

"I don't see why," Berg said.

With a boyfriend like Vigo, Lexie needed a better boyfriend. On the surface, he was the full package: tall, dark, and handsome with a mop of wavy hair and pale green eyes. But he didn't seem distraught or upset or even bothered by the loss. Yes, I could be judgy.

Courtney looked at me through the reflection in the mirror. "Lexie wasn't always late. *Sometimes* she came in a little late. But we all did." She applied glue to a fluttery black lash and stuck it on her lid. "Just that lately, she was unfocused. Like dance wasn't her everything."

"I heard she liked to cook," I said.

"Oh my God, like every day," Courtney said. "Baking was her new thing. Everything baked. Quiche, pot pie, beef wellington. She made *beef wellington*."

"Yeah, and cakes," Vigo said. "Even though no one ate them. Not after you two got sick."

"We weren't that sick. Stop exaggerating," Berg said. He peered out the door as a stampede of footfalls thundered by. "I'm not used to rich food."

"I think it was more than that," Courtney said. "Nothing major. Lexie probably messed up the recipe."

"Except when Lexie did something, she was Miss Perfect," Vigo said.

"That's not a bad thing," Berg said.

"I didn't say it was," Vigo said. "She strived for perfection and didn't want to settle for less."

"This is bullshit," Berg said. He put the Mouse King head over his own and stormed out.

"Whatever, man," Vigo said. "I have to get ready." He got up and went behind a divider screen.

Courtney took a deep breath and dabbed at her eyes with a tissue. "It was not supposed to be like this. Our reunion. We were a team. And now...Nothing will ever be the same."

"Is that why you're staying at the condo?" I asked. "A

reunion?"

"Yeah. It was Lexie's idea. She'd been planning it all semester. When Miss Inga asked us to reprise our *Nutcracker* roles, we were all in. A week together at the condo sounded like so much fun. We haven't seen each other in months."

"You guys didn't go to the same college?"

"No, different dance programs, different entry auditions. I'm at Oklahoma City. Vigo got into UNT and Lexie chose UNC. Berg followed Lexie. Berg always followed Lexie. She was special."

Courtney spun on her chair and grabbed my wrist with such intensity it hurt. "I don't care what it takes, you find the person who did this." She choked back a sob. "They will not live free. They will suffer."

She got herself together with three plucks from a tissue box and turned back to the mirror. I left her to clean up her smeary eye makeup.

In the background, Inga called for places. The performance was about to begin. I made my way to the stage steps, ready to dedicate the performance and name the scholarship in Lexie's honor.

"There you are," Inga Dalrymple said in her shout voice. "I wondered if you were going to bail and make me go out there to do your job."

The dance mom from the night before, the one with striped hair, approached us. "I guess everyone got a promotion," she said. "Courtney doesn't make near as pretty a Sugar Plum Fairy, but at least my daughter is finally dancing in the Land of Sweets." She turned to me. "It's tragic and all, but what's done is done. Might as well make the most of it."

Another mom joined us as the orchestra started playing. Her hair was styled in a chic blond pixie cut. "Did you see who's playing Clara?" She looked positively giddy. "And Shirl isn't even here to watch Courtney dance."

"What kind of mother doesn't watch her kid dance?" the striped hair mom said.

"Courtney won't let her," the other mom replied.

"Won't let her? The day my child doesn't let me go where I want to go, let me tell you..."

"Special performances only," the other mom said.

A new mom walked up. She wore dangly plastic wreath earrings and a matching necklace and the brightest purple eye shadow I've ever seen. "My daughter is the Sugar Plum Fairy, ladies. Pretty darn special, I'd say."

"Go on, all of you," Inga said and made shooing motions. "I know you have seats. Go stick your butts in them." As they grumbled their way up the long interior corridor, Inga turned to me and pointed. "You're on."

With a deep breath, I followed the same path as I had the night before and walked onto center stage. I made my announcement and asked for a moment of silence. The audience was subdued and respectful, and it was dreadful. I noticed my first best friend, Sid Bassi, in the third row, and she motioned she'd meet me in the lobby.

I slowly climbed down the steps and the dancers took the stage. I'm not sure I could ever watch *The Nutcracker* again.

Sid wrapped me in a giant hug. She towered over me by a foot, and her long, dark blond hair cascaded over my shoulders. "Sweetie, I'm so very sorry," she said and kept hugging.

"I needed that," I said. "But you're going to miss the show."

She waved me off. "Seen it a dozen times. Just an opportunity to get out of the house." Sid was a top realtor on the island, a volunteer at the hospice thrift store, on the board at the hospital, and played in a beach volleyball league. She also dated the most eligible bachelor on the island, if not the entire state of South Carolina.

"You hardly need an opportunity to get out of the house," I said.

"Milo's busy this weekend. I can't just sit around binge watching *Alias* on Netflix," she said.

"Vaughn!"

"I know! I started with season one and I'm on five now."

"That first season killed it. Not so much by five. I'm still jealous, though. I'd love to crawl under the covers and live vicariously through Sydney Bristow and Michael Vaughn," I said. "But no time."

"How are you holding up? A lot to deal with a week before Christmas."

"Yeah, and after spending most of last night here, I'm ready to leave."

"Wait. Wasn't Matty your date last night? How'd that end up?"

"With him going home alone and me staying here with Ransom."

She pushed my shoulder. "Stop it."

"I know. And it's only going to get more complicated. My investigations make Matty uncomfortable—"

"And Nick Ransom."

"—and Nick Ransom. But I'm not going to disappoint Mr. Ballantyne. Or the Allens."

"That girl really poison herself?"

"Not likely," I said. "But I'll find out for sure."

"I know you will," she said. "Let me know what I can do." She put her hand up. "I'm not scaling any walls this time, 'kay?"

"Deal," I said and gave her a quick hug.

My phone chirped. Then again. And again. And again.

"Sorry," I said. I hated to be one of those people who checked their phone whilst in the middle of a conversation with a friend, but four chirps was a lot for me. No one ever texted me. They were all from Deidre Burch.

Key under the sea.

Empty.

Dot those i's.

Mums the word.

"Something good?"

"Possibly. But I need your help." I tucked my phone away. "You sure you don't mind missing the show?"

"Absolutely."

"Then let's go."

We snuck out the front doors of the theatre. I'd rather trudge around the outside of the entire building to get to my car than face those backstage moms again. Besides, we didn't have that kind of time.

FIVE

Most of the residential areas on Sea Pine were divided into gated subdivisions guarded by a range of security personnel from intimidating former lawmen who wore guns on their belts to retired folks who'd be just as happy working at Jellystone with Yogi and Boo-Boo.

Though Sugar Hill was a gated residential community, it also housed two hotels, two golf courses, miles of bike paths and beaches, and a handful of restaurants—all with public access. Gaining admittance required nothing more than a smile and a retail destination. Or a resident to call in a pass, which Deidre did for me. It expired in five days and I hoped I wouldn't need it that long.

Once through the gates, I wound down the paved road toward the beach where the hotels fronted the ocean and the low-rise condos had their backs. Palm trees, magnolias, crape myrtles, and oaks were so plentiful, it resembled a mountain-top hideaway, one with high sand dunes and an ocean view.

Deidre Burch's vacation condo was in a cluster development across the short road from a narrow beach path. I'd been there twice before and easily found the weathered wood building. One might think it odd that a resident of Sea Pine Island would own a vacation condo on the same island. But quite a few residents purchased properties for investment rentals. They also came in handy when out-of-towners visited. And when you live on an island, out-of-towners always visit.

"You're sure Deidre left a key in order for you to purposely snoop around her condo tonight?"

"Absolutely. She knew I wanted to look around, and right now everyone is at the performance. I think she likes the clandestine aspect. She texted in code."

"Oy," Sid said.

We climbed the steps to the second floor landing. A hand-painted plaque hung on the door to number fifty-three: The Burch's Sugar Shack. Sid went for the welcome mat, but I went for the sign.

"The mat has palm trees, but the sign has the surf," I said. A brass house key was taped to the back. I peeled it off and opened the door. "As in, *key under the sea.*"

"I'll be the lookout," Sid said. "I'm not up for a B and E arrest tonight."

"The dancers will be at the theatre for hours, Sid. And no one is around."

The sky was a dusky dark blue, nearly pitch. The complex was quiet for a Friday evening. Most folks already out for the night. Though with a population dominated by the already- and the nearly-retired, the restaurants filled by six and emptied by nine. It may have been quiet at the moment, but it wouldn't stay that way for long.

"You'll be safer inside," I said. "Plus, you can help me."

"I'm serious. Orange may be the new black, but I prefer red," she said and curtsied.

"Fine. If someone comes, what's your cover?"

"I'm looking for my missing cat."

"In a ball gown?"

"It's not a ball gown, Valentino. It's an evening dress. I came home early from a night at the theatre and noticed my cat was missing. Obviously, I wouldn't take the time to change. I'd rush out and search."

"Obviously," I said. "I'm going in."

"I'll ring the doorbell if someone comes home."

"Uh-huh." I eased inside and clicked the door shut behind me. "Hello?" I called, just in case. Luckily, no one replied.

It was quiet and dimly lit. A single lamp illuminated the living room slash kitchen combo area: the kitchen and nook opened into the living room creating one combined space. It was generic. A typical vacation rental. Sofa, two chairs, inexpensive end tables, tv and entertainment center. Everything neat and tidy and shipshape. Johnnie Mae did a fine job on the cleanup.

Probably too fine. Not a personal item on any surface. I checked beneath the cushions and on the floor, behind the tv and under the sofa. I moved to the kitchen. The countertops were spotless and devoid of appliances, canisters, or knick-knacks like spoon rests and jars of poisonous berries.

I'm not much of a kitchen person myself. All those sticky ingredients and messy pans. Sixty minutes to make it, another thirty to clean it up, and then five minutes to eat it. The ratio just didn't work for me.

A sheet of paper was on the front of the refrigerator door, held in place with a palm tree magnet. A rehearsal and performance schedule for *The Nutcracker*. Dress rehearsals every afternoon for a week leading up to opening night, then eleven performances including three matinees.

I opened the refrigerator door. Nearly cleaned out. Or maybe it never had anything in it to begin with. Plastic squeeze bottles of ketchup and mustard, an enormous container of what smelled like something gone over. Kale. A variety of salad dressings, all light. No leftovers, either. Maybe Johnnie Mae boxed them up or tossed them out? I checked the trash can. Empty, with a fresh bag in place.

Next I checked the cupboards. Dishes, pots and pans, plastic containers, a pantry. Mostly staples Deidre probably provided. No berries, no exotic ingredients, no leftover cupcakes. Though I doubted any of these dancers ate cake. They probably wouldn't eat cupcakes before a show. Or after. Or ever.

I surveyed the rest of the layout. A master bedroom with a balcony, two smaller bedrooms, two full baths and a half bath, a nice laundry room (especially to someone whose washer/dryer combo is stacked in her kitchen and not in its own room). A linen closet stocked with beach supplies: towels, chairs, buckets, umbrellas, Frisbees.

I started with the master. It was a disaster.

Or half a disaster. Two queen beds were placed on either side of a patio door splitting the room into two separate but equal groups. I wondered who was the Felix Unger and who was the Oscar Madison. I remembered Lexie's dressing room and guessed she was Oscar. Clothes, shoes, hangers, pillows, makeup, bottles, and brushes were flung around her side of the room. On every surface, dangling from the nightstand, the chaise in the corner, and the handle to the sliding glass door. The laundry basket looked to be gorged; the plastic shower carrier placed on top of the lid tilted precariously on the basket's weaved surface.

I tossed clothes, looking for anything important. Which I had no idea what would be important. An old beat-up jewelry box sat on the nightstand amidst the mayhem. I opened the lid and the tiny ballerina twirled a wobbly dance to the music. *Lara's Theme*, maybe? Nothing but cheap jewelry, a handful of plastic rings, three loose keys. I picked up the box and checked underneath. A dry cleaning stub marked RUSH SAT (which to me immediately ruled out Ransom's ridiculous suicide theory, which I wasn't even considering, because one did not rush dry cleaning to be picked up two days after one planned to off themselves) and stack of tickets to *The Nutcracker*. One for every night's performance. Weird, since her friends were in the ballet, and her parents (two of them) would get tickets at the Will Call window. Why the one ticket for each show? Why hide them? I snapped a picture to overanalyze later and gently set the music box back on top.

A charger cord looped around the edge of the nightstand. A second charger? Who used their phone that much? I searched under the bed and in the drawers, nothing hidden, but plenty to be found, just not useful to my investigation. I bumped into the engorged hamper and knocked the shower carrier over. After I righted it, I opened the hamper lid. Might as well be thorough. Sometimes it paid off.

Buried deep inside, nearly at the bottom, was an iPad in a black leather protective case. Now that was interesting. Did she hide it there or simply keep it there? Not as if there were any clean surfaces to set it on. I wasn't complaining. The police might've taken it when they searched earlier if it was in plain sight. On the other hand, who kept their iPad in the bottom of a hamper?

Courtney's side of the bedroom would make Mary Poppins proud. Clothes either folded neatly in the drawers or arranged by color on padded hangers in the closet. Two pictures on her nightstand: one of her, Lexie, and Berg; the other of her and her mother, whom I recognized from the theatre bragging about her daughter, the Sugar Plum Fairy. There was no secret diary tucked into a drawer or a stack of fashion magazines bedside. Though she did have a deluxe bathroom carrier twice the size of Lexie's, neatly arranged with salon shampoos and body scrubs.

I didn't want to misplace the iPad I planned on pilfering, so I stuck it on the countertop by the front door. Then figured I'd walk right past it when I left. I moved it smack in front of the door itself, leaning on the jamb, then resumed my search.

The two smaller bedrooms both held boy stuff. The one on the right was Vigo's. Framed pictures of him and Lexie were on the dresser and the nightstand, at least a dozen of them. I guess those two really liked looking at themselves. The room was messy, though not to the Lexie level by any stretch, and mostly all man things. Man magazines, man hair products, man perfume. Bulky sweats, clunky weights, old-fashioned headphones with the big earmuffs. The only soft touch was a velvety brown teddy bear in the back of the closet. A caramel-colored formal dinner napkin tied around its neck like a kerchief. I recognized it—the signature color of the Wharf restaurant. He had two more folded beneath the bear. As I was closing the closet door, I noticed a poster taped to the wall behind his clothes. Pushing the hanging shirts out of the way, I saw it wasn't a poster, it was a shot-up target. The human silhouette kind. And Vigo was a really great shot. No fancy sharpshooting bullets to the head. They were all center mass, one on top of another.

I went across the hall to Berg's room. His bed was rumpled with one pillow on the floor and the sheet/blanket/spread twisted and bundled and hanging off the side. Same types of man items, though some effort to stay neat was evident. I checked his closet and drawers, but found nothing surreptitiously tucked away or taped to the wall. I even reached between the mattresses. I worried I might find a girly magazine, and that I didn't have enough hand-sani to scrub my hands or my brain, but the space was empty. I opened the trunk at the foot of his bed and found it filled with artist supplies. Charcoals, pencils, sketchbooks.

Berg Guthrie was quite talented. Beautifully detailed drawings of dancers mid-air, sketched in elaborate scenes from forests to castles to ships on troubled seas. Page after page, each dancer was clothed in elegant costumes and headpieces. After about fifteen pages, I realized there weren't multiple dancers. Just one. Lexie Allen. He captured her likeness as if she posed for each rendering. As I neared the end of the book, the content turned dark. Her airy tutu now tattered and torn. In one, she swung from a wood beam, a noose around her neck, her hands clutched to the rope. In another, her head rested in the swoop of a guillotine, the sharp blade merely inches above her. She was impaled in another, shot by an arrow in another, and on the final page, Lexie lay on a cushioned sofa, her arm outstretched, and a tipped-over vial falling from her hand like Juliet Capulet.

The doorbell rang and I jumped. It rang again, then again. "Oh shit, Sid!" I whipped out my phone and started snapping pictures. Another doorbell ring echoed through the condo. I flipped pages, capturing each one. I put my phone in my pocket and the book back in the trunk. Pulled open the shutters at the window. They opened like a door. As I pushed the window lock open, I looked up. Straight at the neighbors in the next building, their window not five feet away. They were playing cards with their blinds wide open.

I slammed the shutter shut and raced across the hall into the master. I slid open the glass balcony door. My skirt caught on the hamper and I remembered the iPad. Hesitated half a second, then ran to the entryway. Muffled voices were right outside the door. The knob rattled. I grabbed the iPad and ran back to the master.

It was now black as pitch outside. The moon barely shone through the heavy cover of palm fronds and oak branches.

I shut the glass door and turned. I was trapped on the balcony. It wasn't a wraparound to the front as I'd assumed. It was a short, private balcony railed in on three sides with the glass door behind me making up the fourth. I peered over the side. Not too high up and the branches were fairly close to the rail. Voices got louder. I climbed one leg over the side. The bark of the branch ripped into my arm and I swore. Loudly.

The voices stopped. I held my breath, then did what needed to be done.

I meowed.

Holding onto the branch, I pulled my other leg over the side of the balcony, and shimmied to the ground, meowing all the way and keeping the swear words to myself. My skirt hooked on a baby branch near the bottom, and it poked my thigh. I landed on my feet with a soft thud.

I duck walked with my head dipped low back to the Mini. Its ice blue color looked bright beneath the street lamp. Note to self: when breaking and entering, do not park directly under the street lights. And don't wear something billowy. I checked for rips and tears, but somehow managed to come away with only stains and smudges on my flowing skirt and once lovely white shirt.

Sid walked down the steps and over to the building next door. I drove around and picked her up.

"Who came home?" I asked. "I was only in there like five minutes."

"More like twenty, Trixie Belden," she said and strapped on

her seatbelt. "It was the Mouse King."

"Berg? Really? He probably didn't stay for the second act."

"What took so long? I was hanging out front like a call girl waiting for a trick to walk by. An expensive call girl, mind you."

"Hey, I'm the one who got all scratched up." I parked behind the building and took out my phone. "Check these out."

The first three pictures were completely blurry. I couldn't even tell they were sketches. The next was a clear shot of my finger.

"Slightly anti-climactic," Sid said.

"There's more." I flipped through two more and then got to the money.

"A death sketch?" Sid said.

"There were a dozen of them, and all of Lexie. Drawn by Berg the Mouse King."

"Wowza. He seemed so nice." She leaned over the phone to get a better look. "I guess he's your number one suspect. You sharing these with Ransom?"

"Um, no. And not only because I shouldn't have seen these. Fruit of the poisoned tree, so to speak."

"How apropos."

"I know what I'm doing," I said and tucked my phone into my handbag.

"You have leaves in your hair."

I plucked at them and tossed a handful out the window. "Now I need to figure out a way for Berg to show me those sketches or for someone else to find them and show me or talk about them or something."

"You'll figure it out," Sid said. "At least you know who your bad guy is."

"There's more than one. Vigo isn't so innocent, either. He had a shooting target hidden in his closet."

"Blank?"

"Shot to shit."

"That's something."

"Might be nothing. He does live in Texas now."

I unlatched my seatbelt and started to get out of the car.

"Where are you going?" Sid asked.

"The dumpster. The trash had recently been emptied. We need to check the bin."

"We nothing. I'm wearing Escada, remember? And you're no fashionista, but you can't dig through grimy cans in that."

I looked at my dirty, but still swanky, ensemble. "I suppose you're right. This is probably salvageable as is. But Johnnie Mae dumped that trash just hours ago. What if pickup is in the morning? I have to check it out."

"You're on your own for this one," Sid said. "But may I suggest you go home and change first?"

"I'm going to need a hazmat suit."

"I'm sure you have one."

Maybe not a standard issue one, but I had something close. I shut the car door and started the engine.

I dropped Sid at the theatre next to her fancy white BMW X6, and sped home for a quick change. Dressed in a plastic jumpsuit I got as a gag gift from Carla three birthdays ago, I loaded into my car. I tossed yellow rubber kitchen gloves and a roll of paper towels on the passenger seat and hit Cabana Boulevard.

With a wave of my security pass at the guard, I drove around to the back of Deidre's condo. Not bad. Only a forty-five minute detour. And hopefully worth it.

I took the brick path between the buildings and followed my nose. No matter how splendid the surroundings—a light breeze swaying dozens of palm fronds, distant waves crashing against the hard-packed sand, the call of the seagulls swooping through the night sky—garbage smelled like garbage. Sour, rancid, and pungent, and that was before I flipped up the heavy plastic lid. A single blue metal dumpster sat directly beneath a street lamp. Again with the spotlights. At least I wouldn't need my flashlight.

With enormous rubber gloves covering my hands, I set the flashlight on the ground, stood on my tippy toes, and peered inside. Two thoughts hit simultaneously: Everybody at the condo complex used white plastic trash bags with those flimsy plastic ties. And there wasn't enough hand-sani in the Mini, my handbag, and my pockets put together to handle this.

Holding my breath like a swimmer diving down to the drain, I leveraged myself with my right hand and swooped in with my left. The bag flew out and I tipped backward, landing squarely on my butt. It wasn't as heavy as I'd imagined. The area was still quiet, but not taking chances, I scurried to the side of the bin out of sight. Luckily, no windows faced the garbage drive.

I said some sort of Hail Mary blessing prayer, even though I'm not Catholic, and got busy on the bag. Nothing in that one or the next four bags as I repeated my stealthy dumpster diving. Many a crime case was broken by a resourceful investigator rummaging through discarded rubbish. But not this case. Or at least this trip to the dumpster. Just five bags of literal garbage. No case-breaking cake mix or deadly fruit. Only greasy black banana peels, a pile of unwashed socks, tomatoes with moldy purple spots, but absolutely no arsenic sauce. A certain grumpy holiday song may have been playing in the car when I parked, but that's the gist.

I did discover how the Post-It industry stayed in business. I probably saw more scraps of paper than any other single item—in a variety of shapes, sizes and textures: colorful, lined, notebook, copy, plus ripped up flyers, bills and envelopes, all covered in hastily and hard-to-read scratch and loopy scripts. Using my advanced deductive reasoning skills (I studied Criminology and have a Bachelor's in Criminal Justice to prove it), I found what might be the trash Johnnie Mae took out earlier: the two bags on the very top of the pile (one contained a crumpled *Nutcracker* program). To make it seem like less of a bust, I snapped several pics of paper scraps with scribbles, along with an empty shampoo container and two smashed cans of Pepsi.

After tossing the rubber kitchen gloves into the dumpster and dousing myself in sani gel, I covered the Mini seat in an old towel and drove out of Sugar Hill. The top thought on my mind: I may have worked on the edge of proper procedure, but I ended the night with two suspects and an iPad. Out of the six thousand hours of training required to get my PI license, I still had more than five thousand to go. After tonight, I could scratch off another ten. Using creative itemizing. More importantly, I wondered about Lexie's friends, and more specifically, if one of them wanted her dead.

SIX

(Day #3 – Saturday Morning)

Lounging in bed on a Saturday morning, or any morning, was one of my favorite leisurely spoils. I could read and think and dream. Sometimes sleep. But just knowing I didn't absolutely have to get up was divine. On days where I did absolutely have to get my butt out of bed before the chickens rose, I compromised. The alarm went off an hour early and I lounged.

Or in this case, ruminated on Lexie Allen while still snuggled safely under a quilt in my jammies. Propped up on pillows, I started filling in my notes. First came Lexie Allen. Her parents were friends of the Ballantynes, and I'd met her several times over the years. Enough to make friendly chitchat at lunches and teas and fundraisers. Courtney mentioned Lexie attended UNC, and I thought Lexie was a sophomore this year, probably nineteen or twenty years old. Liked to cook, lately bake, with unusual ingredients. She occasionally visited an herbalist named Mamacita.

Next, with the help of the worn *Nutcracker* program, I noted her friends.

Courtney Cattanach, best friend and second in line to the Sugar Plum Fairy throne. Shared a dressing room, a condo, and probably a wardrobe with Lexie.

Vigo Ortiz, boyfriend who liked to be photographed. And shoot guns. Not very distraught, in my humble but oh so important opinion.

Berg Guthrie, friend who followed her to UNC. As Courtney said, *always* followed Lexie. As in unrequited love? Stalker? Little brother wannabe? Drew elaborate sketches of Lexie dying in very gruesome ways. Gothic and theatrical.

It wasn't much, but it wasn't nothing, either. I'd only been one day on the case. Oh! I also had my garbage treasure. I flipped through my phone and noted the photographed scraps in the notebook, mostly names and numbers and a pizza place on the island, all written in a script so loopy I expected the i's to be dotted with hearts. As I swiped through the gallery, I saw the pic of *The Nutcracker* tickets and the dry cleaning stub marked RUSH.

What was Lexie dry cleaning that needed a Saturday rush pickup? The laundry room at the condo was fully stocked. In the midst of her current schedule, she'd be at rehearsals all day and then performances at night. No time for a fancy outing wearing the kind of clothes you dry clean. Thinking of fancy outings, I had one that night with Matty. It was the Seabrook Prep Winter Formal. And for this date, Matty wouldn't be going home alone. Though it made me nervous to think about what would happen once we arrived.

I set my notebook aside and reached for Lexie's iPad. It looked new, or at least in beautiful condition. Maybe I was judging that girl on the messy state of her room. Slobby didn't mean she didn't care for her valuables. I didn't own an iPhone, I was an Android girl, but understood the concept well enough. I pushed the button, slid the slider, and a keypad popped up to enter a four-digit passcode.

Could be anything. A good password is easy to remember, something close to home. I grabbed the Ballantyne Foundation phone directory and looked up the Allen's address. They lived at 7439 Cypress Lane. I quickly typed in 7439. The four circles awaiting my numerical entry jiggled, letting me know it didn't work. The last four digits of her phone number? Back to the directory. She wasn't listed, but her parents were. Didn't work.

I needed to be thoughtful. Her birth year might be too obvious, but I tried anyway. Counting backward to figure out her birth year, even though I wasn't quite sure: 1993, 1994. More jiggles. Could be her birthday. Either month and day, day and year, month and year. Again, obvious. And I didn't know that any more than I knew what year she was born. Not a very secure passcode choice for Lexie to make. All her friends and family would know her birthday, probably showed up on Facebook, too.

Last four digits of her social? Favorite holiday? Parents' birthday? Weirdly enough, I knew her mother's birthday. Maybe ten years earlier, I met Lexie Allen for the first time at the Ballantyne Foundation's Annual Kite Flying Brigade on Oyster Cove Beach to celebrate Independence Day. Lexie was shy and sweet and excited. She thought the celebration was for her mom's birthday. She'd never been to a beach party, and like all Ballantyne events, we'd gone all out.

I tried 0704. Jiggle.

Lexie had to have had dozens of special moments and I only knew the one. But her mother later said Lexie talked about that day for months and she hung her kite in her bedroom. It stuck with me because I did the same thing. And mine, too, was decorated with the colors of the flag.

I typed in 1776. An error message appeared: iPad disabled, try again in one minute.

As I waited the minute, I wondered if perhaps I was overthinking it. When the time elapsed, I tried something simple: 1234. Another error message, this time informing me to try again in five minutes.

With time on my hands, I Googled the most common four-digit passcodes. Over ten percent of the population chose 1234. Next on the list: 1111. A jiggle and it disabled. Now the iPad forced me to wait fifteen minutes. I wondered at what point I'd be locked out forever. I didn't have to worry. Turned out Lexie used the fourth most popular passcode: 1212.

And like that, I was in.

Pretty much random luck, which happens now and again. I didn't question it, though I did jump around the room as if I'd won the lottery. Quite satisfying to figure out someone's passcode without their address book or a three-year stint in underground hacking. It somehow felt more clever? interesting? clandestine? knowing the iPad was passcode-protected and I broke it. As if I might actually find something valuable because it had been locked.

Or not so much. As I tapped icons and apps, I barely found a sliver of insight into Lexie Allen. She liked cooking blogs, recipe sharing sites, and streaming a dozen different cooking competition tv shows. Not a lot of dance sites, other than to check the UNC, UNT, and Oklahoma City University dance schedules.

She also visited Amazon about a thousand times. I think she may have been hooked on leaving reviews. Over seven hundred of them. Random products, books of all genres. Some very detailed and long reviews, others short and simple. I wondered if she actually bought any of the items. Maybe I needed to add shopping addict to her bio. Out of curiosity, I looked up how much an iPad cost and was shocked. Who would spend that kind of money for one of those things? Nothing more than a big phone that didn't make calls. One could easily use a computer instead.

I glanced at the clock and realized nearly two hours had passed. With a speed reserved for emergencies, or situations exactly like this one, I showered in less time than it takes most people to do their makeup. I was up, out, and on my way in under twenty minutes. Though slightly OCD (and by slightly, I mean I perform my get ready routine exactly the same, in the exact same order, every single time), I am a professional.

It would be another day without riding my bike to work. My three-wheeler had a basket on back and a bell up front. It kept me stable and free and it reminded me to enjoy my island surroundings. But today involved a visit to the morgue, and there would be nothing to enjoy.

I stopped by the Big House to sneak a box of cookies for Harry Fleet, the medical examiner. He was less growly if I brought treats.

I took in the merry decorations of the entire foyer. A symphony of Christmas carols played in the background. Garland with twinkling lights wrapped around each banister and hung from the antique chandelier. The tree rose straight to the second floor and—I paused.

Adorable painted ornaments covered the entire bottom of the tree. From the long branches near the floor up to about hip height. After that, nothing but silk pine, miniature lights and lonely random popcorn strands.

Carla came out from the kitchen and joined me at the base of the tree. "Yeah," she said. "Kids can only do so much before it's time to eat the cookies, not paint them. We switched to the edible kind and ended up decorating batches for the shut-in delivery. But the kids only ate about half of those. A good day, really."

"Well, crap. So much for being on my game." I looked up to the tippy top. "Where will I get a tree-load of gorgeous themed ornaments before the Palm & Fig? Ones that look planned and special, not like I threw them together last minute?"

"You better think of something. You only have one day."

"One day? The Palm & Fig Ball is in six days, not one. Don't cut me short."

"Chicken, the board meeting is tomorrow. Mr. Ballantyne will get seven calls about a naked tree before the first board member sits down."

Tod walked over with a white pastry box tied with a string. He looked at the tall tree, then at the smattering of ornaments. "You heading over to the Walmart to load up a cart of multi-color plastic bulbs? The kind that come in tubes?"

I took the pastry box away from him. "That's Plan Q and I'm not there yet."

"Plan Q?" Carla said.

"Yes, I'm giving myself time. I'll start with B and work my way down." I sniffed the lid on the box. Even better than cookies. Carla's Christmas caramels. Rich, smooth, and homemade. She individually wrapped each delight in wax paper, and they went faster than a five a.m. Black Friday markdown.

I dropped the box in my office with my handbag. Tod could go get another box, I needed those for Harry Fleet. But first, I needed to trudge up to the attic and check out our leftover Christmas design stash.

Each floor of the Ballantyne manse clocked in around seven thousand feet. Though the attic wasn't quite that large, it was still pretty roomy. I used the hidden staircase in the solarium and climbed the three flights to the dark and dusty attic. It was also dingy, dirty, and dry.

I shuffled through the whimsical and regal accoutrements accumulated over the many years. Our fundraisers and events weren't commonplace black tie functions with expected entrees and ordinary décor. They were noteworthy soirees that engaged the imagination. We weren't just a charity, we were the Ballantyne.

From pirate treasure to pinball machines to a piñata taller than me, I finally found the Christmas section. A bin of wrapping paper circa 1952, three various skirts for a tree much dinkier than the current beauty, and the requisite menorah. Not a single bulb or a strip of tinsel to be found. I dug carefully, mindful not to splatter dust from the ancient boxes onto my hands, arms, clothes, face, or anywhere within three feet of my person. I did not have time to shower and change each and every time I encountered this attic.

An off-site company stored our custom spruce tree, plus the hundreds of feet of garland displayed throughout the Big House. They also assembled and helped decorate. Perhaps they kept a décor stash of their own.

After a detour to wash my hands and face and arms in the ladies room on the first floor, I called the storage company. It was a short conversation. Our locker was empty with no spare ornaments on hand. Though they were available to assist with decorating tomorrow should I need them. I said I should, one way or another, even though their Sunday rate was doubled.

Next I called the lovely boutique I visited yesterday on my way to Mamacita's botanical garden. The owner answered on the first ring.

"Hi, I'm Elliott Lisbon with the Ballantyne," I said. "You helped me with the wind chimes yesterday."

"Oh yes, the alligator lady," she said. "How did the chime work out?"

"It was perfect, thank you. But I'm actually calling about those gorgeous hand-painted ornaments on your feather tree. Can you tell me a little about them?"

"Hand-forged by a local artisan couple. They paint each one by hand, and without a template. Can't find anything like them in the area."

Just what I needed. Something original and hard to find. "Perfect. Any chance I could buy a large quantity and have them delivered tomorrow morning. Like early, early?"

"Of course. How many do you need?"

"Good question. Hang on one sec." I reached behind my desk to the box of sample ornaments our original *Nutcracker* artist had sent over. The invoice was right on top. "Okay, let's see...about seven hundred and fifty for the tree, probably another five hundred for gifts. So about thirteen hundred to be safe."

Silence. I heard the sounds of papers shuffling. "I could do seventy-five today and another fifty tomorrow, if that helps."

It didn't. "Maybe next year," I said.

"We'll need plenty of notice."

I told her I'd get back to her in January and hung up.

Opening the sample box again, I lined up ornaments on my desk. Sugar Plum Fairy, Mouse King, Nutcracker, tiny mice, gingerbread men, gorgeous sweets, swirly lollipops, colorful truffles, candy canes, snowflakes. I arranged them and rearranged them, adding and subtracting, mindlessly playing like a little girl with a new toy on Christmas morning.

"I got it!" I said with a head slap. I swept them into the box, except for the Sugar Plum Fairy, who went in my pocket.

I called the ornament hanging crew to request their services at the Big House in the early morning. I grabbed my handbag and the box of caramels and found Carla in the kitchen. I told her my idea, then let her know I'd be out the rest of the day.

I was feeling pretty darn excited about things when I climbed into the Mini and raced out to Cabana. Then I remembered where I was going.

The medical examiner's office was attached to the back side of Island Memorial hospital. The building resembled a quaint converted home-to-office building with shutters on the windows, thick paneled doors, and a beautifully landscaped entry. Once inside the cubicle-sized lobby, I signed the sheet on a clipboard nailed to the wall and rang the buzzer on the doorframe. Fresh wreaths made from real pine hung on the hooks where pictures normally would be. Orchestral Christmas music filtered through the speaker in the ceiling.

Five minutes later, a lady in blue scrubs popped her head out. "Yes?"

"Elliott Lisbon to see Dr. Harry Fleet," I said.

"Is he expecting you?"

"Sort of. Most likely," I said. "Not an official appointment. More of an informal visit."

She shrugged. "If you say so. Go on back, he's in his office," she said and held the door for me.

Our shoes squeaked on the vinyl floor and I consciously avoided stepping on the lines between the tiles. The entire area smelled stringently medicinal and oddly chemical and I didn't want to think about what the people in scrubs were doing on the other side of those walls.

Dr. Harry Fleet served as medical examiner for not only Sea Pine Island, but the entire county. Over one hundred twenty thousand people. Unfortunately, he was a very busy man. His desk faced the door and he had books piled, stacked, and heaped on every open and flat surface. The wall of bookshelves behind his desk, the desk itself, two visitor's chairs, even the floor. A tall but thin plastic tree sat in the corner, heavy with ornaments. Harry added a new one whenever a child died during the holidays. The tradition started before he became M.E., but he continued it with both sorrow and celebration.

"What?" he growled by way of greeting. He sat behind the desk, scrawling notes on a file.

"Merry Christmas, Harry." I went to set the box of caramels on his desk, but couldn't find a safe spot. I settled for a semi-flat space on top of a heap of files and hoped they wouldn't slide to the floor. "I brought goodies."

"Uh-huh."

"As you know, I'm working on the Lexie Allen case—"

"The Sea Pine Police are working on the Lexie Allen case," he said without looking up.

"I'm *also* working on the Lexie Allen case in my official capacity as PI-in-training for the Ballantyne Foundation." I lifted a stack of files and papers from one of the chairs and sat, keeping the stack safe on my lap. "I knew her, Harry," I said softly. "So did Mr. and Mrs. Ballantyne. She was just a kid. She deserves *everyone* on the case. Even me."

He looked up from his notes. "I suspect poisoning, as I'm sure you know. Won't know for sure until the tox report comes back. The lab rushed the results on the berries from her kitchen. Confirmed as *Atropa belladonna*."

"Deadly nightshade," I said.

"The same. Consistent with her stomach contents. Looked like berries and cake. Won't know until the report comes back after the holidays."

"But no other obvious cause of death? No injuries or wounds?"

"No. Likely poisoning, but won't know until we know."

At least Ransom was honest with me on that front, I thought. Gave me more to go on.

"I know what you're thinking, Lisbon," Harry said.

"What? It can't hurt for me to nose around."

"It will when the Lieutenant finds out."

"He already knows I'm looking into things."

"I bet," he said and went back to his scribbling.

"One more quick question and then I'm out of your hair," I said. Harry was bald. "How likely is suicide?"

He shrugged. "She was nineteen and a drama major. Probably just as likely as an accident. Comes down to whether or not she knew those berries were deadly. Not for me to determine."

"But more than likely a homicide."

"Like I said, won't know until tox comes back and the Lieutenant files his report."

"Thanks, Harry." I stood and put the papers back on the chair. I took the Sugar Plum Fairy ornament from my pocket and set it on his desk. Lexie may have been nineteen, but she was still a kid, and it still hurt.

Harry nodded once without looking up. With a final glance to his memorial tree, I walked out of his office.

SEVEN

I took a spin through the McDonald's drive-thru and sat in the parking lot beneath a shady palm contemplating my next move with a cheeseburger (ketchup only), fries (with bbq sauce) and a Coke. Meeting with Harry Fleet served to motivate me to get this job done as quick as possible. Not that I lollygagged through my other discreet inquiry investigations, but Christmas was coming up fast. People took vacations, businesses closed, daily life shifted. I didn't want this case to get caught in a holiday hold-cycle.

But which lead to follow first: Lexie's dry cleaning stub, Vigo's shot-up target, or Berg's death sketches? I'd basically (or actually) obtained all three through ill-gotten means, so I needed to pursue prudently. A random dry cleaning stub didn't seem like a priority. I might as well chase down a gum wrapper. I had no idea how to investigate a handful of sketches, and that target might as well have been from any sporting goods store in the South. I debated strategies, then went with the closest: the dry cleaning stub.

I tossed my lunch sack in the bin by the entrance, then zoomed onto Cabana toward Oyster Cove Plantation. Outside the gates, on the other side of the boulevard, was a strip center hidden behind a six-foot-tall berm covered in flowering shrubs and short palms. The QuickClean Organic Dry Cleaners was crammed between the Donut Hut and Olga's Tailoring. Though the Hut was closed, the sugary fresh baked scents still lingered in the air. I spent enough time at the Donut Hut to now need Olga's help expanding my waistband. I parked in front of the QuickClean and walked inside.

"Hello, Miss Elliott," said a tall woman with a bleached yellow military haircut. "You pick up?"

"Hi, Olga. Yes, but not for me." I pulled out my phone and slid through the photo gallery until it landed on the dry cleaning stub from the condo. "It's for Lexie Allen. Here's the ticket."

She placed a pair of readers on her nose and examined the photograph. She looked at me over the top of the phone. "Why you have picture?"

"I'm sorry to tell you this, but Lexie passed away on Thursday."

"Oh no. A shame. From the ballet, yes?"

"Yes. A dancer. I'm here on behalf of her family. Would it be okay if I picked up her order?"

"Is only clothes. Nothing valuable." She handed me my phone and went over to the automated rolling rack. With a push of a large red button, the enormous rack rotated around the room and up another story. Hundreds of plastic-wrapped clothes clicked by until she found the numbered slot she was looking for.

She hung it on a rod by the register. "Fifteen ninety-two."

While she swiped my credit card, I checked out what Lexie had needed cleaned so urgently. Two white chef's coats with WHARF embroidered in navy block print on the left chest. "Chef's coats?" I said out loud.

Olga shrugged and handed me my receipt.

I signed, lifted the coats from the rack, and left.

After I laid them flat in my backseat, I buckled myself in. Chef's coats? Did she spill on them? Maybe they were a friend's. It might be logical to get them cleaned for someone very close to her. Otherwise if she spilled on a stranger, she'd just pay for the cleaning. How close was she to this Wharf worker? But wouldn't the

Wharf have their own laundry service? Maybe Lexie borrowed them to wear in her own kitchen. As I drove out of the lot, another thought hit me: what if Lexie stole them?

The north end of the island afforded residents and visitors picturesque vistas of the sound and the Intracoastal Waterway. I turned onto Old Pickett Road and drove three miles to the Wharf restaurant, situated right on the water with an amazing view of the Palmetto Bridge.

The upscale Wharf only offered a fine dining dinner service and a gorgeous spread for Sunday brunch. I was about two hours early for dinner, but I knew from past experience the kitchen would be bustling with prep work.

Two servers were folding the Wharf's signature caramel-colored cloth napkins, placing them on four-tops facing a wall of windows. The waters of the sound gently rolled by, lapping against the trunks of the oaks near the window. It reminded me of the shoreline from the Jungle Cruise.

The clank of pans and pots greeted me as I swung open the wide door to the kitchen. Chef Carmichael barked orders to a staff of ten, all wearing white coats. One cook chopped whole red peppers, one sizzled oil in a pan, and another carried a tray from the steel island to the walk-in.

"Hey, Julia, bring the onions out. White, not green," Chef Carmichael yelled. He was burly and arrogant and made the best she-crab bisque on the island. Or so I've been told. I wouldn't eat it for all the chocolate in Belgium.

"Chef Carmichael, got a minute?" I said.

"Elliott! Are you here about Carla?" he asked. He sautéed some kind of vegetable in a hot pan, flicking his wrist so they flipped like pancakes. "She's been impossible with the fig compote for the short ribs."

The Ballantyne hosted an annual gala the week before Christmas called the Palm & Fig Ball. Distinguished chefs from all over the South bid for one of two spots to co-cater the lavish event with Carla, our head chef. This year, however, we only had one spot open since I'd cut a deal with Chef Carmichael to get Zibby out of a peccadillo in May. He bargained for the other spot, much to Carla's hearty dismay. Carmichael was difficult to work with.

"Carla is difficult to work with, Elliott," he said and squirted oil into the pan from an unmarked squeeze bottle. "She's insisting on crispy lobster dumplings. Unoriginal and uninspired. More appropriate to present lobster consommé. And Chef Newhouse agrees. I'm sending two of my staff to the Big House to start prep tonight and they'll be prepping consommé."

I bet he agreed. Chef Newhouse ran a pair of restaurants in Savannah and had been trying to find the perfect spot on Sea Pine for his third. Chef Carmichael had been "helping" him scout buildings for four years now. Newhouse revered Carmichael to the point of near worship, and Carmichael strung him along like the popcorn garland hanging on the Ballantyne tree.

"I'll speak to Carla," I said. "I'm sure you'll work this out. However, I'm here about Lexie Allen. I just picked up two chef coats with the Wharf's name on them."

"Rory, take this," he said and handed off the crackling pan to a girl with short hair so black it looked blue.

Carmichael and I stood on opposite sides at the far end of a steel island near an industrial sink. "It's horrible," he said.

"You knew her?"

"Of course. She worked in my kitchen."

"She *worked* here?" I asked. "But she's a ballet dancer."

"She's a chef. A star on my team." He waved at the kitchen personnel. Only one person looked up. Rory, the girl flipping pan veggies. She glared as if Carmichael had insulted her and I realized her hair was actually blue. "She will be impossible to replace," he said.

"Did you know her well?" I asked Chef Carmichael.

Rory answered under her breath. "Enough to know she was a better ballerina than cook."

"She was brilliant," Chef Carmichael said. "Loved to create new dishes. They weren't always up to my standards, but she took initiative. Had the drive it takes to succeed in this business."

"Did she ever use exotic ingredients? Like bizarre berries or anything strange or dangerous?"

"Not here at the Wharf," he said. "Why do you ask?"

"Just being thorough," I said. "How long had she worked here? I thought she lived in Charlotte, at UNC."

"Not unless she was commuting. I hired her the first week in November."

"November? As a prep cook?"

"Sous chef. Training, anyway. She'd done prep work for a year at a top Charlotte restaurant. The chef recommended her and I'm grateful he did. A star." He washed his hands and dried them on a towel. "You want to try tonight's amuse bouche? An avocado crab cake on a tomato coulis."

"Sounds wonderful, but I just ate," I said, opting not to mention for the one hundred thirteenth dozen time that I didn't eat seafood. I wasn't sure if it was a chef thing or a Carmichael thing, but my seafood aversion didn't stick in his memory. "I appreciate your time. I have those two chef coats in my car. Would you like them?"

"Yes, yes," he said and pointed to a young prep cook peeling onions in the corner. "Julia, go with Elliott and grab the coats. Put them in my office." He returned to the massive gas-burner stove, tasting sauce from a nine-hundred quart pot. "More salt, Rory," he said.

Julia the cook and I walked through the restaurant and out to the deserted lot. "Did you know Lexie?" I asked.

"We all did. She was nice," she said. "Always worked hard. Friendly, even when she didn't have to be."

"Oh?"

"It's tough in the kitchen. One mistake and you could be out. She covered for me once, saved my butt. That doesn't happen very often."

"What about that other girl, the one with the blue hair? Rory? She didn't seem impressed by Lexie." I opened the driver's side door of the Mini and handed her the chef coats in dry cleaning plastic.

She looked around, lowered her voice. "They hated each other. Hated." She leaned in conspiratorially and spoke so fast, I barely kept up. "Rory felt she deserved the spot on the show over Lexie because she lived in Savannah. Which was kind of rational, but Lexie was the way better cook, so of course the show wants to see who fits best. A cook-off is about the cooking, right? But try explaining that to—"

"Hold up," I said. "What show?"

"A local competition in Savannah. They were both auditioning for a place in the cook-off. It's tomorrow, I think. Rory was mad because she almost had to miss it. She's scheduled to work brunch."

"Are you going?"

"I'm not ready." At my raised brow, she elaborated. "I'm good, but I'd rather get another year of training. When I enter a competition, I expect to win. Besides, those two were practically killing each other over the spot." She winced.

"It's okay, I know what you mean," I said. "One last thing. What's the name of the cook-off?"

"Something like the Stream Kitchen? Like a dream kitchen, but not?"

"Thanks for the info, I appreciate it."

"I don't mean to be rude about Rory, but Lexie was nice to me and I really wanted her to get on that show." She draped the coats over her shoulder and walked toward the restaurant.

Lexie Allen quit school to work as a sous chef at the Wharf and no one knew? Not her bff Courtney, not her boyfriend Vigo, not her death sketch stalker co-ed student friend Berg? And she was auditioning for a cook-off in Savannah while dancing the lead in *The Nutcracker*? That girl had one complicated life.

Said the woman nervously dating two men at the same time. And not just any two men, but a best friend and an old boyfriend. And I had professional relationships with them both. Matty served on the Ballantyne board, and Ransom worked at the Sea Pine police department, the department that signed off on my PI training.

So far neither of my dating/dates had gone smoothly. Adding romance made dinners with Matty awkward. A perpetual teenager's first date where I didn't know how to act or what to say and did weird things like laugh at the wrong moment or too loud or try to fill every natural pause with blather.

It was no better with Ransom. I put up an emotional wall, subconsciously protecting myself. Or fully consciously after he broke my heart twenty years earlier and it still hurt and I never wanted to feel that way again forever and ever amen.

I drove the short distance to my cottage with enough time to doll up before Matty picked me up at six. I hoped Ransom had to work late at the station. If not, he'd be home when Matty arrived. As it happened, Ransom was also my next-door neighbor.

EIGHT

(Day #3 – Saturday Evening)

I took a leisurely shower and put on makeup like a big girl. My dress was snowy white with cap sleeves, a high waist, and fluffy waves of silk organza falling just past my knees. I wore a pretty pair of pink kitten heels to add a pop of color.

With a matching handbag under my arm, I peeked out the window on the front door, waiting for Matty. I didn't know if Ransom was home, and I knew I shouldn't care, but I did. And I did not want to make a big production out of Matty picking me up for this date.

At the exact stroke of six, a shiny black sedan pulled up at the curb. Matty parked, then walked up the drive. Before he could raise his hand to ring the bell, I met him on the doorstep.

"Ready?" I said.

"You look beautiful, Elli," he said and leaned down to kiss my cheek. "And you smell even nicer."

"Thanks, Matty. You, too. Look nice," I said.

He wore a suit the color of a mocha latte with a crisp white shirt and tie. I never saw him in suits unless I visited the campus. His laid-back style usually included Oakley sunglasses and worn surf tees.

It took all my concentration not to glance over at Ransom's house as we walked to the car. Matty opened the passenger side door for me. "Kyra let you borrow the car?" I asked.

"More like insisted." Matty drove a vintage Land Cruiser with a hardtop he rarely kept on. It rode like a Jeep on safari: bumpy, rocky, and rough. It made me feel like I was on adventure with Indiana Jones. "She felt this was more appropriate to take a date to the dance."

"How are Kyra and the new baby?" Matty's firefighter brother and his yoga instructor wife welcomed a daughter over the summer. Their third child in as many years. It suited them.

"She's a doll. Starting to crawl now, getting into things like her big brothers. I'm watching them next weekend so Pete can take Kyra to the mall in Savannah. Play Santa and get the shopping done." Where I thought watching three kids under three would be slightly less pleasant than a trio of root canals, Matty loved it. Though five years younger than me, his biological clock ticked loudly and mine was broken.

We made banal conversation on the drive to the south side of the island. He asked me about Mr. and Mrs. Ballantyne and I asked him how he liked being on the Ballantyne board. It was at least the third time I'd asked him a variation on that question in about a week. Though I doubt he noticed since he kept answering. Our conversations of late were awkward. The easy-going friendship we'd built struggled under the self-conscious weight of our dating.

After what seemed like three hours, but was closer to twenty minutes, we arrived at Harborside Plantation, probably the largest residential community on the island. It had a four-lane entry gate and we zipped through with Matty's school-issued security pass. Tall palms bordered the drive along with enough foliage and ferns to hide the homes scattered amongst two golf courses. At the very southernmost tip was the Harborside Lighthouse, which was red and white striped and postcard perfect.

Matty pulled into a narrow drive just short of the Harborside shops. An embossed plaque on the entry gate said Seabrook Preparatory. He parked right up front. Being headmaster had privileges.

Matty held my hand as we walked into the main building. Dim lights illuminated the quiet hallways. Our footsteps echoed on the tile floor. With a quick squeeze to my hand, he opened the door to the gymnasium. It was all a dazzle with twinkle lights and white balloons and glittered streamers hanging from the ceiling.

The energy was high. School was almost out for the holidays and celebration vibrated all around. As did the music. It began to thump and kids raised their hands high, dancing and laughing to the beat. Lots and lots of kids. Students crowded the gym floor.

Matty and I joined a group of teachers talking about the new curriculum for the next semester. As they spoke, a hot flash crept up my back and settled on my neck. I gave myself a mental high-five for deciding to pin my hair up as if going to the prom. But it wasn't enough. The heat kept coming and I started to feel woozy. Lightheaded. I casually reached out to a nearby table to steady myself.

A mild hot flash rarely made me dizzy. Then I remembered I'd forgotten to eat. Matty had suggested we dine after the dance, which worked for me. As long as I ate a snack, as in a normal dinner meal. Then I'd just eat another one later with Matty. But I'd forgotten my first dinner. I'm not one to skip a meal and I have the tight waistbands to prove it. Even the elastic ones.

"Matty?" I don't think he heard me over the booming music, so I raised my voice. "Hey, Matty?"

He noticed me leaning on the table and came over. "What's up, Elli? You look pale." He put his hands on my arms as if to steady me.

"Do you happen to have a spare candy bar in your desk? Or maybe there's a nearby vending machine?"

He took in my shaky pale state. "I can do better than a candy bar." He grabbed my hand and led me through the crowd.

We wove through teachers and students, talking and dancing, to get to a set of double doors on the far side. They opened with a loud ka-dunk-dunk, and we were in the hall. The air felt cool and fresh, even for a school hallway.

The music faded as we followed corridor after corridor to the center of the school. Seabrook Preparatory didn't have a cafeteria, it had a full kitchen and dining room. Through another set of double doors, this time swinging, we entered a kitchen to make Chef Ramsey envious. Shiny, clean, all sparkling steel: pots, knives, tables.

Matty set me on a stool by the long island, then went to the walk-in refrigerator. He pulled out a tray of lasagna and two containers: shredded mozzarella and an aromatic marinara. He dished up two portions, added the sauce and cheese and popped them into a commercial microwave. He poured a Pepsi—the Mexican in a bottle kind (no high fructose corn syrup in this kitchen)—over a tall glass of ice and stuck in a straw. "This should help."

It did. Sugar and caffeine cooled me down and settled my shakes. The music still beat, though it sounded distant, entertaining folks dancing in another world.

"We still on for shopping tomorrow?" Matty asked. "I've got a huge list."

"Me, too. I haven't started, but Christmas is still almost two weeks away. No need to rush," I said. "Are your parents coming down from Maine?"

"Dad wants to sail to Bimini when they get here. Take Pete's *Fire Escape* down the coast. Mom isn't having it. She doesn't want a moment away from the grandkids."

"And did Kyra suggest they take the grandkids with them?"

He laughed. "You know it. She said they all could go to Bimini and leave her behind. Best Christmas vacation ever. She might actually get some sleep."

The microwave binged and Matty served us the most delicious plates of tangy lasagna layered with fresh ricotta and a sweet basil marinara. The cheese was melty perfection and I covered my entire front side in napkins.

We must have spent an hour talking over pasta and Pepsi. Laughing and sharing. The old Matty and Elliott.

"Ready for dessert, Miss Lisbon?" he asked, and whisked our plates to the sink.

"Why, yes, Headmaster Gannon. And just so you know, the answer to that question shall always be yes."

He helped me off the stool with his hand in mine.

"Thank you for dinner," I said.

"Thank you for joining me. I wouldn't want to be the only guy at the school dance without a date." He twirled me around, then pulled me close.

"Is this the dessert you speak of?"

"It could be." He leaned down and kissed me. His hand still in mine, wrapped around to the small of my back.

The music continued to thump and voices got louder, laughing and talking. A couple came in the door just as we stepped apart.

"Headmaster Gannon," the woman said. "I didn't know you were back here."

"Elli, you know our head chef, Rosa," Matty said.

"Of course. Nice to see you. Matty saved me from a low-sugar fainting spell with a plate of your lasagna. It was fantastic."

"Thank you," she said. "My husband and I are going to sneak a plate ourselves."

We left them to their dinner and went back to the gym. Matty spoke with the dj. The music switched from a thumping techno beat to '80s New Wave and we danced to Siouxsie and the Banshees, Duran Duran, Bow Wow Wow. Better to work off the pasta and make room for dessert.

We took a break for cupcakes and punch. Gorgeous frosted cakes arranged on tiered trays, their blue and white frosting glittering under the twinkle lights. Matty handed me a plastic cup of orange punch and I took a big sip.

The three-year-old inside of me nearly spit that shit out. But I choked it down like the grown-up I am. It tasted funny. Strange. Almost familiar. "Who made this?" I asked.

"Mrs. Ortiz," Matty said. He gestured to a woman in a red floral skirt and holiday sweater. "She's a guest lecturer in the biology department. Loves teas and herbs. Her punch takes some getting used to, but we can't talk her out of making it."

"¡Hola!" Mrs. Ortiz, aka Mamacita, said. "Te ves hermosa, Señorita Elliott."

"Mamacita, what a surprise to see you here," I said.

"You know each other?" Matty said. "Oh right, *The Nutcracker*. I didn't even think about it. Her son is in it."

"Si, si, Vigo," Mamacita said. "He was your favorite student, right, Señor Gannon?"

"Your son is Vigo Ortiz?" I asked.

"Si," she said. "I assumed you knew."

"I did not know." I didn't know if I was surprised or shocked. "I didn't realize Vigo was your son or Lexie was your son's girlfriend or you worked at the school."

"Very tragic. Such a lovely girl." She patted my arm and went to man the punch bowl.

I discreetly tossed my nearly full punch cup in the gray rubber bin next to the table, then dry swallowed the cupcake.

The dj started playing a ballad and Matty pulled me to the dance floor. I swayed out of habit, my mind still twenty feet behind us at the punch table.

I could not believe Mamacita did not mention Vigo to me yesterday. Not one time. Not even a hint that her son had been dating Lexie. Of course Lexie went over to Mamacita's. Probably visited her house a hundred times. Including that garden of crazy.

Matty gently lifted my chin so our eyes met. "Hello? Elliott? Where did you go?"

"I'm right here."

"I've been talking for five minutes and not a single response. Thought maybe you fell asleep on me."

"I'm sorry. I'm not napping, just thinking about Lexie Allen and Vigo Ortiz. It's odd Mamacita never told me her son was Lexie's boyfriend. And even odder...more odd? Odder still? Lexie's boyfriend's mother grows the very berries that killed her."

He nodded slowly. "Definitely a coincidence, but it's a small island and gossip travels quickly. Maybe Mamacita was only protecting her son?"

I swayed to the left, then the right, trying to keep time with the music. "Protecting him from what?"

"Let's not start down that path," he said in a low voice.

I'd questioned one of his students in a murder case a few months earlier and it fractured our friendship. More of a hairline than a full break, but neither one of us wanted to risk another one.

"What did Mamacita say about Lexie?" Matty asked.

"Niceties. Very polite. Nothing to indicate she'd known her personally, practically as family, for an extended time. She called Lexie a nice girl. Really enjoyed going to the garden. That she liked to experiment with ingredients."

"Is it such a stretch to believe Lexie baked the wrong berries into her cake? Or that maybe she committed suicide?"

"Suicide?" I said and stopped swaying. "She was happy and well-liked and had her entire life in front of her."

"Teenagers hide a lot of emotion."

"So she bakes a cupcake to kill herself?"

Matty leaned in and lowered his voice. "She gets dressed up and takes her cupcakes to the theatre. Very dramatic. Something a teenager would do."

"That's ludicrous. You sound like—" I was about to say Ransom, but I stopped myself. "Like you're crazy. Lexie Allen did not kill herself. How is that more plausible than her boyfriend killing her?"

"What possible reason did he have?" Matty asked and dropped his hands from my waist. "I know Vigo. He's a good kid. He's a gentle soul. Not a violent bone in his body."

"You're wrong about that." I'd seen the shot-up range poster to prove it.

Matty ran a hand through his hair. "Elli, this isn't for us to debate. Especially not here."

I grabbed his wrist and pulled him through the crowd of couples and into the hall. "You're right, this isn't a debate. I don't want to fight."

"Me, neither," he said. "Let the police handle this. It's their job."

"It's mine, too."

"Only because you want it to be."

"Why do you not want it to be? Why does it bother you so much?"

"Because you put yourself in danger. You were attacked, Elliott." His normally soft features clenched with frustration and he grabbed my shoulders. "You were almost killed twice in six months working those PI cases. First Leo Hirschorn, then Gil Goodsen, now Lexie Allen."

"But I wasn't killed. I'm right here and I'm fine," I said. "Nothing bad is going to happen on this case. I know what I'm doing and I'm good at it."

He let me go and leaned against the wall. Muffled music and laughter surrounded us and echoed down the corridor. "You don't know what will happen. To you or anyone else. You're out there stirring up emotions and disrupting lives, and why? Because you don't want to accept it was an accident."

"Lexie Allen's life got disrupted. It wasn't suicide or an accident." I didn't add that no one else thought it was those things, either. Even though Ransom didn't admit to me it was murder, I knew him, and that story about an accident was nonsense. I felt like I'd betray Ransom if I told Matty. Which only made me feel awkward for keeping it from him. The space between us may have only been three feet, but the distance spanned an emotional slot canyon, with us on opposite ends, one up, one down, and no tangible way to reach each other.

"Matty—"

All sorts of screams and shouts let loose from inside the gymnasium. The doors flew open and students flooded the halls. They were screaming, laughing, and covered in fluffy white goop.

A panicked teacher came out with her brow all creased and her hands wrung together. "I'm sorry, Mr. Gannon. I left my post for five minutes and someone hit a switch," she shouted over the melee. "It was the punch. It went right through me." Her stomach gurgled loud enough for me to hear and she covered her stomach with her hand.

"The bleachers or the basketball hoops?" Matty asked and jogged toward the doors.

"The hoops. They rigged the streamers to cans of Reddi Whip or something. I don't know how they did it, but, well..."

Whipped cream covered the floor, the tables, the people, and even the balloons. Matty stood on a bench and shouted over the crowd. "Slowly, please, everyone slowly to the exits."

A food fight erupted at the cupcake table and I thanked all things holy I wasn't near the barrel of orange punch in my glorious white dress. I edged toward the door.

The gurgly teacher joined us. "I called the fire department. Some of those rigged cans are still in the rafters and tied to the hoops."

We all looked up.

One hot mess.

"They said they'd get here when they could. There was a big fire over in Summerton. A rig went to help." She shrugged. "Going to be awhile, I think." She turned to help herd students toward the exit.

"I'm sorry, Elli. It'll be a couple hours," Matty said to me.

"Can I do something?"

"I've got plenty of teachers to help, but I'll be tied up untangling this mess."

"Don't worry about me, I understand. I'll get a ride home. But Matty, your job is like mine. It's more than the job description. Sometimes I've got to untangle the mess, too."

We stared at each other in the midst of the pandemonium. He softly touched my cheek, then went into the storm.

I carefully stepped across the slick floor, out the doors, and into the hall. Once outside, I walked along the sidewalk around the school to the front lot. I sat on a bench in the quad and dialed Sid.

"You still home alone for the weekend?" I asked.

"Milo's hosting a poker game," she said.

"And you passed?"

"I've taken the largest pots for the last three games. Milo suggested I skip this one."

"Want to go on a stakeout?"

Sid and I sat in her car facing the rear exit of the Sea Pine Island Community Theatre. She brought two bags of Popcorn Indiana: Kettlecorn for me, Movie Theatre for her. We munched and watched the quiet lot.

"The performance ended an hour ago," she said. "How long does it take for them to change?"

"Can't be much longer," I said. "The little ones left within fifteen minutes. And they wore just as much makeup."

"You think Matty will ever be okay with your PI sideline?"

"He used to be, before the Hirschorn murder in May."

"Which also happens to be the first time he kissed you. Coincidence, Miss Marple?"

I stuffed a handful of popcorn in my mouth and shrugged. Matty's kiss that night wasn't of the goodnight, see you tomorrow variety. It was a throw me down, hands up my dress, let's get it on kind. And I had loved it.

"Matty said it was just a coincidence that Lexie's boyfriend's mother grew a garden of death berries, the same ones that killed her."

"And you don't believe in coincidences?"

"I do. Small ones, not big ones. And a boyfriend living in a house ten feet from a patch of rare killer fruit that took his girlfriend's life is a big one."

"How rare is this killer fruit?" Sid asked and took a swig from a water bottle.

"Rare enough. Mamacita said it grows on the side of the road, but Vigo didn't need to go berry picking in the wild thicket along I-

95. He only had to step outside his back door."

"And the police are sure that's what killed her?"

"Harry Fleet confirmed poisoning, though the tox results won't be back until after the New Year."

"So no surprises?"

"No surprises there," I said and gulped down water from my own bottle. "The surprise came from the dry cleaner. Lexie Allen worked as a sous chef at the Wharf."

"The dry cleaner told you this?"

"I showed Lexie's stub to the dry cleaner who handed me two white chef's coats from the Wharf. Went over to talk to Chef Carmichael and he told me."

"Seriously? She was a chef? And a dancer? And a college student? How old was this girl?"

"Seriously. Nineteen. According to Carmichael, she moved from Charlotte in November to work for him. I don't know if she dropped out or transferred. The only university around here is USC, and I don't think the satellite campus offers a full dance program."

"Probably not," she said.

We each hit the halfway spot of our popcorn and switched bags. "There's more," I said. "Lexie was auditioning for some kind of cook-off in Savannah. Her fellow sous chef, an unfriendly girl with blue hair named Rory, was her main competition. And get this, the competition is tomorrow."

"Get out."

"Yep." I stopped mid-reach into the bag and pointed toward the door. "Here they come."

Seven people trouped out, including Vigo, Courtney, and Berg. They shuffled over to a cluster of cars parked in the first row. We were four spots over to their right and three rows back.

"You think they'll go out?" I asked.

"Nah. Their friend just died. They look kind of solemn."

Sid's car windows were all down, but we couldn't hear what they were saying, only a low rumble of voices as the group leaned on cars, heads mostly down.

"Yeah, probably go back to their condo and order a pizza," I said. We sat in silence and watched the dancers brood. "You're a good friend to pick me up and help me. I know it's kind of boring sometimes."

She waved me off. "No big. I was binge watching tv again. Addicted to *Hannibal*."

"You finished *Alias*?"

"I'm on a Gina Torres kick. Watched all of *Suits*. Fabulous, by the way, thanks for the recommendation. Now I'm on *Hannibal*. Did you know Gina's married to Lawrence Fishburne in real life?"

"I did not know," I said. "Hey, they're leaving."

"Should we follow?"

"Sure, we put in this much time, might as well see it through."

Vigo, Courtney and Berg got into separate cars. Within seconds, red taillights lit up and the cars backed out. They drove in a straight line diagonally across the lot and onto Cabana Boulevard.

"Well, not going to the condo," Sid said after they passed the turnaround and headed toward the south side of the island.

Traffic was heavier than usual, even for a Saturday night. Visitors had been arriving for days, ready to spend the holidays on the island. By next week, every condo, rental, and hotel room would be occupied until the first week in January.

Sid followed and weaved through the cars packing Cabana. We hit the large traffic circle right before Harborside Plantation and followed it all the way around, now heading toward South Pebble Beach. The car parade turned into the drive for Bar Row.

Sid found a spot in the corner and parked facing the entrance. Music spilled over the low buildings, mixed with loud conversation and laughter. A line of cabs waited to the side of the front walk. People with plastic cups zigzagged across the asphalt.

"I'm just putting this out there," I said. "If you die by poison cake, or any means, really, for the whole next week, I'm not going out to the party bar. I'm home eating a pizza."

"Word."

I slipped off my pink kitten heels and swapped them for a pair of flip flops. It was way too chilly for them, but I didn't want to wear my pretty shoes in that sticky sin palace. I took the pins out of my hair and shook it free to make it look more casual. More beachy. More I'm young enough to be hanging out at this place. "Let's do this."

The beefy man at the door stamped our hands (without even asking for ID), and we squeezed onto the patio. It was loud, crowded, and smelled faintly of barf. Four different bars (all with the same owner, I was betting) faced an open patio. Each establishment had its own décor. One had a dance floor, the second a wall of sporting events on flat screens, the third catered to the pool table crowd. The last one was basically a crowded space lined with bar tops and limited seating.

Vigo wore his hair messy and stood about eight inches taller than the average guy, so it wasn't too difficult to tail him. He and his friends went for the dancing bar. A pair of girls waved them over to their table.

Sid and I wedged ourselves between two high tops near the wall, keeping the group within eyesight. Courtney approached Vigo, carrying two drinks in plastic cups, and sat down. They weren't old enough to drink alcohol, but those cups could've held root beer. On the other hand, I didn't know how strictly the bartenders followed the booze law or what kind of IDs Courtney and Co. showed at the door.

A girl with short hair joined the group. She squeezed in tight next to Vigo. He turned and kissed her. Light on the cheek, innocent enough until he put his arm around her and she put her hand on his thigh. They tucked their heads together in conversation. Lots of nodding and talking, her lips close to his ear. Vigo pulled back and handed her his drink. She sipped, then lifted her head to look around the room, as if checking the place out.

"Well, well," I said and leaned close to Sid so she could hear me. The music beat so hard, I felt it in my chest. "That's Rory, from the Wharf. Lexie's competition for the cook-off tomorrow."

"Looks like she was also competition for Lexie's boyfriend," Sid shouted.

"Not anymore," I said.

I pushed my way to the bar and ordered us two of their house specialties. It was half daiquiri, half piña colada, and half disgusting. It was both over-poured and watery at the same time.

We nursed them for nearly two hours. The troupe stayed in the same spot the entire night. Not one got up to dance or mingle or smoke or breathe fresh air. Vigo huddled with Rory like a conspirator plotting world domination, Courtney moped with a trio of girlfriends, and Berg never showed up.

My lower back ached from standing against the wall and my head ached from cheap booze and blaring monotonous music and I would've jumped for joy when they finally left had it not been physically impossible from cramps in seven different muscle groups.

Sid tailed them all the way to their condo, then dropped me off at my cottage. I trudged up the stairs to my room, and after a thorough face and upper body scrub, I threw on an old Dodgers tee and snuggled into bed.

Sid deserved an extra special Christmas gift after tonight. But it was worth it. Vigo went up a notch on my suspect list. His mother grew the same kind of poison berries that killed his girlfriend, and it looked like he had another hottie on the side, who also happened to be competing against Lexie for a coveted spot in a local cook-off. Maybe Vigo decided Rory needed an advantage. And he figured out how to give it to her.

NINE

(Day #4 – Sunday Morning)

The sun had yet to rise when I woke Sunday morning. I rolled over to stay snuggled, but couldn't get back to sleep. I put on a robe and wandered downstairs to my desktop computer which shared its space with my mini Christmas tree. While the lights twinkled and the computer booted up, I grabbed a bowl of cereal and opened the slider to the patio deck. The sound of the waves filtered through the screen while I ate my Cap'n Crunch, then gulped down the sugary milk at the bottom of the bowl.

I typed Stream Kitchen into the Google machine and it returned one billion results. Ish. The third link was the one I wanted. The initial landing page splashed onto the screen. A shiny kitchen with a pair of chefs in white coats gripping panhandles over a gas stove with wicked flames. It didn't look like an afternoon cook-off, it looked like a reality show competition. Surprisingly, there wasn't a lot of information on the show, but the contact information was current.

After retrieving my phone from the charger upstairs on my nightstand, I carried it to the computer and dialed the number. Two rings later, a recorded message informed me that auditions were closed, callbacks needed to be on set an hour before their slot either today or tomorrow, and filming began at seven a.m. sharp.

My phone clock said it was seven thirty-seven. The young prep cook from the Wharf said she thought Rory needed to be there today, but after brunch. Plenty of time for me to zip over and see what was what.

I rinsed my bowl and stuck it in the drying rack, then popped into the shower. I was almost looking forward to the day. Matty and I had shopping plans at eleven, which included lunch, I hoped. I'm not a happy shopper. I'd rather buy via mouse-click than traipse through crowded public retail villages, operating on sensory overload as I simultaneously avoided touching every germy surface while choosing appropriate gifts. But Matty enjoyed the holiday-ness of it. The carols and bells and kids in line for Santa. But the mall had an Orange Julius, so there was that.

Dressed in a festive green linen tunic and long, flowy white pants, I grabbed a floral sun hat, my hipster handbag, a small box of decorations, and hit the road.

I checked in at the Big House to make sure the tree-trimming crew had arrived on time. Two workers were setting up tall aluminum ladders on either side of the tree, while four men unloaded boxes and spare lights. I showed them my personal box for beneath the tree. A surprise to tie the whole thing together. With a sticky bun from Carla's kitchen, I was back on the road and sailing over the Palmetto Bridge shortly after eight.

The tide was low, almost nonexistent. Miles of oyster beds covered the sea floor and their familiar brackish aroma filled the air. The long, low bridge connected Sea Pine Island to the rest of South Carolina. I sped onto the mainland and entered Summerton, a lowcountry town filled with diverse residents, major strip centers, and at the far edges, I-95 which led north to Maine and south to Florida.

I took the back road to Savannah, a town whose popularity grew after the release of *Midnight in the Garden of Good and Evil*. A Southern charmer of an insider's peek behind a genteel society, eccentric residents, and, of course, a salacious murder.

It took thirty-two minutes to reach the Talmadge Memorial

Bridge. I drove two hundred feet over the river and into Historic Savannah. I wasn't going far. The set address on the Stream Kitchen website was for a warehouse near the waterfront.

Parking was limited in that section of town. Somewhat industrial, down from the quaint shops and river boats, but somehow still enchanting. Majestic oaks and magnolias lined the streets, cobblestone walks led to once-stately homes. Even an enormous barge stacked high with metal containers felt quixotic as it navigated the Savannah River.

A plain metal door marked 127A faced a narrow alley and I was able to steer the Mini into a half-spot between the crumbling curb and the sidewalk about ten feet from the entrance. It felt deserted, isolated. Until I entered the warehouse.

Cables and lights and equipment nearly blocked the entrance. Through a pair of overhead doors on the far side, people shouted commands while other people scrambled to answer them. A round table was set off to one side of the entry room, empty chairs pushed back as if a meeting had recently adjourned. Paper plates with half-eaten pastries littered the table along with plastic utensils and discarded napkins. I followed the shouts past the table, through the open overhead door, and into the most wondrous kitchen-like set. It was *MasterChef* meets *The Next Food Network Star*.

Five mahogany islands spanned the room, each at least twenty feet long. Two sets of stainless burners, double sinks, and ovens were installed on each. As were thick chopping blocks and white cutting boards. Each pristine work area gleamed under dozens of can lights.

"We're filming," a man shouted. "This is a go."

A young girl carried a black and white clapper board to the far wall where a fancy logo had been mounted. Stream Kitchen, it said. She slapped down the clapper and rushed out of the shot.

The noise level stayed at shouting, so I assumed the cameras were shooting for background. Another young girl approached me. "Name and slot time?" she asked.

"Elliott Lisbon, but no slot time—"

"Auditions are over. This is a closed set. Unless you're a parent, then I'll need your kid's name and slot time. We'll have bleachers set up next week."

"Definitely not a parent," I said. "I'm here about one of your contestants."

"Press isn't allowed on set," she said, then shouted over her shoulder. "Mark, call security. They've got to man this door better. I don't have time for this." Fran Banks was typed on a lanyard badge around her neck. She wore a headset and clicked the tiny button on the hanging wire. "How much longer 'til the voiceover talent gets here?" She turned to me. "You're still here? Ma'am, I need you to leave. We'll take your credentials next week. Check in with Penny on your way out. We'll put you on the list."

"I'm not press," I said as she tried to hurry me out of the room. "I'm here about Lexie Allen."

That stopped her.

"I assume you heard?" I asked.

"Mark, the producer, he told us yesterday," she said. "Lexie was here, what? Wednesday, Thursday? Hard to believe."

The young girl with the clapper approached us, holding out a Starbucks cup with a cardboard wrapper.

"I asked for this an hour ago," Fran snapped.

"The delivery guy said the line was out the door," the girl said. Her lanyard said *intern* with "Penny" scribbled underneath it. She twisted her hands together. "He said he got here as fast as he could."

"It's cold," Fran said and took another long sip. "Mark!" she shouted into the room. "Dammit, Mark." She clicked the headset button. "Someone get Mark to the front of the set. Now." She turned to me. "You'll probably want to speak with our producer. If I can find him."

"He's out by the—" Penny said.

"Lord, girl, don't lurk. Go get him," she said, and then under her breath, but loud enough for everyone to hear, "Interns. More hassle than they're worth."

Penny spun around and ran into a tall man with curly hair and a faded tee. His badge credentials said Mark Malone. He carefully righted Penny and moved around her.

"What's up, Fran? I've got the lighting crew dangling from the rafter in B."

"This woman is here about Lexie Allen," Fran said. "She's all yours." She hurried off, talking into her headset and shouting to passersby at the same time.

I stuck out my hand, even though I hate the convention, and repeated my intro. "I'm Elli Lisbon, with the Ballantyne. I'm working with the Sea Pine police on the Lexie Allen case."

"Great girl, that one. And she could really cook," he said. A camera rolled by with a large man in a driver's chair. Mark guided me out of the way and over to a food table with picked over fruits and bagels and spreads.

"I've never heard of Stream Kitchen. Can you tell me about it?"

"We're new this year. For the Kitchen Cuisine Channel. Online. Like YouTubeTV or Crackle. Stream Kitchen is the ultimate battle for Southern chefs."

"And Lexie Allen was a contestant?"

"Almost. She came so close," he said. He sounded like a surfer hopped up on coffee and sugar. Speaking of, Penny the intern approached with another Starbucks cup and handed it to him. "Thanks, doll."

"It's not a cook-off?" I said. "I'd heard Lexie was auditioning for a cook-off."

"Her audition *was* a cook-off. She and another local chef here in Savannah. They were battling for the last spot on the show. Turns out the girls were rivals. Couldn't even script it, their catfights were so fierce."

"You mean Rory?"

"You know her? Hellfire, that one. She's on the show now. Has a good shot at winning the whole thing."

I watched Penny linger at the snack table. Lurking, as the headset gal put it.

"What does the winner get?"

"The jackpot. Their own show on the Stream Kitchen, streaming live each week. Showcasing local flavors around the South. Texas BBQ vs. Carolina BBQ, that kind of thing. Plus a blog tour stopping at all the top cooking magazines and a product line of their signature dish."

"Mark! Need you in Studio B," a male voice hollered. "Pronto, man."

He took a big swig of the coffee, then tossed it in the trash by the table. "Sorry to hear about Lexie. She would've been one tough cookie to beat."

Penny still lurked, so I moseyed over, surveying the bagel selection. "Did you know Lexie Allen?"

"Sure, I know all the contestants." She kept her head down and studied a jam jar. "I had to prepare their credentials."

"Even the ones who hadn't made it?"

"Lexie Allen made it. So did Rory Throckmorton. Mark was stringing them along, playing them against one another. Made them audition against each other four times. Today was the final audition. But they didn't know he already decided to keep them both. Tell one today, make a big deal out of it. Then bring the other one back for the first round of competition."

"Why split it up?"

"The surprise, I guess. He really liked to see them fight. And they both really, *really* wanted on the show. It got ugly. And Mark loved it."

Fran's shouting voice got louder and I noticed her stalking toward us. So did Penny, and she scurried away.

With a quick wave to Fran, who ignored me, I carefully stepped through the warehouse. With its massive can lights, thick cables and bustling crew, it reminded me of backstage at the theatre. Lexie would've felt at home there. Too bad she never got the chance.

I needed to find out more about this Rory Throckmorton. First I see her out snuggling Lexie's boyfriend, then I discover she was in a heated battle for a reality show. Maybe Rory didn't want to wait until the producer made his decision on who would join the competition. Maybe she made it for him.

TEN

(Day #4 – Sunday Afternoon)

I flipped open the protective cover on my phone and saw a missed call and a text message, both from Matty. He canceled our shopping date. Still handling the whipped topping debacle from last night's dance. Parents to be called, damages to be assessed. And school let out for the holiday break in a matter of days.

I was secretly relieved to not have to go shopping. I'd much rather shoot down my list as if on a game show where the contestant who finishes first advances to the bonus round. I always bought thoughtful gifts, mind you. It just didn't take me all day to do it.

Oh! Speaking of shooting. I had just passed the exit for the only gun club within a hundred miles. I hit the gas, changed lanes and took the next exit. After a quick u-turn, I was in the lot seven minutes later. Rory may have jumped to the top spot on my suspect list, but Vigo was the next name down.

Newly built in the last year, the Summerton Gun Club boasted over forty-thousand square feet of indoor shooting luxury. I'd personally never been there, but it could be seen from the highway in every direction. The building itself was imposing with a stucco exterior trimmed in fieldstones. Automatic doors whisked open as I approached, and a girl at the counter greeted me before I got both feet on the entrance rug.

"Welcome to the Summerton Gun Club. How are you doing today?" She wore a hunter green polo with an elaborate SGC crest embroidered on front.

"I'm fine, thank you." I looked around. Wood-beamed rafters two stories above, a gourmet coffee café near the lobby, and a solid ten-thousand square feet of retail space. "I don't know where to start."

"I'm happy to set up a tour," she replied. "Or you can walk around on your own. We also have range masters available to answer questions."

"I'll look around first, if that's okay."

"Take your time. I'm here if you need me."

Racks of shirts, pants, and bags dominated the center of the store. All with the gold SGC logo emblazoned on them. There was even an entire row dedicated to children, including gun cases and carryall bags. In splashy pinks and blues. The store was mostly empty except for a handful of green polo-ed employees, all friendly and clean-cut in a former military, off-duty cop kind of way.

Glass cases filled with firearms lined three of the walls. On the left and back walls were the handguns, on the right were the long guns. Special glass cases set to the side held even more. I browsed, but stood away from the displays, not getting too close. I'd never fired a gun, never wanted to own one, either. I'd once had a gun pointed at me during a case and it still unsettled me.

I ended up in the far corner near a wall of windows overlooking a block of shooting lanes. Tables and chairs were set up for observers alongside racks of accessories like goggles and fanny packs and earplugs. Several people stood in the shooting booths, firing handguns. Targets hung from clips at different distances down the lanes in the concrete room. Kind of crowded for a Sunday mid-morning.

I wandered toward a check-in counter, not sure how to get the information I needed. Perhaps Vigo wasn't such a great shot. Perhaps anyone could hit the target. No one said you had to place your paper target at the farthest distance.

"May I help you?" a young man in a green uniform shirt asked me.

"I hope so. I've never been here before, but a good friend of mine recommended it. Said you're the best facility in the state."

"You're not a member?"

"A member of what?"

"We're a membership club, but we're also open to the public," he said and handed me a brochure.

Memberships started at two hundred dollars a month and went up to seven grand. For a shooting range? It included access to their VIP lounge and exclusive restaurant. Like a country club, but with guns.

"You can bring your own firearm or rent one of ours," he said, barely interested in our conversation.

"I can rent a firearm? For how long?"

"By the hour. You need to buy your own ammo."

"How much does all this cost?"

"Depends on the firearm. For you, probably a nine mil Glock. It's fifteen an hour, plus rounds. The lane is twenty an hour."

I'd never once considered owning a gun, even though many private investigators carried them. I thought a concealed weapons permit only required a class and a fee. Maybe a qualification test. I made a mental note to check with SLED, the South Carolina Law Enforcement Division.

"Okay, I'll start with that," I said. I took my PI pursuit seriously. Probably a good idea to try one before I took the class. And it might help me get over my trepidation from my last encounter with a gun to actually hold one.

"Driver's license?"

I handed him my license and took out my credit card. I wondered if I could expense it to the Ballantyne. I didn't see why not, since my training was part of the program.

"My friend comes here all the time. The one who recommended you," I said. "Maybe you know him? Vigo Ortiz?"

The kid slid my license through the plastic reader attached to his computer screen, then stuck it in a slotted tray. He handed me a pair of goggles, massive earmuff noise protectors, and a paper target. "Don't know him."

"Maybe this isn't the shooting range he was talking about," I said and inspected the equipment. I squinted behind him to the bin he pulled them out of. I could barely make out three words, though I noticed one of them was "clean."

He put a gun on the counter with a box of nine millimeter rounds. I knew that because it said so on the box. "Lane thirteen," he said. "Through the first door, then the second, through that room, all the way down on the right. Check out on your way out." He went back to tapping on the keyboard.

"Could you look him up in the computer? My friend? It should say whether or not he comes here, right?"

"Sorry, ma'am, we don't give out personal information. We're a private club."

"But it's also public."

"Not the information."

I gathered the gun paraphernalia and dropped it at a side table near the range entrance. I discreetly slathered hand-sani on the puffy ear muffs and goggles. Not everyone's definition of clean matched mine. As it dried, I realized the kid just handed me a gun and bullets and told me to go shoot. No instruction, no training, no supervision. I didn't know how to hold a gun properly, how to load it, or where to find the safety. I'd seen training videos during my ballistics classes in college, but that was twenty years earlier, and we studied the bullets after they were fired, not before. I didn't even know what to do with the target.

I opened the folded paper. It was nothing like the one in Vigo's room. His was a person outline, this one had two black round targets, one on the left, one on the right, each with three concentric circles. Like the Target logo, only black. Maybe Summerton wasn't the shooting range Vigo went to.

I picked up my gear and headed back to the check-in counter. The kid was gone. I hung around for a few minutes, but he didn't return. I wandered to an alcove around the corner from the range door. On one side was a bank of observation windows overlooking another set of shooting lanes. On the opposite wall were eight different targets hanging in frames. Different shapes, circles and squares, and bright colors like lime green and hot pink. Each frame had a price sticker ranging from one to three dollars. The last target on the bottom row was identical to the one in Vigo's closet, minus the bullet holes. It was three bucks.

Below the target frames, several sheets of paper were pinned to the wall. A competition practice roster. I looked closer. A hall of fame of sorts. Initials with some kind of score system. Number two in the under-twenty category: V. Oritz with a target symbol next to his name, the same shape and color as the one I saw in his closet.

"Hey, Lieutenant," a voice said from around the corner. "You teaching a class today?"

"Not today," a familiar voice said. "I'm here to see someone."

I peeked. The counter kid had returned and was chatting with Ransom, who was walking my way.

I ducked back, my arms still loaded with gun supplies, and tried to act casual.

"Well, Elli Lisbon," he said. "What a surprise."

"Who ratted me out? One of those employees wandering around is Sea Pine police, right?"

"Yeah. A range master. He got skittish when he saw you rent a gun." Ransom looked down at the bundle in my arms. "The Glock. Nice choice. You plan on shooting it?"

"That's why I rented it. Figured I should practice before I take my CWP class."

He nodded toward the target wall. "Thinking of trying something fancy your first time out?"

"Actually, I was. Then I noticed something interesting." I gestured with my elbow to V. Oritz on the competition score sheet. "Name number two. He's Lexie Allen's boyfriend."

He glanced at it. "Oritz? You mean Vigo Ortiz?"

"Close enough, and notice there's the—" I stopped before I

mentioned the target I'd seen. "Pointing out it's unusual. Lexie gets killed and her boyfriend happens to be an excellent marksman."

"She was accidentally poisoned, not shot."

"Still going with accidentally?"

"You'll need a better suspect if you're going to convince me otherwise."

"I'm working on it," I said.

"So I hear. I've received calls from Chef Carmichael at the Wharf, Olga at the QuickClean, and Inga Dalrymple from the dance studio."

"Inga? Why?"

"She noticed you hanging around the theatre parking lot after hours."

"Apparently I'm the only one on the island who believes in discreet."

"With you getting that much notice, I wonder how discreet you're being, and what you're up to."

"I'm discreet and I'm onto something good," I said and shifted the awkward bundle still in my arms.

"Have you ever shot a gun, Red?" He took the gun and ammo from my arms, set them on the table. Then the goggles, ear muffs, and paper target.

"I have not." I prepared for battle. When it came to my discreet investigations, no way he wanted me shooting guns. He didn't even want me talking to the dry cleaner.

"Let me help you. I've got some time."

"You're going to help me?" I asked with so much incredulity in my voice, it cracked.

"Unless you'd rather I didn't."

"No, no, I'd love it. Thank you." I was grateful and relieved. I wasn't sure I could gracefully return the gun five minutes after I rented it, without even firing a single shot, in front of Nick Ransom. But no way was I going to waltz into a shooting range and figure it out on my own.

Ransom picked up the gun, slid the top part back, showed me

the empty chamber. "If it was loaded, the round would've popped out. But you can see it's empty." He squared my shoulders until I faced the wall. The observation windows on my right, the target display on my left.

"Left foot forward, right foot back, knees slightly bent," he said. "Wait, you're left-handed, right?"

"Yep," I said and switched my stance.

He put the gun in my hand. "Keep your finger flat on the side, off the trigger until ready to fire. Hold your arm straight, right hand cupped on the butt." He moved my hands into position and stood directly in front of me. "This is for stability." He smacked the end of the gun and I stumbled back. "That's what it's going to feel like when it fires." He hit the front of the Glock several times until I stayed planted. He stood behind me, put one hand on my hip, the other pointed to the sight on the end of the barrel. "Center it between the two markers on the back of the gun. Now gently pull the trigger." He waited while I lined everything up. I hesitated, then pulled the lever until it clicked.

After about five minutes of gun-smacking and sight-aligning, he put the goggles over my eyes, the big muffs over my ears, and picked up the target. "Let's see how you do on the range."

The muffs made me feel as if I were underwater. Sound was muffled, but it also echoed. It was disconcerting. He opened the first door for me, waited for it to close, then opened the second, as per the posted instructions.

The acrid air hit me first. Tangy, sharp and unmistakably gunpowder. I'd never smelled it before, but recognized it immediately. Like burning firecrackers. Discarded shells littered the concrete floor. A gun went off and I flinched. Even with my ears fully covered, the shot was ridiculously loud. Four men stood in separate half-booths, feet planted, firing down their lanes. I jumped at every single shot.

Ransom went into an adjacent room. Smaller, only six lanes, but just as occupied. Two men and a couple. We entered booth thirteen. Ransom tapped on the clear glass dividers. "Bulletproof."

He sounded distant, as if we were in space wearing astronaut helmets. My breathing sounded labored, deliberate and loud in my head.

He placed the gun and ammunition on the table at the front of the booth. He took my handbag and hung it from a hook underneath the table. He clipped the target to a shot-up white rack. Nothing fancy, just regular black binder clips, one on each side, then pushed a button on a keypad mounted to the sidewall. The target zoomed backward five yards.

A bright muzzle flash startled me. The guy next to us started shooting his rounds in succession, blowing holes in his target, every two seconds, one after another. The constant explosions rattled me, put me on edge. Like in a haunted house, waiting for the next ghoul to jump out.

Ransom placed the bullets into the clip, then hit it against his hand. "To settle them," he said and put the magazine into the gun. "This doesn't have a safety." He leaned in close. "It's live. Keep it pointed down range and your finger off the trigger until you're ready."

I lifted the gun. It was heavy. My entire body started to shake, deep inside. The gun had no safety. Why no safety? What if I accidentally turned and it fired? Another round of gunshots blasted in succession, this time from farther down the lane. Then the man on the other side of us started to shoot.

"Why no safety?" I shouted at Ransom.

"It's okay. Just point it at the target, finger on the side like I showed you." He took a large step back, standing behind me and to my right.

I faced the target, arms outstretched. Left finger resting on the barrel. Right hand gripped beneath the gun. Markers lined up with the left target. I stood and stared. The gun grew heavier with each second. Finger on the trigger. Pull.

The force blew the gun toward the ceiling and I stumbled backward. Ransom steadied me and I quickly set the gun on the table. The blast was five times more powerful than Ransom's hand-smacking the barrel.

He looked at the target. "Very good. Especially for your first shot," he said and rubbed my arms. He gently squeezed my shoulders and leaned forward. "BRASS. Breathe, relax, aim, stop, squeeze. Watch me."

I stood two large steps behind him while he stood at the booth table. Explosions continued from the other lanes. Spent shells flew through the air, bouncing onto the floor. A man at the far end looked at me, then back at his target. He fired. Again and again. The acrid smell never left the air.

Ransom lifted the gun. He waited a beat, then fired. Three times. Three hits.

The couple two lanes over switched places. They leaned close to talk. The man pulled a long gun from his bag.

Ransom waved me over. "Try again. Remember to breathe."

I reached for the Glock. No safety. How many guns in this room didn't have safeties? It bothered me. The gun again heavy in my hand. I didn't like it. I didn't like any of it. It was awful. A crazy person once threatened me with a loaded gun. It wasn't half as frightening as this.

I breathed in. I breathed out. I tried to relax. Waves of trembles rolled from my shoulders to my hands. I was surrounded by strangers. Mostly men, mostly alone. Shooting guns. Loading, aiming, firing. All to perfect their shot.

Why does someone need to be a perfect shot with a handgun?

I aimed. The explosions around me continued. So did my trembles. I started over with B.

Breathe.

Relax. Practice. It's only practice. Target practice. As in practice makes perfect.

Aim. Guns kill people versus people kill people versus people with guns kill people.

Stop. People who shoot at target practice makes perfect.

Squeeze.

The bullet exploded from the barrel. I worried the gun would fly from my hands. I gripped it tight as I stumbled into Ransom.

"You've got five shots left," he said. "Breathe."

The dampened sounds made me feel as if I was drowning. From deep underwater to far outer space to now I was drowning. The man next to us looked over while he loaded his clip.

I set the gun on the table next to the box of ammunition. "I don't like this," I said to Ransom.

"What?" he said and leaned in.

"I'm done," I shouted. "Too loud." I gestured to the observation window. "Outside. You finish."

I calmly unhooked my handbag and left. Through the door into the next room, through the next door, waited for it to close, then out the range door. I whipped off the ear muffs. Ripped off the goggles. Took two very deep, long breaths. I placed the gear on the rental counter with shaky hands and walked to the observation glass viewing Ransom's lane. I sat on a stool and watched.

It was quiet. Safe. Like watching television or a movie. Removed from the reality, the actuality of the action. The brass casings flew haphazardly over Ransom's head with each shot, harmlessly falling to the floor. After firing the remaining bullets, he swept up the spent shells using a thin broom propped in the corner. He packed up and turned to leave. He stopped to talk to the range master. They watched the other shooters for a moment, shook hands, then Ransom left.

By the time he returned the gun and unused ammunition and found me at the table, my shaking had all but stopped.

"You okay?" he asked softly.

"Sure," I said. "Just loud in there."

He grabbed my hand and helped me from the tall stool. "Let's go outside."

Fresh air never felt so delicious. Clean pine and moist soil. I felt lighter, more at ease, with each step I took. We walked along the sidewalk around the side of the building to our cars. Side by side. My ice blue Mini convertible, his silver Mercedes McLaren racer. Apparently he was much better at investing than I was.

He leaned on the hood of his car. "Bad memories?"

"Some. I know how serious that situation was. How close I came to getting shot. But that gun did not seem nearly as dangerous as the one did today. I can't explain it."

He pulled me closer until I stood between his legs. He tucked my hair behind my ear. "Talk to me, Red."

I breathed in through my nose, out through my mouth. "It was the noise. Those repeated blasts. And the smell. It was everything. I've never been so uncomfortable, so unsettled." The tremors started again and I tried to shake them off. "Anyone could turn and shoot you. Shoot me. All those loaded guns. No safeties. I don't know who's standing next to me. Maybe I look like his ex-wife or his boss, both of whom he hates, by the way."

Ransom wrapped his arms around me and pulled me close. "I admit I didn't like seeing you with a gun. I like you better out here. In the sunshine."

"Me, too." He felt strong, and I felt safe and protected. I rested my head on his shoulder.

"Christmas is next week," he said. "I think Mimi is going to invite you to dinner."

I was happy my face was still hidden in his hug. Mimi Ransom, his mother, intimidated the crap out of me. She was a lovely Charlestonian who rode horses at the stables and raised funds for the charities and she'd recently helped me out of a jam, for which I was grateful. But the last time I ate a meal in her home, I knocked a pan of sugared carrots onto her gorgeous silk dining chairs. And that was before I fell over. On my way out, I drove through her prize roses and into the mailbox. I may have been nervous to meet Ransom's parents.

"Sounds lovely," I said. "But the Ballantynes are due home from their humanitarian trip to Guatemala soon. Not sure what we've got planned."

"I'm sure we can squeeze something in. We haven't celebrated Christmas together since college."

I stood back and punched his shoulder. "We didn't celebrate it then, either, hotshot. You left me the week before."

His phone buzzed in his pocket. He checked the number, then slipped it back. "I've got to run."

"Pretty darn convenient, Nick."

"Yeah, I do what I can." He placed his hands on both sides of my face and kissed me. His lips were soft and sweet and I lost my train of thought. It felt good to let go. To let the wall ease down, if only by a brick or two. To imagine a second chance at that Christmas celebration. The kiss deepened. His hands moved to my waist, then my hips. He pulled away after another soft kiss and rested his forehead on mine. "Have dinner with me tonight," he said. "I'll grill those kabobs you like. Drink some wine, walk on the beach..."

I nodded and he kissed me again. Quick this time, one on the lips, one on the forehead, then opened my car door. "You be careful out there. I know you're searching for suspects."

I smiled. "I've got a good one, too."

"Oh? More than a kid who likes target practice?"

"Yep..."

"Ah, the 'something good' you're on to?" Slightly arrogant tone, completely patronizing smile. "Not like you'll find out anything I don't already know."

"Is this an I can do anything you can do better moment?"

"I'm a pro, Red."

"Well, I'm a pro-in-training. I find things out. Like Vigo Ortiz's mother keeps a garden where she grows the deadly berries."

"Mamacita. Yes, we've met. Gorgeous tomato plants."

"Then there's a certain set of sketchbooks filled with Lexie Allen—"

"The death poses," he interrupted. "Bergin Guthrie. He's a choreographer and those are for his new routine. Lexie even helped him with the sketches. Her idea. I found that out two days ago."

"So did I," I said, my competitive fire burning bright. "What about her rival at the Wharf?"

"Check. Rory Throckmorton, the other sous chef. Though rival is overstating. Both are young cooks, up and comers, but it's not as if they're fighting over a head chef position in the Wharf kitchen."

"Ah, but did you know they were vying for the one coveted spot on a national cooking competition show? And the final audition was today?" By the surprised look on his face, I knew I had him. "Cooking, Lieutenant Ransom. As in food, as in berries, as in poison berries."

"A cooking competition? Today?"

"Yep."

"They really were rivals," he said. "Elli, that's good information."

"I don't mean to brag, but you know, just doing my thang." Silence. Did I just say thang? "Anyway, you owe me now, Ransom."

"What's the name of the show and where is it taping?"

"Say it."

"I owe you. Now tell me."

"I'm serious. Anything big breaks in this case and you share with me. Deal?"

"Scout's honor."

"You're no scout."

"We could go camping and I'll show you. Though they don't issue badges for some of my skills." He leaned down and kissed my lips softly.

My competitive fire began to smolder. "The Stream Kitchen in Savannah. Mark Malone is the producer." I rattled off the address and he jotted it in his notebook.

"I mean it, stay out of trouble," he said. "I can take this from here."

"Take what, Ransom? I thought it was an accident."

He paused, then smiled and walked around to the driver's side of his slick racer. The wing door floated open. "I have to go. See you tonight, after the board meeting?"

"Absolutely."

I sank into my seat and my lips still tingled. I felt pretty darn good. Ransom finally confirmed Lexie's death was no accident.

Even if confirmation by omission. My investigative skills might actually impress Ransom and solve his case. My case. Lexie's case. At least I hoped so. But man, he had way better resources. He already knew about Mamacita and Berg. He didn't even ask me how I knew about those sketches and I just blurted it out like an amateur. A choreographer, huh? I didn't even know that part. What kind of dance was Berg planning? And wasn't that a convenient explanation?

ELEVEN

(Day #4 – Sunday Afternoon)

The clock on the dash said 11:43. Time enough to grab a quick lunch on the island and hit the library when it opened at noon. With my hair hatted and the top down, I cruised through Summerton and over the Palmetto Bridge. It was brisk and clear and ideal for an island holiday. The sun glinted off ornaments dangling from the garland wrapped around the palm trees lining Cabana Boulevard.

I called Sid while I drove. "You available for lunch? I'm thinking Molly's by the Sea."

"Can't, but I'd love to. Broker's open house all day. You can swing by here. We've got those prosciutto-wrapped arugula skewers you love. The ones with the buffalo mozzarella. And pitchers of mimosas. I'm at the Zimmerman house in South Pebble Beach."

My stomach growled and I glanced at the clock again. "I shouldn't. Last time I attended one of your broker's opens, I stayed five hours and ended up napping in the guest house." I pulled into the Sonic lot and studied the menu board. "What about tomorrow? I'm thinking of going to Berg's parents' house, get some insight into those scary ballerina death sketches."

"Are we breaking in?"

"I hope not. I'm wearing seven Band-Aids as is."

"You think his parents will offer insight? Maybe drop a dime on their kid?" she said, then hollered away from the phone. "The lilies on the dining table, the hydrangeas in the living room."

"Yeah, probably not. Ransom said Berg's a choreographer now, that's what the sketches were for. But I don't know if I believe him. Berg or Ransom."

"Ransom? I thought you weren't sharing with him."

"I wasn't. But then he got all competitive with his I'm better at this than you, and I couldn't let him think that."

"But it's true, sweetie."

"I'm aware. But he doesn't need to know."

"I'm pretty sure he knows."

I pressed the speaker button on the Sonic menu and ordered a chili cheese dog, fries and an orange slush.

"I'm offended. You're opting for a chili cheese dog rather than my canapés?"

"I'm on the run. You know I eat poorly when I'm on the run."

"Uh-huh," she said. She hollered away from the phone again. "Use the Tiffany pitchers. The coordinating glasses are in my car."

"I'll let you go. Good luck today."

"Thank you. And you enjoy your poorly executed lunch," she said. "We'll catch up later."

"Definitely. I didn't even tell you about the guns."

"Guns? What guns?"

"Apparently, I've got pretty good aim."

After an abbreviated snapshot of my shooting range experience, we said goodbye, and five minutes later a carhop on roller skates glided over with my meal on a red plastic tray. It may not have been filled with canapés, but it was darn delicious. And only took fifteen minutes from order to eaten.

With a quick dash down Cabana, I arrived at my next stop: the library. It was located on the north end of the island near Oyster Cove Plantation and shared the Island Civic Complex with the police station. It was basically a two-room library, with the children's portion taking up more than its fair share.

A couple sat together on one of the park benches that bordered the courtyard entrance. I recognized them as Lexie's parents. They held hands, lost in their own thoughts, each staring into the garden of palms and pines.

"Mr. and Mrs. Allen," I said softly. "I'm so sorry for your loss."

Mrs. Allen looked up at me with sorrow in her watery eyes. "Elliott," she said, then wiped a stream of tears from her cheek.

"We're here to meet Deidre," Mr. Allen said. He moved his stare from the trees to the automatic doors about thirty feet away but made no move to get up and go inside.

Deidre had mentioned helping the Allens pack up Lexie's things from her condo. It didn't seem they were ready to undertake that task.

"I'm here for Deidre, too," I said. "Perhaps I can help."

Mrs. Allen patted the bench beside her. "No, dear, we'll get there. We need a little more time."

I sat down and wrapped my arms around her frail shoulders. I worried a strong breeze would blow her away. "She was a lovely girl."

Mrs. Allen pulled back and sniffled. "A dream child. Polite and kind, and so talented. My girl could sing and dance like an angel. And cook. Oh, could she cook. She was looking forward to the cooking show. Thought she could win it."

"You knew about that?" I asked.

"Yes, but she swore us to secrecy, didn't she, honey?" Mrs. Allen said to her husband.

He nodded and looked out at the palms, his gaze unfocused and distant.

"She loved to dance," Mrs. Allen said. "She was a natural. But cooking held a life's worth of passion for her." She almost laughed, a memory touching her. "She tried every recipe her little hands could find. And she could fry anything and make it taste gourmet."

"Chef Carmichael at the Wharf raved over her," I said. "He said she excelled in Charlotte and he was honored to have her join his staff."

She smiled and squeezed my hand. "It was a hard decision for her to leave dance for cooking, but the right one." She paused and tears rolled down her soft cheeks. "Even though it was food that took her life."

"We'll find out what happened to her," I said.

"We know. The captain assured us. But accident or deliberate—part of me can't fathom who would hurt her—it doesn't matter. She's gone. She's just gone. It doesn't seem fair we only had her for eleven years."

"Only eleven years?" I asked.

"We adopted her when she was nine, took her in at eight," she said. "We never had children of our own. She was our first foster placement. She didn't have an easy childhood, but she was an easy child. We fell in love at first sight."

"She was a lucky girl, Mrs. Allen. You were wonderful parents."

She squeezed my hand again, then leaned on her husband's shoulder.

A slight breeze rustled the palm fronds and the seagulls cried in the distance. I left the Allens to remember their daughter and went inside the library.

Deidre Burch manned the information desk along the back wall. She helped a guest locate the romance paperbacks, then turned to me. "How'd it go?" she said in a low whisper. "Under the sea, if you know what I mean."

I slipped a key from my handbag and handed it to her, discreetly palming it and shaking her hand. "Mission accomplished. Appreciate the assistance."

"Don't mention it," she said and raised her voice a notch. "What can I do for you?"

"A book on poisons. Reference section, I presume?"

Deidre perched her readers on her nose and her fingers clattered on the keyboard. "Looks like we've got one currently on the shelf."

"How many others have been checked out?"

"None. We only have the one book. In the entire library." She wrote down the author and section numbers and pointed me in the right direction.

Three aisles and two turns later, on the middle shelf, I found a squat lime green book with an intricate scroll pattern pressed into the hardcover. *Wicked Plants: The Weed That Killed Lincoln's Mother & Other Botanical Atrocities.* I thumbed through the pages until I found deadly nightshade. Less than three and a half short pages, mostly tales of how people a hundred years ago mistakenly ate the lethal berries. Accidental deaths from children to adults. An accident wasn't too farfetched, at least during a time when folks still foraged for food and women couldn't vote.

I took the book to Deidre to check me out. "Can you look up its history and tell me who borrowed it in the last three months?"

"Will it help the murder investigation?" she asked using her indoor voice.

"Murder? I think the police still classify it as an accident."

"Uh-huh. Your Detective Ransom doesn't understand how small this island is. He's doing too much investigating for an accident." She held up the book on poisons. "By the look of it, so are you." She swiped my library card and studied the screen. "As for this book's history. You, today. Before that no one checked it out."

"How about farther back?"

"I mean literally no one ever," she said and handed me the book. "You're the first. Due in three weeks. Though you'll probably get more information online."

"Thanks, Deidre." I tucked the little green book into my handbag. "The Allens are out front on the bench. I think they're trying to work up the energy to come inside."

"Those poor people. They arrived two hours before we opened. I don't think they'll ever have the energy. I've been out twice and I'm packing up early, going to leave in ten minutes," she said. "You find who did this, Elliott Lisbon."

I walked out of the lobby and into the courtyard. The Allens sat on the same bench. Mrs. Allen's head on Mr. Allen's shoulders.

Their hands were clasped together and their eyes were closed. I silently vowed to them, to Deidre, and to myself: I would absolutely find out who did this. No worries on that front.

I needed a drive. An hours-long, head-clearing, wind-whipping drive to work it all out. I flew over the bridge, down the highway, and north onto I-95 toward Charleston. I felt the Allens' loss deep down in my soul. I lost my parents, one after another, twenty years earlier. And the holiday timing reminded me of losing Ransom at Christmas, just a few months before my parents died. The back-to-back-to-back losses sucked the air out of me at the time, and I had felt like an object floating in space. No rope for me to hold onto and nothing to tether me to. It took years before I felt grounded again.

Mr. and Mrs. Ballantyne kept me attached. Growing up, my family spent summers in Summerton. My parents were close friends of the Ballantynes and frequent charity event attendees. The Ballantynes treated me like a daughter, sometimes even more than my own parents. They loved me and cared for me, but in our family trio, I was a third wheel. With the Ballantynes, I had a home. They trusted me with their foundation while they traveled the globe, and wanted me close when they returned to the nest. Losing them, either of them, would create a void so immeasurable, it hurt to breathe just thinking about it.

By the time I crossed over the Ashley River and entered downtown Charleston with its architecture, residents, and cemeteries all dripping with Southern charm, my soul felt lighter. I still called the Ballantyne home, my friends loved me, and I truly had a very rich life. I needed to be thankful. I spent the next hour and a half walking the picturesque streets, encountering mannerly shopkeepers, and purchasing one-of-a-kind gifts for Christmas.

At the end of the day, I returned to my cottage to quickly unload my bounty before hustling up to the Big House for the final board meeting of the year, then dinner with Ransom. I expected it to be quiet and quick. The meeting, not Ransom. Nothing on the board's agenda. No one really wanted to spend the evening talking business points this close to the holidays. But I wanted to get there early, be ready when the board members arrived to see the tree.

I parked out front, close to the steps, and walked inside.

The magnificent spruce was gorgeous. It reminded me of every Christmas I spent at the Big House as a child. Mr. and Mrs. Ballantyne would put the most whimsically-wrapped gifts with huge ribbons under this tree. They'd give me books and puzzles and games and they played them with me. Afternoons spent assembling puzzles and laughing over board games.

The most special Christmas memory was of the very first game they ever gave me, even though I was a little too old. It was Candyland. My parents had even joined us, and we all played for hours, heading to Gum Drop Mountain and avoiding cherry pitfalls.

This year's Ballantyne tree looked like Candyland come to life.

Vibrant ornaments from *The Nutcracker* commissioned set sparkled on the branches. We used the glittered candy canes and sugared plums, jumbo bon bons, and dazzling peppermint twists, plus the long strings of popcorn looped around the tree, and mixed in between, were the ornaments the children had painted. Seven different iterations of Candyland boxes were displayed on the fluffy white tree skirt. From my own vintage games collection.

I squealed like a child on Christmas morning.

"It's delightful," Carla said as she walked up. She set a tray of coffee mugs on a table near the foyer door. She poured a steaming cup of cocoa from a large urn, plopped a fresh scoop of whipped cream on top, sprinkled it with shaved chocolate and handed it to me.

"So are you," I said and sipped. "This is the best part of the whole meeting."

"Wait 'til you see the red velvet mini bundts with strawberry cream cheese frosting," she said. "Don't know how I pulled it off in that kitchen. The first delivery for the Palm & Fig arrived today. I've got more pans than I have hooks, tables, and bins. I don't know what I'll do when the food gets here on Tuesday."

"Oh, speaking of, Chef Carmichael said you're having a mild disagreement over lobster," I said and followed her to the kitchen.

"Those were his words? Mild disagreement?"

"He may have used other words," I said and ogled the array of sweets on the steel island in the center of the room. Rows of mini bundt cakes topped with healthy dollops of frosting, colorfully decorated cake balls on sticks, and decadent square petit fours. "We'll talk about Chef Carmichael after the meeting." I helped myself to a cake stick. Moist chocolate cake covered in smooth vanilla frosting. I may have moaned.

"Don't you worry about Carmichael," Carla said. "I'll fix the disagreement."

I eyed her skeptically and scraped the stick clean. I knew how Carla handled her disagreements with Carmichael. One in particular ended with her flinging etouffee at his head after he slung his own crawfish into said etouffee.

Two kitchen assistants were sorting pans and pots on the far counter beneath an enormous hanging rack. "Girls, let's get these into the parlor before Elli eats them all," Carla said.

Each grabbed a large sheet tray and turned. Julia and Rory from the Wharf. They both wore their chef coats, sharply pressed and bright white.

"Nice to see you again," I said. Julia looked nervous as if I might mention our private talk, and Rory gave me a half nod.

I helped them fill the trays and ate a pair of petit fours. Lemon cream and raspberry mousse. I was licking my fingers when Nick Ransom walked through the swinging door with two uniformed police officers.

"Rory Throckmorton," Ransom said. "We'd like to talk to you."

Well, that was fast, I thought.

Julia looked at me and I think she thought the same thing. Her bottom jaw dropped until her lips formed an O and she stepped away from Rory.

"Me?" Rory said. She had been about to take her tray of desserts into the foyer when Ransom came in. She stood there clutching the large tray, almost holding it out to him, a barrier between them.

"Yes," Ransom said and looked around the room. It was a generously-sized commercial kitchen, but it felt cramped. Carla, Rory, Julia, Ransom, two officers, and I shared the space with the island, the pastries, stacks of pans and pots, and cases of supplies for the Palm & Fig. "We'll give you a ride to the station," Ransom said.

"The station? Like the police station?" Rory asked. She glanced over her shoulder at me, then at the back door, then over to Ransom. "Why me?"

The kitchen door swung open and Jane Walcott Hatting, chair of the Ballantyne Board, marched in. She wore a perfectly tailored designer suit with a silk scarf. "Elliott, why are you hiding in the kitchen?" She noticed the pastries and rolled her eyes. "Carla, will you be displaying the desserts or have we opted for a self-service cafeteria operation? Shall I instruct the board members to pop into the kitchen on their way to the parlor?"

"Jane," Ransom said by way of greeting.

Jane looked startled, then noticed the assorted police personnel surrounding Rory. "What's going on, Lieutenant?"

The kitchen door swung open again and nearly smacked Jane's backside. Tod took one step in, then backed right out.

"Let's take this out of the kitchen," I said and put my hand on Rory's tray. "I'll take this. Julia, we'll put these in the parlor."

Jane led us into the foyer, which was filled with board members admiring the tree. Deidre and Matty manned the cocoa station, filling mugs of warm chocolate from the urn. Julia took her tray to the parlor and I handed mine off to Tod.

"Aunt Zibby!" Rory cried and ran into Zibby's arms. She was easy to spot. Her hair was still pink, but this time it was topped with a stunner of a cloche hat with a wide velvet ribbon and a cluster of fluffy pink feathers.

"*Aunt* Zibby?" I said.

"My dear Rory, what a delight to see you," Zibby said and

hugged her tight. "You smell like sugar and rain."

"Aunt Zibby, the police are here," Rory said. "For me."

"Don't be a silly, dear," Zibby said. "That's Elli's beau. He's probably here to put the angel on the topper tree."

My face flushed red and I didn't dare look over at Matty.

"Ma'am," Ransom said to Zibby. "We *are* here for Rory. We'd like to talk to her down at the station."

"Do you have an arrest warrant?" Jane asked.

"An arrest warrant? No."

"What kind of warrant do you have?" Matty asked. He'd abandoned his post near the entrance and now stood next to Jane.

There were approximately twenty people in the foyer between the towering spruce and the double-oak entry doors. Ransom and his two officers stood with their backs to the tree, facing the crowd. Jane and Matty faced him, semi-blocking Rory and Zibby on the front line, while every board member behind them locked onto the dramatic scene unfolding before them. One member quietly refilled her cocoa cup, never taking her eyes from the spectacle, while two others moved closer.

Ransom glanced at me standing to the side, clearly between the opposing clusters. "A search warrant," he said. "Which we executed this afternoon. We found quite a bit of interesting evidence in your kitchen. Including *Atropa belladonna* berries."

"What?" Rory said.

"What's *Atropa belladonna*?" Jane asked.

"It's the deadly nightshade plant," I said. "It produces poisonous berries. That's what killed Lexie Allen."

"But that was an accident," Matty and Jane said at the same time.

"It was homicide," Ransom said.

"I don't have deadly nightshade," Rory said. "Why would I have deadly nightshade?" She turned to her Aunt Zibby. "I don't understand. I don't have deadly nightshade."

"The evidence suggests otherwise." Ransom nodded to one of the officers. "It's enough to bring you in for questioning."

"Wait," Matty said and put a protective arm in front of Zibby and Rory. "She doesn't have to go if she's not under arrest. You don't want to talk to her. You want to interrogate her."

"Are you an attorney now, Gannon?"

"I don't need to be. She has rights."

"Would you like me to read them to her?"

"Hold on, Ransom," I said. "You're moving very quickly. Six hours ago you claimed Lexie's death was an accident. Now you're questioning Rory as a suspect in a homicide?"

"That's how investigations work," Ransom said. "We got good information from an inside source and we acted on it."

Jane narrowed her eyes and looked between us. "What 'good information' led you to obtain a search warrant?"

"We received a tip about the Stream Kitchen," he said. "Rory and Lexie were battling to be contestants in a cooking competition. Two of them, but only one spot left on the show. It got ugly. We think deadly."

"The show? This is about the show?" Rory said. She looked from Jane to me to Ransom and then back to me. "You! You were on the set today," she said. "Fran grabbed me the second I got there and told me some reporter for a charity was there from the island. An older lady with crazy red hair, she said."

She connected that dot fast. "Older lady? I am not *older*." I tamped down my frizzies and tucked them behind my ear before I realized I was doing it. "And I never said I was a reporter."

"But you told the police I killed Lexie so I could be on Stream Kitchen?" Rory's fists were bunched up so tight, I thought she might punch me. "Are you crazy?"

"You did this?" Jane said. She stepped forward and raised her voice. "You implicated Zibby's niece in a murder?"

"I only shared what I found—"

"Filming starts tomorrow," Rory said. "Tomorrow! If they hear about this, they'll give away my spot."

"Which you conveniently now have, since Lexie Allen isn't alive to compete for it," Ransom said.

"I earned that spot," Rory said. Her face was sunburn red and tears watered her eyes. "How could you do this?" she said to me.

"I didn't do what you—"

"Rory, we need to go," Ransom said, and then to Jane, "You're welcome to come with us. But you should know, it doesn't look good."

"Damn right I'm going with you," she said. "I'm calling Gregory Meade on the way." Jane turned to Zibby. Her hat was askew and her earrings didn't match. "Zibby, you ride with me, okay?"

Ransom and the officers led Rory from the foyer. The crowd of board members parted down the center. Moses couldn't have created a more perfect path.

"I'll need my pocketbook," Zibby said. She put her hand on my arm. "You'll help us with this hodgekapotch, right? It's your specialty."

"I'm on it, Zibby," I said.

Jane stuffed her portfolio into a slim briefcase. She stalked past me, then spun back around, pointing her pen at my face. "You better be on it. And you better not screw this up again."

"I didn't screw anything up last time. I nearly got killed helping you."

"It wasn't nearly enough," she snapped. "I can take care of myself. But you've put Zibby right in the middle of it. You need to get it together." She stormed out leaving a wave of silence in her wake.

"Okay, then," Tod said from the very back of the group. "The board meeting is postponed until further notice. Can I get an amen? I mean, a motion?"

"These meetings sure are more exciting than my bank meetings," one member said.

"No kidding," another said. "I skipped my grandma's potluck dinner to be here. I'd never miss one."

"This is the second time Jane's been dragged out by the police..."

Carla helped Tod usher board members from the Big House with pastry boxes and paper to-go cups for their coffee and cocoa.

I lingered near the Christmas tree, holding a fallen ornament in my hand and a hint of confliction in my heart. The tree turned out to be a childlike dream, but Lexie Allen would never celebrate another Christmas morning. I'd impressed Ransom with my investigative prowess, but I ended up hurting Zibby Archibald.

Matty walked over and put his hand on my shoulder. "Are you okay?" He looked composed in his casual linen suit and loafers. Soft and cozy and calm.

"Yes," I said. "No. I don't know. I didn't know Rory was Zibby's niece. I feel terrible for Zibby."

"And Rory," he said. "She's the one they're questioning."

"Matty, I swear to you, I didn't do anything wrong."

"I'm not accusing you, Elli. I'm just worried about you and Zibby and Rory."

"Me, too," I said. "I shared information, solid information, on an important case. I'm a cooperating investigator. I did the right thing."

"Are you trying to convince me or you? Because it didn't look like the right thing to me. It looked like Rory's life is falling apart and you loosened the pieces."

"Someone killed Lexie Allen. Don't forget that. And Rory is a good suspect."

"Maybe not good enough. An arrest record will change her life."

"So will killing someone."

"Dig with care, El. The end may not justify the means and you'll have to live with the decisions you make."

He squeezed my shoulder and kissed my cheek. He thanked Carla for her desserts, asked if she or Tod needed anything. With a wave to me, he left through the tall door. No mention of our canceled shopping trip or thoughts about rescheduling it.

Fifteen minutes and two trips to the kitchen with half-empty cocoa cups later, I sat behind my desk. Carla and Tod were in the chairs across from me. We each had a pair of red velvet bundts on a shiny white plate in front of us. I took a hunk with my fork and shoved it in my mouth.

"Jane's pissed," Captain Obvious said.

"Yeah," Carla agreed. "And Zibby's heartbroken. Or will be when they explain Rory's going to prison for murder."

"Don't say that!" I said. "Zibby is family."

"Which makes Rory family," Tod said. "Is she a Ballantyne? I've never met her."

"Me, neither," I said. "Maybe on George's side? She could be an Archibald."

Vivi Ballantyne and Zibby were cousins, but Rory could've been related to Zibby's late husband. "Her last name is Throckmorton. So by marriage?"

"I don't think it matters," Carla said. "Vivi adores Zibby and has since they shared their first Shirley Temple doll."

"What am I going to do?" I said.

"Chicken, you found one suspect, you'll have to find another," Carla said. "Prove the chef with killer berries in her kitchen didn't do it."

"Before Mr. Ballantyne returns on Thursday," Tod said.

"The same day as the Palm & Fig Ball," Carla added.

"Well, shit," I said.

"Ballantyne Ballerina Killed with Cake," Tate Keating said. He leaned in from the hall, gripping the doorframe. As crime reporter for the *Islander Post*, Tate fancied himself a true newspaper bloodhound, sniffing out scandals and secrets, then splashing spectacular headlines across the front page. "Care to comment?"

"Nope," I said. "That headline is complete sensationalism, Tate. And not true, in case you're interested in facts and truth."

"Your opinion," he replied. "But I'm not holding back, Lisbon. I went easy on you last time."

"'Whack Job Whacks Wife at the Ballantyne' was not going easy!"

He tipped his imaginary newsboy cap and left, whistling his

way down the hall.

"Don't even think about it," I shouted, then took another heaping forkful from my plate. "I'm going to need more cake."

TWELVE

Tate Keating not only thought about it, he did it. I tapped my way to the *Islander Post* home page on Lexie's iPad the moment I woke up. I didn't want to waste time booting up my computer. He embellished and hinted and stayed a thread's width inside the lines of liability.

> *With a Ballantyne ballerina dead and a Wharf chef hauled down to the police station, it's going to be some kind of Palm & Fig Ball on Thursday night. One of Sea Pine's finest, Lieutenant Nick Ransom, interrupted the latest Ballantyne Foundation board "meeting" of fancy desserts and exotic drinks to personally escort one of their Palm & Fig chefs to the police station. Rory Throckmorton, protégé of the Wharf's famed Chef Carmichael, is lead (dare we say: only) suspect in the murder of Lexie Allen. Who also happened to be the star of* The Nutcracker, *sponsored by, you guessed it, the aforementioned Ballantyne Foundation.*

I skimmed the rest of the article. Apparently Tate hadn't figured out the connection between Rory and the Ballantyne. But he would. I threw on a robe and marched downstairs, dialing Jane's cell as I stormed. She didn't answer. I left a message asking her to meet me at the Big House with Zibby and Rory in an hour. I threw open my front door and crossed over to Ransom's porch in bare feet.

He answered my pounding with a cup of coffee in a sturdy blue carry cup. Steam drifted from the tiny drink opening. "Good morning, Red," he said. "Sorry I had to cancel dinner last night."

"Nothing good about it, Ransom," I said with my finger in his face. "You owed me."

He glanced at my crazy pillow-creased mop hair and worn tee. "Care to come in? I made pancakes with apple bacon."

"I don't want your apple bacon, I want you to keep your word. You promised the next big break in this case, you would tell me. I think arresting someone is a big break."

"Just as well. I'm on my way out," he said and joined me on the porch, shutting the door behind him. "We didn't arrest someone. We were only questioning someone."

"*Questioning* someone is a big break. A search warrant. A main suspect."

"I couldn't tell you. You're too close to this," he said. "Your loyalty lies with the Ballantyne, not the police. That's your life and your job."

"So is this. PI-in-training means part of my job is working with the police. I can be discreet and not blab police business all over the Ballantyne board." I felt a flush remembering my blabbing braggart ways got me into this mess, but plowed on. "I share loyalty, Nick Ransom."

He leaned on the porch railing and sipped his coffee. His freshly-washed hair was still damp and his pressed shirt was crisp from the cleaners. "If I told you we were going to search Zibby's niece's apartment and bring her in to the station, *before* we did it, you're telling me you wouldn't have felt duty-bound to tell Zibby? Or Jane? Or Mr. Ballantyne? You wouldn't have warned Zibby, given her a heads-up?"

"You knew she was Zibby's niece? And didn't share that either?"

He softened his voice. "I found out during the search. I couldn't tell you. I didn't want you in that position."

"You still owe me," I said and stepped closer. Then remembered I hadn't brushed my teeth and stepped back.

"I don't know what other big break we'll get on this one," he said. "I have it pretty well wrapped up."

"Well, I'm duty-bound to prove Zibby's niece didn't kill anyone."

"This isn't your case. Don't get involved."

"If you haven't figured it out by now, you better. The Sea Pine police cooperate with the Ballantyne Foundation inquiries and investigations, which means this is my case." And with that, I walk/stomped back to my cottage.

Bragging never works out. It reminded me of the scene in *Beaches* when Bette's character is a little girl and she brags about this big audition, trying to impress her rival. When she arrives at the audition, the rival is there and wins the part. If she would've just kept her pie hole shut, it would've been smooth sailing.

This was all my fault. Me and my pie hole. I wore my discretion oath like a sparkly crown on a pageant queen. I never took it off. Discreet inquiries required me to be discreet. It was right there in the title. Nick Ransom was under my skin and I felt competitive. Why did I brag to him about Rory and the Stream Kitchen? To prove I was better than he was? Or to impress him? Neither option made me feel good about myself.

I showered, brushed (hair and teeth) and dressed lickety-split, then sped to the Big House. I plopped into my desk chair as the handset on my desk rang.

"Oh, Elliott, you're there," Chef Newhouse said when I answered. "Thought I'd leave a voicemail."

"Good morning, Chef, nice to hear from you. Carla is quite excited about all the deliveries. Says you three have an amazing menu planned for the ball."

"Yes, um, that's why I'm calling," he said and cleared his throat. "I won't be able to participate this year. I know it's short notice, but it can't be helped."

I jumped to my feet as if he were standing in front of me. "What? The Palm & Fig is in three days. You can't cancel on me now."

"I've given this a lot of thought, but I made up my mind, and I won't change it."

"You made up your mind? There isn't some emergency forcing you to cancel?"

"I would think it's an emergency to you," he said. "It's your reputation, too."

"What are you talking about?"

"The article in the *Post*, of course. I'm afraid I can't be associated with such a controversial organization. It would ruin my reputation."

"So will canceling at the last minute, Chef Newhouse. Everyone is expecting you to be here."

"Not after that article. You'll be lucky if anyone even attends the ball now."

I bit back a gasp. "I'm offended. The Ballantynes will be offended. This year's ball will be our most successful. You'll regret this."

"I doubt it. But maybe it'll be different next year," he said and hung up.

"Oh, it'll be different next year, buster. You won't even be considered," I said to the empty room. "Of all the pompous, arrogant, lousy, crappy, irresponsible, ridiculous—"

"Tough morning, chicken?" Carla said. She walked in with a breakfast burrito on a plate and set it on my desk. A smattering of guacamole covered a warm tortilla stuffed with chorizo, eggs, cheese, and fried diced potatoes.

"Chef Newhouse just canceled. He canceled!" I took a delicious bite of burrito heaven and sank into my chair. "With three days until the ball. Three days!"

Carla waved her hand at me dismissively. "I don't need that self-important hack in my kitchen. It'll run more smoothly without him."

"We need a replacement, Carla. We can't let the *Post* influence the entire island. Everyone will whisper if he's not here. His name is all over the invitations."

My phone rang before she could argue.

"Elliott, you're there," Chef Carmichael said. "I was expecting your voicemail."

"It's nine-thirty on a Monday morning, why wouldn't I be in my office?" Sure, I was no early bird, but jeez.

"I have a conflict for the ball," he said. "It seems—"

"Don't you dare, Carmichael."

Carla leaned on my desk. "Is he backing out, too?" she said. "Fine by me."

It was my turn to wave her off.

"Too?" Chef Carmichael said. "What's Carla talking about? Newhouse canceled?"

"Yes, he also had a fake conflict at the last minute," I said. "I'm serious, Carmichael. You begged for this job—"

"I'm serious," Carla said. "I'm practically running the entire menu and staff as it is."

I continued to wave her away, my arm flailing like a panicked kid shooing at a swarm of hornets. She started to smack back.

"You pleaded with me, Carmichael," I said. "I pulled a dozen strings to get you this gig and you are absolutely not abandoning ship. Besides, Rory is one of your own. Canceling implies you have no faith in her."

"I want head chef status," he said. "It'll be just me and Carla, but I'm lead. And we announce it to the *Post* and print it on the menu cards."

That was quick. I glanced at Carla and she read my face like a fortune teller with a tarot card. "What's he saying?" she asked with squinty eyes.

"Not going to happen," I said. "Equal billing, no

announcement, and you bring extra staff to work in the Big House kitchen."

"She's already got my best sous and my best prep. That's all she's getting. I've got a restaurant to run."

"See you tomorrow," Carla called into the handset. "Thinks he's going to negotiate status," she mumbled.

"I'm not budging on the consommé," he said and hung up.

"This is serious, Carla," I said. "The ball is in three days."

"I don't need Newhouse. And I barely need Carmichael. Though his staff has been nice. We've got a thousand shrimp that need peeling..." she said as she left my office. She popped her head back in. "Jane, Zibby, and Rory arrived, by the way. Breakfast in the parlor."

Jane Walcott Hatting, she of the snappy disposition and wicked heels, was a high-end antiques dealer in Savannah and ran her auctions with an iron gavel. Her family was old Savannah money. The kind who still hid it in the walls in case the Yankees ever stormed back.

She was chair of the board, I was director of the Foundation. We never saw eye-to-eye, more like we stood toe-to-toe, on every issue for the Foundation. Mr. Ballantyne felt it gave us a more rounded organization. Different perspectives, different styles, different ideas. As ridiculous as it sounded, he was right, and it worked. And that was the absolute one thing Jane and I had in common. Our faith, and loyalty, to Mr. and Mrs. Ballantyne. And protecting the Ballantynes, both the family and the Foundation, was pure instinct.

I grabbed my notebook and a pen, then joined them in the parlor, the official boardroom in the Big House. A polished mahogany table was dead center in the room with eight high-back chairs on each of the long sides, and one on each of the short ends. Jane sat in her massive chair at the head of the table just inside the parlor doors, Rory and Zibby to her right.

"Good morning, Elli," Zibby said. She looked bright and confident as she spooned butter into her coffee. "Our own Kinsey

Millhone is on the case."

"Morning, Zibby," I said and grabbed the seat to Jane's left. "Rory, Jane. Thanks for meeting me on such short notice."

Along with their breakfast plates, there was a platter of fresh fruit and a coffee urn on a crocheted hot pad on the table. And a single can of Pepsi next to a cup of ice.

"I need to know everything you told Lieutenant Ransom, Rory," I said. "He's convinced you killed Lexie Allen. Tell me why."

Rory glowered at me as if she'd rather tell a jury her story than tell me.

I poured the Pepsi (I prefer my caffeine cold and fizzy) while Zibby leaned over and spoke to her in a gentle voice. "Now, Rory, dear, you must trust us, me and Jane. We told you, Elliott is on our side. This nonsense is nothing more than a misplaced monkeyshine. She'll prove you're blameless and all will be right again. Indeed, Elli?"

"Indeed, Zibby," I said. "The very best I can. But first things, Rory. Convince me that you're blameless. Start at the station. Why is Lieutenant Ransom convinced you did this?"

Rory gave in with a loud exhale and pushed a tomato around her plate with a fork, her breakfast barely eaten. "It was awful. He really thinks I killed her. He said they found deadly nightshade berries in my apartment. But I don't know how. I never bought those berries. I swear. I've never even seen them."

"You never cooked with them? Maybe someone gave them to you?"

"No, never. I know what deadly nightshade berries are. Nobody in the world would cook with them."

"Did the police have any other evidence or witnesses or anything?"

"Not that they told us," Jane said. "But we didn't stay long. Gregory Meade took over and the questioning shut down."

I took a quick note. Gregory Meade was a prominent criminal attorney in Savannah. He worked closely with Jane when she was accused of murder some six months earlier. Ransom questioned her in this very room. It was déjà vu all over again.

"How do you know Lexie and her friends?" I asked Rory. "They seem pretty tight and have been since childhood. What's your connection?"

"That group isn't as close as you think," Rory said. "Besides, I don't really know them. They don't matter."

"You looked pretty close to Vigo Ortiz," I said. "And considering you're being questioned for killing his girlfriend, I think it does matter."

"She's not really his girlfriend," Rory said.

"That's what you pull from that statement?" I said. "I know you gave him a teddy bear with a Wharf napkin."

"How do you know that?" Rory said, looking at me with squinty eyes.

Zibby patted her arm. "She's very good."

Jane pulled out her portfolio and tapped her pen on it.

"I've been investigating Lexie's death since Friday. I know a lot of things. The police know a lot of things. Work with me. The bear was from you, right? Not Lexie."

"We're just friends," she said.

She sounded sincere and scared and defiant. She was barely older than a teenager. A kid desperate to protect secrets no one cared about. Or maybe it was something more. I saw her tucked in close to Vigo at the club the other night. Though I left that part out. "What about the rest of Lexie's dancer friends? Courtney and Berg?"

"I didn't know them, and I didn't want to know them."

"Well, it's you, and it's them," I said. "That seems to be the whole picture."

"And Lexie's mother is in prison for murder," Jane said. "*That's* the picture, Elliott."

"What are you talking about? I saw her and her husband yesterday."

"Not Mrs. Allen," Rory said. "That's her adopted mother. Her real mother is in jail."

"I didn't know that," I said.

"I thought you said you knew a lot of things? It's your job to find this stuff out," Jane said. "Jesus, Elliott, what exactly are you doing?"

"Murder? Who did she kill?" I asked.

"It was like fifteen years ago," Rory said with a shrug. "I doubt she killed her daughter, too."

That double revelation left me staring at my notes trying to compose myself. Jane was spot on. I'm supposed to know these things. I moved to the island permanently fifteen years ago, but it takes time to earn confidences. Plus, Lexie was from Beaufort, which was far away. Not in miles, but in social circles. Sea Pine had enough of its own drama. Its residents didn't need to borrow it from Beaufort.

Back to the facts: Lexie was adopted and her birth mother was a murderer. But I agreed with Rory. Doubtful she killed her own daughter, especially from prison. Besides, the police questioned Rory. Found evidence implicating Rory. They were building a case against Rory.

"Let's get back to the deadly nightshade berries," I said.

"I told you, I don't have any. Whatever the police found in my apartment, they aren't mine. I had *black* nightshade, not *deadly*," Rory sighed and put her napkin on the table, twisting it with her fingers. "The competition kept getting tougher. Mark, the producer, he wanted us to be more and more original, push our boundaries, he said. Lexie and I weren't cooking with poison. We weren't trying to kill ourselves." She looked right at me. "I didn't kill Lexie. She wasn't my favorite person, but I didn't hate her."

"That's not what I heard," I said.

"I'm not saying anything else," Rory said. "I don't trust you."

"We won't disclose your private information," Jane said, then looked at me. "Starting today."

"Firstly, Jane, Rory working at the Wharf and competing for a spot on the Stream Kitchen was not private information. Secondly, I figured that out by myself, not because it was told to me in confidence. Lexie Allen was very close to us." I circled my hand around the table. "All of us at the Ballantyne. It's important we find out what happened to her so her family can be at peace."

Rory continued to twist and pull at her napkin.

"The Sea Pine Police, especially Lieutenant Ransom, are quite good at what they do, Rory," I said in a softer tone. "I may have told them about you and the Stream Kitchen, but they would've found out. And I don't mean eventually, I mean immediately. They aren't some small town Barney Fife-led organization."

"What is Barney Fife?"

Maybe I am older, I thought. "Never mind that. Whatever you tell me, I'll keep it quiet as long as I can, but the police will find out on their own."

"If I tell you, you'll keep it confidential like?" Rory said.

"Yes, absolutely." I left out the part about me not being an attorney and privilege didn't extend to PIs-in-training and charity board directors. But I was balancing concern for two young women, both close to the Ballantyne. One dead, and the other accused of killing her.

"Lexie and I were competitive. We met at the Wharf and both wanted to impress Chef Carmichael. Who had the best knife skills, created better flavor profiles, demonstrated molecular gastronomy techniques. Even whose coat fit better. Everything in cooking is a competition. When the Stream Kitchen opportunity came up, we both wanted that, too." She paused and took a long drink of her coffee. "We auditioned with like thirty other locals and our cooking stations ended up next to each other. I don't know, something happened, like a pan got bumped, and she snapped at me. I snapped back. It's like that in the kitchen. But we knew each other. It was normal. I don't think we would've been that way if we were strangers. You know, you try to be polite and all that."

"Okay," I said. "But what's so secret?"

"The producer loved the arguing. Immediately I noticed the cameramen spending more time on our station. Lexie noticed it, too." Rory took another big swig of her coffee, then held her cup in her hands. "We played it up. By the start of the third audition, we knew we were in. We'd fight like mean girls, then put up the best looking dishes on the set."

"This is great," I said, relieved Rory might not actually be guilty. "It helps you, Rory. The police think you hated each other, and that's your motive. But when they find out it was fake, they won't have anything."

"Except the poison berries in her apartment," Jane said.

"If she didn't put them there, then someone else did," I said. "I just need to point this out to Ransom."

"They can't find out," Rory said. "You said this was confidential." She turned to her Aunt Zibby, grabbed her arm. "Please, tell them they can't tell anyone. It'll ruin everything."

"Rory, the police think you killed someone," I said. "A tv show can't be more important to you than going to prison."

"I didn't kill her no matter what they think. But they'll kick me off the show for faking the fights with Lexie. Then Chef Carmichael will fire me. My career will be over."

"Why would Carmichael fire you?" I asked.

"Competition in his kitchen is more fierce than on the show. Chef wanted us on Stream Kitchen. Publicity for the Wharf. Now Lexie's dead and I'm accused of killing her. Which is crazy because I had a better shot of getting on the show with Lexie as my rival. Together we'd get double the air time, the interviews, everything. Now? Who knows? And that show is the only reason Carmichael hasn't already fired me. It's bigger than tv. It's online."

She had a point. I knew Carmichael, and he'd definitely keep her in his kitchen as long as it helped him. But even the faintest trace of scandal would get her chopped.

She laid her head on Zibby's shoulder and cried. Zibby patted her and hugged her and whispered reassurances.

I glanced at Jane and whispered, "I'll keep this to myself as long as I can. But at some point, it may become necessary to share it."

"Then don't get to that point," Jane said.

I waited until Rory's tears stopped and Zibby kissed the top of Rory's blue-haired head.

"What about a different motive?" I asked. "We have to think like the police. If we take the cooking competition out of the equation, we're still left with the girlfriend competition. You say you and Vigo are just friends, that Lexie wasn't really his girlfriend. What's that about?"

Rory sat up in her chair and pushed away her plate. "Nothing."

"It's not nothing. Were you jealous? Did you want Vigo to be your boyfriend? Maybe he wanted you, too, and took Lexie out of the picture."

She snorted and wiped drippy mascara from beneath her eyes. "That's ridiculous."

"Not really. That's what the police will think, I can tell you that much. You're the likeliest in the group."

"More like that kid Berg," Rory said. "Lexie had him trailing her around, hanging on her every word. He loved her so much, he almost hated her. She tortured him. It was her idea to get that stupid condo and live with Vigo. Throw it right in Berg's face and act like she didn't know he was in love with her."

"If you're making a list of suspects, don't forget Inga Dalrymple," Jane added. "She pushed for the performances to continue immediately after Lexie died. Without a single missed performance, not even the day after. It didn't ring an alarm with your crack detective skills, but she's just as likely as Rory. That makes two suspects more viable than Rory. Certainly even you can do something with that." Jane snapped her notebook closed and stood to leave. "I want to know everything you find out, the minute you find it out."

Zibby came around the table and hugged me. "You'll get this peccadillo tidied before Santa jingles into town."

Rory and Jane didn't look so sure.

I left them in the parlor and headed straight to my office. My phone rang and I almost didn't answer it. Feuding chefs? Inquiring reporters? It was neither.

"Elliott! Are you there?!" Mr. Ballantyne shouted.

"Yes, sir, I'm here," I shouted back.

"We're at the station," he yelled. "The trains just pulled out."

He sounded as if he was standing next to me, the line was so clear. He shouted anyway. Mr. Ballantyne was like Jimmy Stewart in stature and nature, with a dash of Errol Flynn on adventure.

"How are you? Coming home Wednesday?" I asked.

"Absolutely! Four p.m. arrival. Unless we come home sooner. Vivi is distraught over Zibby and her darling Rory."

"Us, too, sir. Jane and I just met with them both. They are doing well, and I'm dedicating every minute to helping them."

"Exactly the words I needed to hear," he said. "I spoke with the Allens this morning. They don't believe Rory could've done such a thing, and I agree."

"Me, too, sir," I said. "I'll get to the bottom."

"Before the week's end, I hope, Elli, dear," he said. "We're off to the next station. Adios and Godspeed!"

The week's end! It seemed a ridiculous goal, but Christmas was coming and no amount of bemoaning would stop it.

Rory was the police's main suspect (but not necessarily mine), and her being Zibby's niece provided me with strong motivation to find the police a new main suspect.

How did I not know Lexie's birth mother was locked up for murder? Or that Berg was practically stalking Lexie? Or that Lexie and Rory didn't actually hate each other? Lexie had two distinct factions in her life: cooking and dancing. I couldn't neglect one for the other. Time to put the spotlight back on the stage.

I needed gossip and I knew right where to go. Those snippy dance moms. I tucked my notebook into my hipster and left the Big House. Rory had a point about Berg. Perhaps he decided to act out those sketches. Vigo shouldn't be overlooked either. He had Rory on the side and Berg fawning over Lexie, who got all the attention. Vigo could've gotten sick of it. He had access to Lexie, Rory, and those berries. And why not Courtney? Maybe she wanted a promotion in *The Nutcracker*. She certainly got one. Courtney &

Co. knew her best. They were closest to her and if *Forensic Files* taught me anything, it was that people are nearly always killed by those closest to them.

Inga Dalrymple's Dance Studio was located in Palmetto Plaza off Cabana next to the Bi-Lo grocery. Johnnie Mae greeted me when I walked in. She sat behind a tall counter, but at a low desk. I peered over the ledge. Papers, books, CDs, and pens were scattered as if someone dumped a stuffed banker's box onto the surface. Complete disorganization. It made my teeth itch.

"Hi, Johnnie Mae, nice to see you again."

"You, too," she said. "Elliott, right?"

"I didn't know you worked here," I said and inwardly cringed. It seemed "I didn't know" was my most popular phrase this week.

"My third day on the job." From a distance her frail figure and gray-haired bun painted a picture of an aging senior, but up close, even past her sad eyes and pale skin, she couldn't have been older than fifty. "I'm here part-time, at least through the holidays. The last gal quit without notice. Up and left."

"That sucks," I said.

"I don't have much experience," she said. "But I couldn't leave Inga. She's a mess. The kids are unfocused, and the moms haven't had this much to gossip about since Amber's mother left town with her Pilates instructor. At least, that's what I heard." She grabbed a stack of file folders. "Sit here and you hear everything."

Voices drifted from around the corner. Distant, but distinct. Women cackling and biting and snarking. Just what I was hoping for.

"Is Inga in class? I wanted to catch a quick word," I said.

"It wraps in twenty, but you can wait with the moms," Johnnie Mae said. "Inga won't mind."

"Thank you, I think I will."

I followed the hen-pecking down the hall to an open door about twenty feet away, and then up five short steps. Three moms passed me on my way up and I entered a loft-like room. Two bleachers covered in carpet faced a wall of windows that overlooked a long studio. Seven little girls in white leotards and tights were forward-flipping on a line of blue padded mats, while up here in the observation room two mothers sat on separate benches.

I recognized them from the theatre. One mom with striped hair whose daughter was promoted to the Land of Sweets, the other with the blond pixie cut.

The talk faded when they saw me. "Are you a new mom?" the one with the pixie cut asked. By her scrunched up face, I figured being new was not welcome.

"I'm Ellio—"

"You're the lady from the Ballantyne," the striped-hair mother said. "I saw you from backstage." She turned to the benches behind her with her arms wide. "The night Lexie Allen died in her dressing room. I was there, you know."

"I know," pixie cut said, smacking down her arm. "The others left, remember? To go get coffee? It's just you and me in here."

"I hope I'm not interrupting," I said. "I came to talk to Inga about Lexie, but she's still in class." I looked through the glass and saw Inga clapping at a student. Not in the praise way, more like the pay attention right now way.

"Not at all," stripes said. "We're just so broken up about Lexie. She was such a sweet girl."

"Very sweet. Everyone loved her," pixie said.

"I'm Nora, by the way," said the striped-hair mom. "This is Francine." The two moms looked similar, yet completely different. Like two versions of the same person in different income brackets. Both blondes wore skirts and blouses. Nora was mid-level, as evidenced by her strip center salon highlights and cotton button-down. Nice, but off the rack. Francine was executive level. She wore her short hair swanky and glossy and donned a designer-cut tunic.

"Nice to meet you," I said.

I sat on the lower bench next to Nora and watched the tumblers below.

"You knew Lexie?" Francine said.

"Yes, she danced *The Nutcracker* for the Ballantyne's production the last three years," I said.

"To have her best friend carry on for her is amazing," Francine said. "Though Courtney's not nearly as pretty as Lexie."

"No kidding. Lexie was a stunner," Nora said. "Lucky break for Courtney."

"Instant promotion, right?" I said. "I think the police might be wondering about that."

"Really?" Nora said and scooted an inch closer. "That's not how it works, though. At least not for this production. Too small."

Francine laughed. "Yeah, but if we were talking Jacksonville or even a Charleston production...a whole new ball of wax."

"Besides, Courtney has several auditions lined up after the holidays," Nora said. "Much bigger than community theatre."

"The Sugar Plum Fairy really has just the one dance," Francine said. "Now, my Winnie is playing Clara, she's the real star. In practically every scene."

"Winnie doesn't get up on her toes like she should," Nora said. "Inga stuck her with the role of Clara, who basically sits through most of the performance. Not like my Queenie in the Land of the Sweets."

I'd never witnessed such brazen insulting behavior—directed toward someone else's child, mind you—dealt so casually. By both women, straight to their faces, without any reaction.

"Lexie's been with the studio since she was little, right?" I asked, getting the conversation on track.

"Both her and Courtney. Thick as thieves those two," Nora said. "All the way back to kindergarten. Always up to something."

"Courtney was the better dancer," Francine said. "But Inga favored Lexie. Everyone knew it."

"Well, of course she did. Everyone did," Nora said. "How could you not after what that child went through. No one begrudged her the lead."

"What did she go through?" I asked.

"You don't know?" Francine said.

"I heard her mother went to jail," I said.

"Prison," Nora said and scooched another inch closer. "For murder."

"Twenty years hard time," Francine said. "Surprised it wasn't more."

"It should've been," Nora said. "Killed her neighbor and abandoned her child."

"She killed her neighbor and abandoned Lexie?" I asked.

"Yes, indeedy," Nora said. She tucked her striped-hair behind her ear and geared up to tell the story. "Lexie's mother, her real mother, lived in this duplex in Beaufort—"

"In an alley," Francine interrupted. "Real cheap seats, you know? No garages or driveways, just these side-by-side houses crammed together. Pelican Alley, of all things."

"Courtney's mother still lives there," Nora said.

"No surprise," Francine said.

"I went over there once, and never again would I let my daughter in that neighborhood," Nora said.

"Your kids are too young to have gone there," Francine said.

"It was for a work thing, when I was younger," Nora said. "Never mind, that's not the story. Anyway, Lexie's mother was a drunk. What was her name? Something apropos..." Then with a finger snap, "Truby Falls!"

"More like Truby staggers," Francine said.

"Seriously. Anyway, Truby Falls was a drunk and smoked like a chimney. Never bothered to read the warning on the side of the pack."

"She should have, might have saved her life," Francine said.

A flurry of little ballerinas rushed into the studio below. Some picked up the tumble mats, some tied their hair into tiny buns, others ran up to Inga.

"Let me tell the story," Nora said. "Now one night, Truby gets drunk, and it's late, and she's smoking, and she passes out. Burns down the duplex."

"Not the whole thing," Francine said. "Truby saved herself, of course. Passed out, she said, in the bathroom after puking. Yeah, right. But the living room went up in flames and burned through to the unit next door."

"I'm telling this story, Francine," Nora said. "It burned through to the unit next door. By the time the fire department arrived, Truby's neighbor was dead."

"Where was Lexie?" I asked.

"Across the alley at Courtney's," Nora said. "They all woke up with the sirens and the trucks. Poor Lexie sat on the lawn and watched the police take her mama away."

"Poor Lexie? Poor neighbor lady who ended up dead," Francine said. "Lexie got adopted and she was better off for it."

"Ain't that the truth," Nora said.

That was a hell of a story and I'd never heard it. Made me think I spent too much time isolated on the island. This all happened in Beaufort. Only a thirty-minute drive through the lowcountry, Beaufort was like a tiny Charleston, minus the money and history. It had a petite downtown of shops and galleries on the water and was gateway to dozens of smaller islands and even poorer people.

"I think Inga's waving at you," Nora said to me.

I peeked into the studio below. Inga was pointing toward the door.

"Thank you, ladies, for keeping me company," I said. "Good luck with *The Nutcracker*. Maybe I'll see you at the theatre."

They stayed silent until I hit the bottom step. Then they practically spoke over each other. I couldn't quite make out what they were saying. They'd reduced their volume to whisper level.

I met Inga in the hall. "Do you have a second to chat?"

"Not really," Inga said. "But make it quick and I'll tell you what I can."

She grabbed a messy stack of folders from the front desk and led me to a squat bench outside the front door.

"Tell me about Lexie," I said. "She's been here since she was little?" I knew the answer before I asked the moms upstairs, but it was the easiest question to start with. To get people talking, sometimes you needed to lob an easy one across the plate.

"She was a dream. As a student and as a kid. A good kid," she said as she shuffled papers. "My star. She was going to dance on Broadway someday. She studied dance at UNC, but I coached her on school breaks."

"She quit school," I said. "She was working as a sous chef on the island. That was her new passion."

Her head snapped up. "What are you talking about?"

"Lexie dropped out of college to pursue a career in cooking. She was very talented."

"That's ridiculous."

"I spoke with her mother yesterday. She said Lexie loved dance, but she loved cooking more."

"Well, isn't that a kick in the teeth," Inga said. "You give your everything to make these kids into something special and they just abandon it. Damn parents. They ruin their children. Let them do whatever they want without consequences."

"Lexie wasn't exactly a child."

"She was a child. Her and her friends. They weren't grown up, but they thought they were. Thank God they aren't all abandoning my hard work. Vigo's class is touring with a revival of *La Cage aux Folles*."

"But Vigo's here. Why didn't he go on tour?"

"He wanted to study dance at UNT," Inga said. "After watching him as the Cavalier this week, it was the right decision."

"He and Lexie always been an item?" I asked.

"Mostly, when they were in high school." Inga pulled a folder from the pile and rifled through the contents. "They were in different classes here, but we did a competition using both teams. They were partners and it stuck. They were good for each other. Almost all of my dancers go on to be national performers."

"I heard Courtney has some really great auditions lined up after the holidays."

"And she should," Inga said. "She was always better than Lexie technically. The kid has great focus. Even though she doesn't interpret the choreography the way Lexie could. You believed her when she danced."

"Berg seems to be an up and coming choreographer."

"He's good. I let him choreograph some smaller pieces over the years," Inga said. "But he needs more emotion, more focus. Use his loner status to his advantage."

"Loner? I thought he, Courtney, and Lexie were inseparable."

"More like he follows Lexie around like a lovesick puppy. I told him to use that unrequited love to fuel his choreography."

Well, it fueled something. Though at least I had confirmation he really was a choreographer.

"Look, those three were tight," she continued. "And no jealousy between them. Which is unusual in this business." She re-stacked the folders and stood. "A lot of other dancers around here would've liked to see Lexie knocked down to get her roles."

"I thought that's not how it worked."

"That doesn't mean the other dancers liked having her around."

Someone didn't like having her around, I thought as I walked back to my car. And they used her love of cooking to make it happen.

THIRTEEN

(Day #5 – Monday Afternoon)

The biggest pieces of evidence, or only evidence as far as I knew, were the deadly nightshade berries found in both Lexie's and Rory's kitchen. Sometimes you follow the money, sometimes you follow the evidence.

People had answers, but I needed to ask the right questions. Was Mamacita's the only place to get deadly nightshade berries? How long would it take to grow the plants yourself? Were any nightshade berries missing from Mamacita's garden? What about those deer she thought busted in? And where was Berg when that happened? Where was Vigo?

Zibby said to take a gift when visiting Mamacita. I wasn't sure if she meant every single time I went, but better safe than sorry and all that, so I made a five minute detour into the Bi-Lo for a box of cupcakes. Store-bought wasn't close to Carla-made, but I didn't want to take the time to swing by the Big House.

I drove up Cabana to Marsh Grass Road and cruised along until I saw the Gullah Catfish Café and the dirt driveway. I wound around the back to Mamacita's worn trailer. The sun had begun its afternoon descent. It still shone through the branches, but the temp had dropped to the low sixties. The leaves on the tall trees rustled in the light wind, and a cat screeched in the distance.

I walked up the wobbly front steps and knocked on the metal door. It shook with each knuckle-wrap, and I swear I saw a curtain move, but no one answered.

"¡Hola!" I called. "Mamacita? I brought cupcakes." White snowman-shaped sprinkles covered the thick mound of red frosting. The super sugary kind you can only get at the supermarket. "Me torta para usted?" I tried to peer inside, but the curtains covered the windows frame to frame.

With plastic container in hand, I followed the foliage path along the side of the trailer to the main garden around back. I tapped on the chain link fence. It rattled and jiggled, but no one appeared. The padlock on the metal flip handle was undone, the bottom square part twisted away from the slim top tube part.

"Mamacita?" I called. "You out here?"

I surveyed the garden perimeter on both sides and tried to track the fence to where the deadly nightshade plants were cordoned off. The brush was too thick and I was in ballet flats. I kept a ton of emergency supplies in the Mini, but they fell into the beach category not the hiking category.

Though I wouldn't need hikers if I took the path *inside* the wild garden. I gently lifted the handle and slipped through the gate. The paths went in seventeen crazy directions and I felt as if a white rabbit with a pocket watch might skitter by. I remembered Mamacita taking me to the far left corner, so I followed the maze the best I could. I cut through two flower patches and found the low wooden picket border.

Deadly nightshade lined the outer chain link fence. I carefully stepped into the plot and leaned closer. The metal fence was bowed inward and loose on the bottom. Only the skinniest of arms could reach through one of the link openings, but the leaves practically touched them, so one probably wouldn't need to reach through. It was nearly impossible to tell if someone had snatched a handful of berries from one of the stalks. How many berries would kill a person? Five? Fifty? I knelt to check the backside of the plant and the right leg of my shorty pants got caught on a picket. I pitched forward and grabbed a stake for balance, but a plant was wrapped around it.

I screamed a most unladylike string of swear words and yanked back. I tipped over the picket and landed on my butt. Thorns from the plant had stabbed me in a dozen places. My hand was bruised and bleeding and I'd ripped my pants. But I still gripped the cupcake container.

Then the barking started.

Loud, sharp, vicious. I scrambled up and slowly backed away like I was taught as a child. Except I couldn't see where the barking was coming from. Maybe I was backing into it.

Thirty feet away, directly to my right. From behind the greenhouse. An enormous black Rottweiler stormed straight at me. Its teeth bared. Its legs pumping.

I ran.

Deep barks chased me through the flower beds. I skittered on the dirt path, but kept running. The gate was dead ahead. Had I latched it?

Over it or through it? Over it or through it?

I slammed into the gate. Flipped the latch. Flew through it. I stumbled and rolled. Flat on my butt. I shoved the gate shut with my feet and kept them there.

Two dogs, at least five hundred pounds each, barked their ever-loving heads off. Drool dripping with each sharp roar. I scrambled forward onto my knees and shut the metal latch. My hands shook. My entire body shook. And each bark made me twitch.

I'd landed on the cupcake container. They were smooshed. The plastic lid cracked and broken. I picked it up and mumbled something about knocking and cupcakes and bringing the requisite gift for Mamacita and how the hell could deer get close to this place, much less humans?

I scurried back to the Mini. The barking continued and the chain link fence rattled. I tossed the cupcake container on the passenger side floor. Stuck the key fob in the slot. Foot on the brake, shift into reverse, gas that sucker. I zoomed down the dirt drive and onto Marsh Grass Road as if chased by the zombie apocalypse.

I gripped the steering wheel with jittery hands as adrenaline rushed through my system. My legs started to vibrate and I had to pull over on the dusty shoulder. I closed my eyes and rested my head on the seat back.

After five minutes of swearing I'd never break in anywhere ever again, I lifted my head and took a deep breath. I saw Vigo in my rearview. He rode a motorbike and turned into the Gullah Catfish Café drive. With a five-second get-it-together pep talk, I whipped the Mini around and went back to Mamacita's.

I caught up with him walking toward the garden on the side of the trailer. "Hey Vigo, you got a second?"

"Sure," he said. "What's up?" He checked out my appearance from dirty and scuffed ballet flats to ripped and frosting-coated pants. "You okay?"

"Sure, yeah," I said. "I, ah, well, nothing really. Just a tiny accident."

The dogs went bonkers when the saw me. Barking, growling, jumping on the metal fence.

"Hey, girls, what's wrong?" He opened the garden gate and petted the two wild crazy terrorizing dogs. They licked him, and he laughed, then the dogs sat by his feet, one on each side. Panting and drooling, but keeping an eye on me. "Don't worry about these two. They're harmless."

"Uh-huh," I said. "Is your mom around?"

"Nah, she ran up to Savannah for the day," he said. "Won't be back until after sundown. One of those cemetery things." He said it casually, as if I'd know what the heck he was talking about.

"Sure, sure," I said.

"I'm sure she would've liked to have seen you. Because of Lex and all."

"Did Rory tell you I'm helping her? Helping both her and Lexie, really."

"Man, it's been a rough week for Rory," he said. "And Lex, too, right? For all of us. Anything I can do, you just ask."

"Was Lexie your girlfriend?"

"Wow, right to the point," he said. "I like it. Lex was more than that, she was my best friend."

"And Rory?"

"She's totally my best friend, too." Vigo knelt down to the dogs' level and scratched one of their necks. "But she didn't understand Lexie or our relationship. Rory and I are both competitors, I guess, but dance is different. We compete for trophies and solos and roles, but we're a family. Cooking isn't like that. It's always cutthroat. Really breeds insecurity."

"Can you tell me anything that can help Rory?"

"She didn't kill Lex," he said and shrugged.

"If you think of anything, please contact me." I reached into my handbag for a card and held it out to him. One of the dogs eyeballed me and growled.

Vigo laughed. "Come on, girl, it's okay." He took my card and slid it into his pocket without looking at it.

"I'll catch up with your mother later."

I still felt wobbly as I drove onto Marsh Grass Road, a mild undercurrent humming through my system. Like I'd gulped seven cups of coffee in ten minutes. My brain was buzzy and I felt disorganized.

Not just because of the dogs. But also because I hadn't yet gotten any real answers.

I reached for my phone.

"Hey, Parker," I said when she answered. "It's Elliott."

"You okay, El? You sound funny."

"I'm good, just rushing around, you know how it is," I said. "Anyway, do you still have the cupcakes from Lexie's dressing room in evidence?"

"Why?"

"Can I take a look?"

"No."

"Will you send me a picture?"

"Why?"

"I'm curious to know how many berries were in the cake. Can you tell me that?"

"No."

"What can you tell me?"

"I can tell you that you're getting better at this. You almost ask all the right questions."

"Almost? What did I miss?"

"Ask the Lieutenant," she said and hung up.

No problem, I thought, and dialed Ransom. If I wanted answers, I'd need to keep asking questions. Ransom finally picked up on the fifth ring.

"Debating whether to answer?" I asked.

He laughed. "What's up? I'm in the middle of something."

"Me, too," I said. "I'll keep it quick. How many deadly nightshade berries did Lexie ingest?"

"Hot on the trail, are we?"

"Yep."

"About five, from Harry's estimate, but it's only an estimate."

"That's not very many," I said. "That's all it took?"

"Yeah, about that. They work fast, not like arsenic where one poisons slowly over time."

No one would ever notice if five lousy berries had been plucked from that plant in Mamacita's garden. But what right question was I not asking, as Parker said? "Was there a specific variety of Nightshade?"

"Just the *Atropa belladonna*," he said. "I gotta run, Red."

"Wait! What am I missing, Ransom?"

"Me?"

"You're a who, not a what."

"You could still miss me."

"Seriously, Ransom, it's been an upsetting day and I need you to toss me a bone. A nugget. A morsel. When it comes to these stupid berries, what am I missing?"

"That bad, huh?" he said and paused two beats. "Okay, but only because I owe you. You're missing the where part of the berries."

"Where? Like where they were found?"

"Where they were grown."

"Mamacita's, that's where," I said. "I thought that was established."

"The game warden reported dozens of belladonna plants out at Stickly Island. The ground had been trampled. Rory didn't need to go to Mamacita's. She could've gone to Stickly."

Stickly Island Nature Preserve ran north off Sea Pine Island right before the bridge to the mainland. The four thousand acre refuge housed a variety of wildlife from herons to alligators, and though it was mostly salt marsh and tidal creeks, a hundred dozen different types of plants called it home.

"By that logic, anyone could've gone to Stickly," I said. "It's public land."

"Yes, but Rory considerately provided pictures of her and her Aunt Zibby out there hunting for their conservation group."

"Are you kidding? She gave you pictures?"

"Not directly. They're on their website. Rory and Zibby are standing in the same area as the belladonna plants. Going to be tough to argue that one."

"That's a stretch. It's still public. And you still owe me," I said and hung up.

I put the Mini in gear and pulled out onto the road. Here I am risking my life to examine a single deadly nightshade plant and there's an entire forest of them two miles away. But who knew about them? Just because Rory visited the preserve didn't mean she was foraging for poison berries. And it didn't mean she was the only one who knew those berries were out there.

FOURTEEN

(Day #6 – Tuesday Morning)

In case you must know my every move, I drove straight home and ordered pizza delivery. I ate an entire sausage, mushroom, and black olive all by my lonesome and polished off a six-pack of Dos Equis. There were only three bottles left in the paper carton, but I polished them off all the same.

Every dot connected to Rory. Conveniently so. If she didn't kill Lexie Allen, she was the perfect patsy. How did the real culprit know about Rory's trips to Stickly with Zibby? Realistically, they didn't need to. Rory connected to Vigo who connected to Mamacita who connected to a garden patch of poison. Just dumb luck Rory got an extra dot connected to Stickly.

The next morning, the sun barely brightened my bedroom from the skylight in the ceiling. I grabbed Lexie's iPad and tapped my way to the *Islander Post* home page. Nothing but a follow-up article rehashing Tate's speculation on the Ballantyne and ballerinas. No mention of Rory being related to Zibby Archibald or Vivi Ballantyne.

I tapped from icon to icon. The weather. Google News. Amazon. I scrolled through Lexie's reviewer page. A long bio including her dancing performances and college years, and a recent photo. Happy, smiling, lovely. Her silky blond hair pulled back into a long pony, barely a wisp of makeup. The opposite of Rory

Throckmorton, with her severe-cut neon blue hair and thick eyeliner.

I browsed through the hundreds upon hundreds of reviews Lexie left. Random products, in every category. I read one, then another, then another.

> *Product: A designer espresso machine (3 stars)*
> *Title: When You Need a Pick Me Up*
> *It was a looooong day at school. Needed 3 espressos to make it thru. Classes tougher and I'm losing interest. Working at night is wearing me down. I understand the saying about burning the candle at both ends. I feel like the flaming wicks will melt me away leaving nothing but a charred and empty string. Totally need something to get thru it. Maybe 7 espressos. This machine can handle it.*

By the fifth one, I realized these weren't reviews. These were diary entries. The text wasn't actually a review of the product itself as much as it was a vague reference to her day.

> *Product: Pink herringbone luggage set (5 stars)*
> *Title: Congrats to me!*
> *I got the job! I'm moving up and moving on!! Time to pack my bags. These are just what I need. I earned them but it took sooooo much out of me. I feel validated. I can do this and I'm good at it. Go me!*

Kind of clever. Public, yet private. She never had to worry a snoopy roommate would stumble upon her most intimate thoughts. She wrote them online for the world to read, but no one knew it. Just pop on over to Amazon, match a product to a mood, and journal about the day.

My cell rang while I was in the middle of one of Lexie's five star days.

"You better get down here," Tod said. "Jane just threatened

Carmichael who threatened her back. Looks like the Palm & Fig is off."

"It's not off," I said.

"That's what you think," he said and hung up.

Using my speedy yet efficient routine, I was dressed and out the door in fifteen minutes. I parked on the side of the Big House and entered through the mudroom. Two kitchen helpers I didn't recognize were scrubbing what looked like clean pans. They kept their heads down and their hands busy.

Muffled shouts got clearer as I pushed through the swinging door. I walked to the foyer where Carla and Tod stood by the tree, ten feet from Jane and Carmichael. They faced each other on the wool rug: Jane livid and Carmichael smug.

"You cannot suspend Rory from the Wharf," Jane said. "I'll make sure you regret this."

"And I'll abandon the Palm & Fig," Chef Carmichael said.

"Win, win," Jane said.

"Hold on," I said. "Carmichael, you can't walk out now. Your reputation is on the line as much as ours."

"Except you don't have much reputation left to protect," he said.

"Watch it, white coat," I said. "Don't let the newspaper fool you into thinking we have no pull in this town."

Carla stepped over to Carmichael and pointed a wooden spoon at him. "I'm done. You in or you out?"

Carmichael glanced at her spoon and tilted his head, as in thinking.

"I don't have time for your antics," Carla said. "This negativity is not infusing my food with love. You're making a sour Christmas, so make a decision." She poked his shoulder with the spoon handle and marched back to the kitchen.

"I expect Rory back on the job," Jane said. "Tonight. She'll be finished at the set in time to be here for prep."

"If she's not in jail," Carmichael said.

Jane ignored him and clicked her way toward her office.

Carmichael shrugged and headed to the kitchen.

"See?" I said to Tod. "The Palm & Fig isn't off."

"Don't be so sure," he said and waited until the swinging door to the kitchen stopped moving. He lowered his voice. "Inga Dalrymple was found nearly beaten to death this morning."

"What?"

"She's at Island Memorial in a coma."

"What?"

"Call came in right before you arrived. And you can thank me for waiting to say something until after Carmichael left. He'll abandon ship when he finds out. Not possible for one person to kill a ballet dancer and a different person altogether to attack her teacher four days later."

"That doesn't mean Rory did it."

"So you say."

Tod postponed the set up crew for the Palm & Fig while I rushed to Island Memorial. I didn't want to deal with the volunteer at the main desk lecturing me about police business and family members only, so I called Sid. She was on the board of directors for the hospital and spent many a day off in meetings on various floors.

Sid phoned down to the desk. After scribbling my name on the visitors' log, the volunteer slapped a name sticker on my chest, and directed me to the ICU on the third floor. Once off the elevator, the hallways were bright and busy. Mornings were the worst time to be a patient, especially when you needed rest. The staff was chatty and loud and catching up with daily duties. Lights shone and carts rattled and machines beeped and bonked from dozens of open doors.

Technically, I wasn't allowed to visit a patient in ICU, since I wasn't family. I slow-walked behind a nurse and busied myself with hand-sani (wholly unnecessary because hand-sani dispensers were mounted ten feet apart on every wall) until the nurse smacked the metal square door opener on the wall. I may have been faking my way into the unit, but the look of worry on my face was genuine. Somebody beat Inga Dalrymple so bad, it put her in a coma.

Two doctors spoke near the nurses' station. Their faces were solemn, and one kept looking over at the two police officers stationed by a patient room at the end of the hall, presumably Inga's. I passed an alcove with chairs and two sofas. A full coffee service counter lined the near wall. A stainless Keurig with a stocked K-Cup stand, a variety of flavored creamers, and packets of sugars, both real and artificial. A platter of muffins sat untouched next to rows of bottled water.

Courtney, Berg, Vigo, and two other people took most of the seats in the room. The two new guys resembled Sheldon and Leonard from *The Big Bang Theory*. So much so, I did a double take. I think it was the retro tees layered with hoodies. One thin and lanky, the other short and moppy with black glasses.

The group didn't notice me as I passed, but Ransom noticed me walking toward him. He was talking to the two officers posted outside Inga's room and gave me an encouraging head nod as I approached. A "no visitors" sign was posted in bright red letters on the door.

"Hey, Elli," Ransom said. "News travels fast." He led me to a chair grouping three rooms down the opposite hall.

"Is Inga going to be okay?"

"Unknown. Someone found her in the wardrobe department bleeding from the head. Looked like she'd been there all night."

"At the theatre?"

"Yep. It's a dangerous place to be these days," he said. "Especially with your client around."

"Rory isn't a regular at the theatre, Ransom. Dancers are."

"Maybe, but a witness says Rory was there—"

"What witness?"

He looked at his notes as if he didn't know. More likely deciding what to tell me. "Courtney Cattanach," he finally said. "She says Rory was at the studio yesterday arguing with Inga Dalrymple."

"About what?"

"I can't get into that," he said. "But I can tell you it does not look good for Rory Throckmorton. I'm sorry, Red." He tapped my knee with his notebook and started to rise. I grabbed his wrist to stop him.

"I know you're hesitant to share with me, but we both know I can walk down this corridor and talk to Courtney and Berg and Vigo."

He eased back into the chair. "I can walk down there and tell them not to talk to anyone but the police."

"Sure, but they'd never be able to do that. They're kids. They've probably already told their same stories to ten people and posted it all over Facebook."

A guy in scrubs passed us, pushing a tall rack on wheels. Each rack row held multiple food trays with metal domes. He stopped at the door to our left. "Hey, good lookin', your French toast is here."

Ransom sighed and leaned toward me. "Courtney Cattanach was packing up her car after rehearsal at the studio and saw Rory and Inga arguing through the big plate glass window out front. It looked heated. She didn't know what they were saying until Rory followed Inga outside and into the lot. Courtney didn't hear everything, but she did hear Rory threaten Inga."

"She threatened her?" I asked. "Like an 'I'll kill you' threat?"

"No, Rory said 'you'll regret this' to Inga."

"Maybe she misheard."

"Bergin Guthrie heard it, too. Courtney says he was standing right next to her."

"That's a long way from killing someone," I said. "And that was at the studio, not the theatre. And just because Courtney says Berg heard it, doesn't mean he did."

"I know, but it's early in the investigation. I'm on my way to talk to him now," he said and stood.

I stood, too. "Rory didn't do this, Ransom. Don't jump to conclusions."

"I don't jump to conclusions, Red, I form them."

"Well, you're forming the wrong one."

His phone rang and he checked the caller ID. "I gotta take this." He clicked a button and ducked into the closest patient room.

I pulled out my own phone and checked the time: 9:37 a.m. Ransom was on the phone, then he needed to talk to Berg, who was only a hundred feet away. Not much of a head start, but it was something.

I dialed Sid. "You still in the hospital? And free for the morning?"

"Actually, I am. Something up?"

"Meet me in the lobby."

I sped through the ICU security doors to the elevator in the fastest walk just short of a jog. I punched the button five times, just to be sure.

As I rode to the first floor, I realized I hadn't needed to sneak into the ICU after all. Seemed like anyone could waltz right through those security doors. Of course, no one was allowed into Inga's room. At least I hoped so. As it happened, I agreed with Tod's assessment: the same person who killed Lexie attacked Inga. And all my ballet dancer suspects were huddled a mere corridor away from her already injured body.

Sid waved from the sidewalk beneath the porte cochere at the hospital entrance. "What's going on with the dance instructor?" she asked.

"She's in a coma," I said.

"The medical part I knew. I meant the criminal part." Sid walked toward her car on the left and I walked toward mine on the right. We stopped in the second row.

"Let's take mine. It's faster," I said.

"It's not faster and mine's more comfortable."

"We're going to Savannah, not Seattle. It's like thirty minutes from here. And I drive faster."

She rolled her eyes and followed me to the Mini.

"You tell me the medical and I'll tell you the criminal," I said.

"I checked with the ICU station. Inga was brought in around

six this morning. She lost a lot of blood and never regained consciousness."

"Is she brain dead?" I said.

"No, but her brain is swelling. They're trying to get it down. In the meantime, she's under police protection. No visitors, not even family."

"Good to know." I fastened my seatbelt and hit the gas, reversing out of the spot. "Someone hit her over the head at the theatre. No witnesses, but lots of speculation." I gunned it again and we were speeding down Cabana. My turbo beat her turbo any day of the week.

"What's the rush?"

"We need to talk to Rory and get her story before Ransom does. He's tied up with Berg, but won't be for long."

"You can't think Rory killed Lexie over a spot on an internet cooking show, and then what? Tried to kill her instructor, too?"

"I don't think it, but Ransom does. Or some version of it." I whipped into the left lane and sped around a slow moving SUV packed with kids and a distracted mom. "Rory said they both landed spots on the cooking show, which eliminates the motive to kill Lexie."

"Do you believe her?"

"I do. Besides, it's too diabolical and Rory's young."

"Well, she didn't need to kill her, she just needed her out of the audition," Sid said. "Food poisoning would've done it."

"Interesting theory. That would be really embarrassing for Lexie," I said. "For her to get food poisoning from her own food, so severe it lands her in the hospital. If she missed the audition because of that, she'd be out."

"Maybe Lexie was purposely poisoned, but accidentally killed."

"Maybe. But if not by Rory, then by whom?"

FIFTEEN

(Day #6 – Tuesday Late Morning)

We crossed the long Talmadge Bridge and drove onto the storied streets of Savannah. Classic red velvet bows were tied onto gas lamps and merry green pine wreaths hung on wrought iron fences. I maneuvered the Mini toward the waterfront, then cruised down the alley next to the warehouse kitchen set. Cars were jammed in jellyroll tight, bumper to bumper. There wasn't a patch of concrete, even on the sidewalk, for my compact convertible. I ended up in the lot across the street behind a bar slash bistro.

"You coming with?" I asked Sid. I stuffed my phone in my pocket and swung my handbag over my head cross-body.

"You know it," she said.

We jogged across the street to the plain metal door. As before, it was quiet outside, but loud and chaotic inside, only times ten. A zillion can lights lit the entire soundstage. Bright and hot and dazzling. The polish on the stainless appliances shone and the glass fixtures sparkled.

At least ten people shouted directions, barked orders, hollered cues. Thick ropes of cable snaked and slithered over the concrete floors. We ducked around crew members, carefully avoiding the attention of the big dude near the entrance, keeping to the edges. I nodded at Sid, indicating the long buffet table filled with leftover breakfast pastries and fruit. "We'll blend if we loiter by the food."

I grabbed a handful of napkins, stuck a croissant on a plate with a scoop of cut cantaloupe and wandered to a group of cheftestants. Sid joined me and we stayed on the perimeter. I counted eleven chefs in matching white coats. Stream Kitchen was stitched on the left chest of each coat in red script. They were buttoning and fidgeting, but not really talking. Competitors. Except Rory wasn't in the group.

We hung back and Sid ate her breakfast selections. "Let's switch," she said.

She handed me her empty plate and I gave her my full one. I was starving, but no way I was eating food off a buffet. It'd been sitting there for hours, exposed to whatever was floating in the dusty dirty grimy warehouse air, and worse, every person in there probably hovered over some section of the table, breathing their germyness all over the food platters.

I surveyed the enormous soundstage. "I don't see Rory."

"Do you think Ransom arrested her?" Sid whispered.

"No, but maybe he detained her before she got here. He said he was headed to talk to Berg, but that doesn't mean he didn't send Parker over here."

"Anita Alvarez," a voice shouted. "You're up. Station one."

A woman about thirty with long wavy black hair hurried over to the mahogany island at the top of the set and stood behind the far station. Two cameras on wheels moved within a foot of her face. The pots and pans in front of her were steaming and frothing and sizzling. She posed with one hand on a pan, then with her arms crossed, then holding a butcher knife. She never smiled.

"Curtis Bolton," a voice shouted. "On deck. Station two."

While a guy jogged over to the spot on the island next to the first chef, I walked behind the group on the side. I scanned the room and recognized Penny, the intern from my earlier visit. She held a paper cup of coffee in each hand. She took a hesitant step forward, then stopped. Then again.

"Hey, Penny," I said in a low voice. But with all the bustle, she couldn't hear me. I tapped her on the shoulder.

She jumped and squeezed one of the cups. The lid popped off and coffee splashed out. "Oh!"

"I'm sorry," I said. "Here, let me help." I took one of the cups and handed her my stack of napkins.

"Don't worry, this isn't the first cup I've spilled today. I'm just happy this time the coffee's cold." She mopped up her hand and sleeve, then stuck the wet napkin wad into the topless cup. "You're the reporter lady."

"I'm not a reporter. I'm the director of the Ballantyne Foundation on Sea Pine Island." At her blank expression, I added, "I'm a friend of Rory's." A small fudge, but close enough.

Penny the intern took several large steps back until we were hidden in the shadows. "I really like her," she said. "But she's in big trouble."

"I know. That's why I'm here."

"That's great. Where is she?"

"I thought you could tell me. I need to talk to her."

"But that's why she's in big trouble," Penny said. "She's not here."

Two more names were called. Goodall and Lockerbie. They were moving down the alphabet at a pretty decent clip.

"How late is she?" I asked in a whisper shout.

"An hour, at least. If they call her name and she's not on set, they'll release her from the contract." She leaned in close, our foreheads almost touching. "Without a warning or anything."

"What are they filming?"

"These are the intro shots. You know, when they run the opening credits. This is only the first series. They have three other scene changes after this."

Someone tapped me on the shoulder, then it was my turn to jump.

"What are you doing here?" Rory asked.

"Rory!" Penny said. "You made it!"

"Made it? I've been in makeup," she said. "Someone dumped coffee on one of the chairs in wardrobe and I sat in it. Soaked my uniform through. By the time I got a replacement for both the pants and coat, I was the last to hit makeup."

"Oh, wow," Penny said. It was slightly less bright in our corner of the warehouse, but her face looked pink with embarrassment to me. "That's terrible," she choked out. She looked around, left to right. "Glad you're okay, Rory. I better get back." She scurried away through the mob of crewmen near the last island row.

"What's going on, Elliott?" Rory asked. "I don't have a lot of time." She, too, looked around. "If Fran catches you here, she'll freak."

"Inga Dalrymple was rushed to the hospital this morning," I said.

"Really? What happened? A heart attack?"

"Someone bashed her over the head at the theatre late last night and now she's in a coma."

She stepped closer and whispered, "And you think I did it?"

"No, I don't think you did it, but Lieutenant Ransom does," I whispered back.

"That's crazy. Berg was the last one at the theatre last night."

"How do you know that?"

"He's always the last one. I met Vigo and his dancer friends at the bar. We always go out after the performance. Except Berg, he never goes. The police should suspect him, not me."

"Well, the police have two witnesses who saw you arguing with Inga yesterday at her studio. They also heard you threaten her."

"I didn't *threaten* her, threaten her." She put her hands on her face, then pushed back her hair. "Is she going to be okay?"

"She's in ICU and not allowed visitors," I said. "But tell me why you argued. Was it about Vigo or Lexie?"

"Why would it be about Lexie?"

"Then Vigo."

Another name was shouted over the crowd and echoed across the room.

"Inga works him too hard and doesn't give him time off. He was late to rehearsal because of me, because of this," she said with a hand wave around the room. "I went to the dance studio to explain, but it was like talking to a dictator ruling her own country. She wouldn't even hear me out. And *she* threatened to replace him. That woman is a monster."

A stagehand walked by handing out squat bottles of water. We each took one.

"Look, I know I sound harsh. I'm sorry she's in the hospital," Rory said.

"There has to be more. Your explanation doesn't make sense. You're too old to go running to Vigo's teacher. What was your threat about?"

"It makes sense to me and I don't care if you don't believe me."

"I don't believe you. And trust me, I'm more gullible than Lieutenant Nick Ransom. He won't take the time to cajole another explanation out of you. He'll just cuff you and interrogate you from a jail cell."

"He will not," she said. "Jane said he's not as tough as he comes off."

"He arrested her pretty as you please, and right in front of a crowd. Tucked her in a squad car and dragged her to the station." I took a swig of water and pointed the bottle at her. "I love your Aunt Zibby like she's family, so I will help you until I no longer can. But you better start helping yourself before you're the one tucked in a squad car."

"Carly Shamas," a voice called. "Station one."

"Fine," Rory said. "Inga Dalrymple was going to ruin Vigo's life and I needed to stop her."

"Well, she's stopped now."

"Now I'm on a killing spree? I lose an argument with someone, so I just kill them? Who does that?"

"Actually, it happens a lot. People would rather kill someone than deal with them. Divorce, neighbor disputes, hiding secrets, money troubles..."

"Rory Throckmorton," the booming voice shouted. "You're on deck."

"I gotta go." She pushed her way through the minglers to our left.

"Wait, Rory," I said and followed her. "Why were you fighting Vigo's battle?"

She never turned back, just kept pushing through.

"I'm here to help!" I called.

I may have raised my voice on that last line a bit too much. I caught the attention of two stagehands and the beefy security man near the door. Sid grabbed my arm, and with a wink to the security guy, she and her tall self rushed me out of the warehouse.

"Well? Did she do it?" Sid asked.

"I don't think so," I said. "But she isn't telling me what's going on."

"Something's going on?"

"Yes, definitely. With her and Vigo and this whole group."

We waited for traffic to pass, then crossed the street.

"Want to get a drink?" I asked.

She made a production out of checking her watch. "It's a little early, don't you think?"

"Perhaps," I said, and pulled open the door to the bistro bar. "Lunch, then?"

The hostess let us pick our own table out on the patio. Which was really a strip of sidewalk in front of the bar with rickety two-seaters. She handed us sticky plastic menus, took our drink order (one Pepsi, one iced tea lemonade), and left us to decide our meal choices.

I'd picked a table facing the alley of the warehouse. I wanted to see if, or really when, Ransom showed up. It was eleven thirty. I figured he'd be there in less than an hour.

My phone rang right after our sandwich platters arrived.

"Elliott, dear? It's Zibby Archibald." Zibby was old school Southern gentility. She always introduced herself on the telephone. No matter how often you spoke with her or explained caller ID.

"Hi Zibby, how are you?"

"Good, dear. Having a nice visit with Lily Parker," she said and lowered her voice. "I'm in the kitchen getting her a raspberry punch. She's asking about Mrs. Dalrymple, the dance teacher. Is Rory in more trouble?"

"I'm not sure. But I'm keeping a close eye on the situation. I'll take care of her."

"Okay, I trust you. I better go. You tell Rory I love her."

My heart started to crack.

"Parker is at Zibby's asking about Rory and Inga," I said to Sid after I clicked off. "I don't know what I'll do if Ransom shackles that girl and books her for murder."

"Yeah, that'll make for an awkward dinner date."

"That, too."

Sid pointed to the alley with her fork. "Maybe Rory's boyfriend's come to get her out of town."

Vigo Ortiz maneuvered his motorbike around two parked cars and stopped short of the set door.

"Don't even think it," I said.

Five minutes later, Rory and Vigo slipped outside and hurried down the alley. They ducked behind a car.

"Be right back." I jogged across the street with my head low and quietly dipped behind a car on the opposite side of the alley from where Rory and Vigo stood.

I tiptoed closer. I could barely hear their conversation, so I duck-walked another car down, loose rocks crackling under my shoes.

"—the cove beach by the condo," Vigo said. "You know where."

"Tonight? Why tonight?" Rory said.

"Because it has to be tonight, and you know it. Be there at midnight exactly."

Rory looked over at the closed warehouse door. "Why didn't you just text me?"

"You're on police radar now. They're probably monitoring your calls or checking your call history. We can't take chances that this gets out."

"Fine, I'll be there."

"Berg will be there, too."

"Vigo!" Rory said with a light stomp of her foot. "He's going to find out."

"He won't find out. I'll be careful and it'll be okay."

"I don't think so. Someone nearly killed Inga last night."

"I know. I've been at the hospital all morning."

"The police think I did it." Rory again glanced at the warehouse door. "They know about my argument with Inga. And if they know that, then how long until they find out the rest?"

Vigo hugged her quickly and then pulled back. He kept his arms on top of her shoulders. "The performances will end, holiday break will be over. I'll go back to school, and you'll be a cooking rock star. The investigation will die out, and no one will find out. I promise."

"My Aunt Zibby's friend is all over this. She just left."

He laughed. "She's a little Chihuahua. Out of her league."

"This isn't funny, Vigo. If your mom finds out, she'll be devastated. She loved Lexie."

"Look, don't stress so much," he said. "I better get back to the hospital before someone notices me missing."

"Is the show canceled tonight?"

"No," he said. "Inga would kill us if we did that."

"Whose idea was this anyway?"

"Courtney's."

"Which makes it a bad idea. Who made her boss?"

"She did," he said. "About thirteen years ago."

They walked to his bike and hugged, then Rory went through the steel door and Vigo sped off.

I crossed the street and joined Sid at the table. "Those kids are hiding something," I said. "And it can't be good."

"Yeah? What's up?" Sid asked and took a drink of lemonade.

"Vigo isn't impressed with me. He likened me to a Chihuahua humping a pug."

Sid spit lemonade across the table and onto my linen tunic.

"Sorry, sweetie. He really said that?"

"I'm paraphrasing," I said and dabbed lemonade splotches with my napkin.

"What are they up to?"

"I don't know. Something down at the beach. Clandestine, don't tell anyone, for your eyes only. That kind of thing. And a specific mention about Berg being there and finding out their secret."

"You think they'll confess and then kill Berg?"

"I think they're teenagers and their whole lives are clandestine. Probably going to do nothing but get wasted and make out around a bonfire. Want to go?"

"Well, when you put it that way."

"They could also confess and kill Berg."

"I can't either way. Milo and I have a date. You'll have to sweet talk someone else into going."

"I'll go to the beach alone," I said as the waitress approached. She cleared our plates and refilled our drinks, while Sid and I smiled and nodded and waited for her to leave.

"Don't you need backup?" Sid asked.

"Only if I get caught."

SIXTEEN

(Day #6 – Tuesday Late Night)

Sid and I waited three hours for Ransom to show at the warehouse, but he never did. I didn't know whether to be happy or wary. We drove back to the hospital and went our separate ways. I alternated between the ICU floor, the police station, and the Wharf restaurant. An entire afternoon in circles. No arrests, no interrogations, and Inga's condition never improved.

I made an appearance at *The Nutcracker* that evening, which was the most solemn performance ever danced in the history of Christmas. The audience crackled with nervous energy, between the death of the Sugar Plum Fairy and the attack on the producer, while the dancers themselves looked exhausted and strung out.

Ten minutes before the curtain closed, I slipped away and drove to my cottage. Vigo told Courtney to meet at the beach at midnight exactly, which meant I needed to arrive much earlier to remain unseen.

I dressed in all black, from my tennies to my fedora. Then I changed. All black worked in dark alleys and secret caves. I was headed to the beach. Better to blend with the sand and sea grass if I went beige. Plus my floppy canvas sunhat looked more "I'm just hanging out" and less "I'm here to spy on you."

With a flash of the paper security pass, I drove through the

Sugar Hill Plantation gate just after eleven p.m. The moon was slightly more than a sliver and didn't help illuminate the road any better than the random street lights did.

The public beach access path was directly across the road from Deidre's condo. I figured the group would park there and walk across, which meant the Mini needed to be someplace else. I chose a lot three buildings down from the condo, but on the ocean side of the road, between a pair of SUVs. I tucked my phone in my pocket and hid my handbag behind the driver's seat. I grabbed a beach towel from the trunk and quickly followed the sidewalk to the wood plank path to the sand.

I walked casually, but quickly, then stopped when I hit the last plank. The tide was so low, the water had receded nearly two hundred feet. The hard-packed sand stretched beyond where I could see. Wisps of moonlight glinted off the tiny tide pools left behind.

So much for hiding on the bank out of sight behind a sand dune mound. Not that I wanted to snuggle amongst the dirty buggy scratchy sea grass, but spying and eavesdropping required cover, and the beach before me was akin to standing in the middle of a football field. Flat and open in every direction. I could still hide behind a sand dune, but they could end up hundreds of feet away.

I scurried back to the Mini, ditched my hat, and rifled through the trunk. I emerged with binoculars, a thick sweatshirt, a fold-up chair in a bag, and a loggerhead turtle migration book. Yes, I had one with me. I also had a museum handbook, a golf course guide, a lighthouse pamphlet, two yacht club brochures, a clipboard, and seven maps covering the states of South Carolina and Florida. A PI-in-training needed undercover materials.

Using my deductive skills, I reasoned Courtney and Co. probably wouldn't gather close to the plank path. They'd walk toward the water either to the left or right. I strung the binoculars around my neck and the chair bag strap over my shoulder and walked toward the water. When I turned back, lights from a bank of condos shone brightly on the right side. I chose the left.

I set up watch about ten feet in front of the dunes. I found an abandoned stake near the grass and used it as a prop. Loggerheads laid their eggs in the summer and the hatchlings headed out to sea in the fall. Little turtles were already swimming their way to warmer waters this time of year, but I hoped no one would realize it. Tall sea grass rustled in the wind all around me. I was partially hidden, but also partially exposed.

It was a no-go. Extremely plausible midnight turtle watching cover story or not, one glance at a stranger and they'd keep walking until I was no more than a dot near the dunes. I quickly packed up, tossed everything behind a sand mound, and hurried into the grass.

I'd barely settled in when I heard them approach. For a clandestine meeting, they weren't very stealthy.

"I thought we needed a full moon," a girl said.

"Did you bring the feathers?" a guy asked.

"I've got everything we need," Courtney said. I couldn't make out her features, but I recognized her voice. It looked as if she was carrying a box larger than an upright suitcase.

With talk of feathers and a full moon, maybe this was a ritual. Vigo did mention Mamacita was in Savannah for some kind of cemetery thing.

Four more people stepped onto the beach from the walk and joined the others. I was wrong about the group straying far from the path. They gathered twenty feet in front of me and slightly to my right, straight in front of the beach walk.

"Did you tell anyone?" Courtney said. "Or did anyone see you arrive?"

The group answered one collective "no."

"Good," she said softly, almost too softly. I could barely hear. "This is a private ceremony."

I didn't move or breathe, hoping no one would notice me tucked in the thin grass stalks. With the tide far away, its muted roar provided a steady, yet faint, soundtrack. The wind blew at higher speeds on the beach, adding to the eerie and romantic calm of the late night.

It was freezing and bitter cold. No one so much as glanced around. Not another soul was on the lonely beach. Two lights blinked off from the condo complex on the other side of the path.

Courtney knelt on the sand and took the lid from the box. The remaining five members stood behind her, all with their backs to me.

I lifted the binoculars and tried to focus in the black night.

Courtney handed each member of the circle something. They held it in their hands, individually, and began to chant. Courtney clicked a butane lighter and passed it from person to person.

Candles.

And flowers.

They weren't chanting, they were singing. A song I didn't know. A sad verse of love and loss and meeting again someday.

Through the binocular lens, I made out Courtney, Berg, Vigo, and Rory. I also recognized the two *Big Bang* lookalikes from the hospital. The Sheldon one stood next to Vigo. He placed his left hand in Vigo's right. They held hands through the song, then squeezed them tight as it ended. They dropped them the instant it was over.

"So that's the big secret they're trying to hide," I said under my breath.

"What's that?" Ransom said.

I yelped and he put his hand over my mouth.

"Shhhh," he whispered close to my ear.

Carrying flowers by candlelight, the group slowly walked forward toward the sea.

I smacked Ransom's hand away from my face and punched him in the arm. "What are you doing here?" I whispered.

"Your stakeout skills are slipping."

"They didn't see me."

"No, but I did."

I rolled my eyes with great melodrama, but it was wasted in the dim moonlight. We shared my binoculars and watched the dancers place their flowers into the ocean, one by one. It took ten minutes for them to return to their original circle where Courtney's box sat on the compact sand.

Berg stopped halfway back. He knelt, and stood, then knelt again. Pacing and kneeling across a twenty-foot span of sand.

Courtney hugged the *Big Bang* Leonard and wept, Vigo hugged the other girl. Their soft cries were carried along the coast by the chilly winds sweeping across the flat shoreline. Berg finally returned alone. He passed the group without stopping, nearly marching toward the wood walkway. Once he hit the first plank, he ran.

The rest of the group gradually broke up. They handed their candles to Courtney. She packed them away and followed the trail back toward the condo.

"What was that about?" Ransom said.

I stood and dusted grit and bits from my pants. "Now we're sharing?"

"Of course, Red. We always share."

"I don't think so."

Ransom took my hand. His warm strong hand engulfed my freezing cold fingers. He tucked a towel under his arm and led me toward the calm ocean water. We stopped halfway to where Berg had been pacing and kneeling.

Berg had drawn Lexie in the sand. He placed a flower ring on her head and she was dancing with a dolphin.

We continued closer to the water's edge and sat on the towel on the damp sand. I rested my head on Ransom's shoulder. He wrapped his arm around me. We'd been on that beach, or one nearby, twenty years earlier. In love. Forever ahead of us.

Flowers flowed with the gentle tide, slowly washing out to sea, reminding me forever wasn't always ahead.

"Why only seven words on my answering machine when you left?"

"You counted them?"

"It's not that hard to count to seven." *Not our time, Red. You take care.* I was young and thought he was the love of my life. I replayed that message until the tape wore thin.

"Recruiting happened fast. The government is like that. I barely had time to pack." He stroked my hair, softly running his fingertips through the strands. "I thought about that message all the way to Quantico. Part of me regretted not saying more. But we were kids. I didn't know where my training and assignments would take me. Details I could never share with you."

"Or you could tell me, but then you'd have to kill me?"

He laughed low. "Something like that." He lifted my chin up toward his face. "Someday you'll forgive me." He placed his hands on my cheeks and kissed me. Slowly, softly, deeply. My insides sparked and I held onto his shirt, gripping it with my fists. I'd missed him and his kiss and his love my whole adult life. It was comforting and invigorating and suddenly ice cold.

The tide was returning. Seawater crept up to my shins. It was only romantic if you didn't mind sand in your pants and your hair and freezing water soaking your feet.

Ransom helped me up. The moment washed away like the flower rings in the sea. He held my hand as we walked back past Lexie dancing in the sand. With the tide rising, she'd be gone by morning. But really, she'd be gone forever.

SEVENTEEN

(Day #7 – Wednesday Morning)

Melancholy enveloped me through the night and into the early morning. Lexie (murdered so young), Ransom (what might have been), Matty (our friendship felt broken), my parents (distant when alive, but now gone forever). I burrowed deep beneath my quilt and wallowed in my blue state. It didn't help that I'd chosen a New Age Pandora station on Lexie's iPad to fall asleep to. Wispy Irish ballads mixed with sorrowful instrumentals and I never wanted to get up.

My alarm sounded, and I was forced to roll over to smack the off button. I tapped the Pandora icon and made the melancholy stop.

The Ballantynes were to arrive home today. I missed them and was looking forward to spending the holidays together. They always brought me peace. But Christmas would be less bright with the death of their dear friend's child. Even worse if Rory Throckmorton was in jail for her murder. Rory, Vivi Ballantyne's cousin's niece, the main suspect.

I shook off my blue and padded downstairs in bare feet. I poured a bowl of cereal and took it and my notebook out to the patio. It was brisk and refreshing. Morning joggers ran close to the shoreline while owners let their dogs splash in the sea.

I needed to make a list of the loose ends. I skimmed to the

beginning pages of my notes. Three things from my search of Lexie's room: the iPad (an oversized non-phone), the dry cleaning stub (two chef's coats), and a stack of single tickets, one for each *Nutcracker* performance (importance unknown). Who were the tickets for? A boyfriend? Considering I saw Vigo holding hands with a boy on the beach, he probably wasn't actually her boyfriend, just like Rory said. Then who was? I added the tickets to the list of loose ends, but really, how could I figure that one out?

Thinking of *The Nutcracker* led me to the attack on Inga. Pretty brutal, and it had to be connected to Lexie's death. Inga argued with Rory, but much earlier in the day. According to Rory, Berg was likely the last person at the theatre. Was he the last one to see her unharmed? Why didn't I think to ask Ransom last night on the beach? I flushed and touched my tingly lips. That man was a damn distraction.

I continued with more note-skimming and page-turning. Lexie's birth mother, Truby Falls, was serving a twenty-year sentence for murder. She killed someone, so then maybe someone killed her daughter? Definitely a loose end for my list.

Rory's other connecting dot: the nightshade berries at Stickly Preserve. That might've been enough for Ransom and his team of detectives, but I couldn't get past the links from Mamacita to Vigo and on to Rory and Lexie. Vigo's mother just happened to have a bushel of the exact same deadly berries, and she also talked to Lexie about them? And the same week, deer trampled Mamacita's garden in the exact spot where the nightshade plant grew? I added two more things to my list: Berg's whereabouts for Inga's attack and Mamacita's garden.

Which first? Murdering mother, death sketch drawing dancer, or killer berry growing Mamacita? My final decision: Mamacita, the most accessible. Second, the mother who was in prison somewhere in the State of South Carolina. Third, Berg. I could catch up with him later. I knew exactly where he'd be.

I called Tod. My day at the Ballantyne was booked from breakfast pastry to midnight snack, but Rory came first.

"I won't be in until later," I said when Tod picked up. "Can you postpone the set up crews again?"

"You planning on setting up the Palm & Fig as the guests arrive? Perhaps we can hand each a chair and a knapsack with their table settings to take up to the ballroom."

"Don't be melodramatic, Tod. I'll get it done. Tomorrow," I said. "Today I need to absolve Rory before the Ballantynes get home. Or at least find reliable evidence against someone else."

"The Ballantynes arrive at four p.m."

"I know. I'll be there. But I have to get Rory out of the fire before they arrive."

"That gives you eight hours. You better get moving," Tod said. "I hope you're dressed."

I glanced down at my Kermit pjs. "Obviously I'm dressed."

Once I showered and put on big girl clothes, I headed to Mamacita's with a promise to myself if she wasn't home, I'd leave without snooping (thereby eliminating any imminent dog attacks), and with one quick detour to the Bi-Lo for added insurance.

The Gullah Catfish Café was jammed for breakfast. Cars were parked cattywampus from the dirt shoulder to the dirt drive around back. A line of hungry diners poured from the open screen door. My sunroof was open and the smoky scents of grilled sausage and crisp bacon accompanied me all the way to Mamacita's trailer.

Vigo sat on the rickety porch steps. The two dogs rested at his feet. Until I walked up. They sat at attention like gargoyles guarding the castle gates. They growled as I approached, but this time, I came prepared.

"Morning, Vigo," I said and held out a package of raw hamburger. "This is for you and your mother."

"Hey, cool," Vigo said. "Let me put them inside. My mom's out back." The dogs danced with excitement and Vigo talked to them as he led them through the front door. He hadn't raised a single questioning eyebrow. Clearly not the oddest gift he'd received.

He returned two minutes later and settled back onto the steps. "You're still here."

"I know this is sensitive, but I saw you at the beach last night," I said softly. "With the other boy, holding hands."

His easy smile and relaxed expression faded slightly. He glanced over his shoulder, then stood. "I don't know what you're talking about." He walked over to his motorbike. It was parked next to the Mini in the small turnout.

I followed. "Rory is protecting you, right? That's what all the secretive behavior is about."

He put on his helmet and snapped the strap without saying a word.

"Vigo, you said Lexie and Rory were your two best friends," I said. "One is dead and the other is accused of killing her. Rory will go to prison."

He swung his right leg over the bike and sat down. He stared out into the distance.

I leaned against the Mini's driver door and waited.

Distant birds called high atop the tall trees. The morning air smelled of fresh pine and burning wood and grilling breakfast meats.

"My family wouldn't understand," he finally said. "I'd be an outcast in the Hispanic community. They're not very accepting of gay men. Mama is old world." He gestured toward the exotic garden. "*Old*, old world."

"And Lexie? How did she end up being your girlfriend?"

"She didn't want to hurt Berg's feelings. She knew he loved her, but she didn't love him back. In high school, Mama kept setting me up with nice girls. So Lexie and I made a deal. We became a fake couple. No one knew."

"Rory knew."

"Yeah, she's known a long time. And then Inga found out. Me and Danny, we met at her studio—"

"The boy from last night?"

"Yeah. At an after-party last week, Inga took a bunch of pictures and posted them on Facebook. In one of them, in the background, you could see me and Danny holding hands. It was like for a second."

"That's what Rory was arguing about with Inga? She wanted Inga to take the picture down?"

"Inga already took it down. She noticed it right away. But Inga told me to tell my parents because she wasn't going to lie for me. I don't think she would've told anyone, but I got scared."

"And Rory was protecting you."

"She's a good friend. So was Lexie. They both looked out for me." He started the bike and revved the engine. "I didn't look out for either of them." With one more rev, he skidded in the dirt and rode away.

I followed the landscaped trail to the garden. Mamacita was right inside the gate. She wore an enormous straw hat on her head with the pull strings on the chin strap tight against her chin.

"¡Hola!" Mamacita said when she saw me. "Como estas?"

"Bien," I said. "Como estas?"

"Oh, muy bien," she said. "Have you come to tour my plantas?"

"No, no. Not today, but soon. I just have a quick question about the deer."

"Ay, the deer," she said. "They creating havoc for all the island."

"Do you know if there was a migration going through or a special time of day they're more active?"

She eyeballed me from beneath her hat.

"Information for the Ballantyne and the Stickly Island Preserve coalition," I said. "That kind of thing."

"Si, si," she said in a skeptical tone that belied her agreeing words. She took off her colorful canvas gloves and put her hands on her hips. "Lemme think. Last week, when you and me saw the trample...ay, it was the second time."

"When was the first?"

"Oh, Tuesday, the week before."

"Are you sure?"

"Si, si. The only day I wasn't in Savannah. Had to be early evening or maybe later afternoon. I was out here until three or so.

Came out again at seven. Though the perros were barking like four thirty. Right in the middle of my novellas. Maybe the deer startled them and they started barking?"

"Maybe," I said. "What exactly did the deer eat?"

"Anything they wanted. I don't count the plantas and berries."

"Thank you, Mamacita. I brought hamburger and gave it to Vigo, before he left." To make sure she knew I brought a gift.

"Gracias," she said.

"Adios," I said and walked back to my car.

I thought back to *The Nutcracker* schedule on the refrigerator in Deidre's condo. Tuesday that week, and every day that week, they had dress rehearsal at four. The entire cast should've been there. Should've didn't mean they were.

I dialed Parker and she answered on the first ring.

"Make it quick, Elliott," she said. "I'm at the hospital and not supposed to use my phone outside of police business."

"This is police business," I said. "Anyone acting suspiciously?"

"No one's held a pillow over Inga's face while I've been on watch, if that's what you mean."

"Did you interview Berg? I heard he was the last to see Inga the night she was attacked."

"We did. And Rory, too. Yesterday. You're falling behind."

"When did you interview Rory? I was all over the island yesterday and hardly let that girl out of my sight."

"Hardly isn't good enough," Parker said. "I gotta go, El. Good luck."

"Wait! What about Berg?"

"Still investigating. But it's Rory you need to worry about. Now I really gotta go," she said and hung up.

Next I called Rory. Then Jane. No answer. Since Rory was at the beach late last night, and Parker didn't mention arresting her this morning, Rory wasn't in custody. Yet.

I checked my watch. Almost ten a.m. Time to track down Lexie's birth mother.

Most modern PIs do everything online these days. But my

years of fundraising and board member herding taught me that personal meetings net better results. I needed to talk to someone at the county courthouse and get the scoop, the file, and interview Truby Falls in prison. Face-to-face.

I drove the thirty minutes to Beaufort. It was situated across the bay from Sea Pine, but since I wasn't piloting a boat, I had to take the long way via highway roads. It was a quiet drive and I kept my sunroof open. It was too chilly to put the top all the way down, but I loved the fresh briny air as I traveled across a number of long bridges, the river water barely covering large patches of lowcountry.

The county courthouse was a beauty of pillared majesty with wide front steps. Two mighty flags fluttered in the wind, high on tall poles. The patriotic red, white, and blue familiar to every county courthouse, and the deep blue background with a white palm and moon native to South Carolina.

An elevator ride up, an elevator ride down, three hallway turns, four backtracks, and five lines later, I presented myself to a clerk behind a glass window.

"I need information on an old case," I explained for the sixth time in an hour. "Truby Falls was the defendant. House fire on Pelican Alley eleven years ago."

A nice lady in a polyester suit and plastic glasses tapped her fingers on the keyboard in front of her. Her monitor was the size of a boulder. I imagined lines of text blinking from a rectangle cursor slowly ticking across her screen like a typewriter.

"You'll need a FOIA request," she said. "It'll take a while because it's a closed case." She pulled a stack of forms from a folder.

"Can you tell me which prison she's in? I'd like to visit her. Today, if possible." I didn't have weeks to wait for a Freedom of Information Act request to get processed. Faster to pop over to the prison and get details from Truby herself. See if she had enemies vengeful enough to kill.

"All visitation requests must originate from the inmate," she said. "You'll need to get those forms from her. Once she's put you on her list, and you return the forms, they'll be processed. Each prison will have different visitation rules. You'll need to contact her attorney."

"That's it? There's nothing you can tell me?"

"Nope. But you can always go online. Search the case files, do an inmate search. Find out where she's housed, how much time she received for which charges, see what programs she participates in, if any." She slid me a stack of FOIA forms and wished me luck.

I sat on the courthouse steps and started the Google machine on my phone, but it was way too small and it frustrated the crap out of me. I thought about the iPad with its built-in cellular access, but I'd left it at my cottage. I went to the library instead.

Located near the water and the lively downtown, the county branch of the library was on a small side street nestled amongst clapboard houses with shutters on the windows and rocking chairs on the porches. Huge palms and magnolias lined the streets with Spanish moss hanging low on the branches.

After flashing my library card, I sat at one of the far computer terminals. It'd been over an hour since I left Sea Pine Island, and in less than five minutes online, I found Truby's case. She was convicted off Second Degree Arson (ten-year sentence), Malicious Injury to Property (five years), Burning Personal Property to Defraud Insurer (five years).

That's why that dance mom said "yeah, right" when talking about Truby getting sick in the bathroom. The police found evidence of arson and fraud. Truby must've faked the whole thing for the insurance money, and someone died in the process.

I clicked over to the Department of Corrections database. That took much longer. Fifteen minutes on the inmate search and no trace of Truby Falls. Though I was surprised how thorough the database was. I could search everyone with a last name starting with a B. Page after page of inmates popped up, with a link to each inmate's profile. The detail amazed me. The record showed a recent photo, their full name and age, plus their entire record of charges and sentences. Below that it listed every instance when they left the facility and why. Court appearances, trips to the infirmary, furloughs, their job history inside the prison.

Interesting resource for my PI-in-training career, but didn't help me with my current case. I cleared out of the search and left the library, driving the mile or so back to the courthouse. After two wrong turns inside the building, I stood in line for the same clerk who assisted me earlier.

"Hi again," I said when it was my turn. "I found the information I needed on the court case, but I can't find her in the DOC database. Truby Falls."

She click-clacked along her keyboard. "You'll have to contact her attorney." She wrote a name on a slip of paper and slid it through the half-moon window opening.

"Can't you help a girl out?" I asked. "This woman I'm trying to track down? Her daughter was murdered last week. Lexie Allen over in Sea Pine Island." I showed the clerk my temporary credentials, which amounted to not much more than a typed piece of paper with my name and application level for PI status. "You can contact Corporal Lily Parker at the Sea Pine Police Department to verify."

"Well," she said and looked around. "I've known Lily for years. I guess it can't hurt." She gestured to her screen. "Not like this isn't public record."

"Thank you so so much," I said as she scrolled the wheel on her mouse.

"Truby Falls was released about a month ago," she said. "That's why you can't find her. The database is for active inmates only."

"What? She received a twenty-year sentence, and that was like ten, eleven years ago."

"Ten years. She was arrested eleven years ago, spent a year in jail during trial. Out now with time served. Only the arson charge carried the class B felony, the other two were much lower. She qualified for accelerated release."

"Is she on parole? Can you tell me her parole officer's name?"

"Nope. Time served. No parole."

"Holy cow," I said. "Where is she now?"

"Anywhere she wants. It's a free country and she's a free woman."

I sat in my car for ten minutes trying to absorb the new information. Truby Falls was not in prison. Her daughter was dead. Did she know? Did she care? Did she kill her? Did she leave town? Maybe an old neighbor would know.

Since I was already in Beaufort, I used my phone GPS to locate Pelican Alley. It was near the water on the other side of town from the library. I drove through downtown. It was decorated for the holidays with red bows on street signs and white lights in all the trees. Shoppers vied for parking spots along the curbs while sale banners hung in the windows.

I followed the map lady's voice commands, even though I doubted she knew where she was going. She directed me inland, away from the coastal summery roads I'd associated with a name like Pelican Alley.

I saw the dilapidated street sign and drove down the narrow street. Though the term street was generous, my Mini navigated without trouble. I didn't know Courtney's mother's address, but I figured out which duplex was hers by the wooden *Nutcracker* display in her compact yard. The Sugar Plum Fairy had a printed picture of Courtney taped over her face.

A woman wearing purple eye shadow and matching plastic grape earrings answered my knock. She'd been at the theatre the night after Lexie's death, talking to the other moms. Or bragging to them.

"Yes?" she said.

"Are you Courtney's mom, Mrs. Cattanach?" I asked. "I'm Elliott Lisbon with the Ballantyne Foundation."

"Oh, the Ballantyne, of course. Come in, come in," she said and opened the door wide. "It's pronounced natch, Catta*nach*. But you can call me Shirl."

"I'm sorry to drop over unannounced, but do you have a minute to talk?" I followed her into an area smaller than the front half of a single wide trailer.

"Of course," she said. "Can I get you a sweet tea?"

She didn't wait for my reply. She went into the kitchenette and poured a cup from a plastic pitcher. "You here about Courtney in *The Nutcracker*? She's amazing. Do y'all put on other shows?"

"I'm actually here about Lexie Allen."

She handed me the glass and gestured for me to sit. I didn't want to. The living room couldn't have been more than a hundred square feet and felt claustrophobic. Knickknacks, trophies, pictures, tabloids, and beauty products crammed every semi-flat surface. The place wreaked of old cigarettes and everything looked as if a yellow film coated it.

I smiled and sat at the very edge of the sofa. I took a sip of sweet tea and bit back the urge to spit it into the glass. I'm classy that way.

"Poor Lexie Allen," she said. "I knew that girl since she was practically a baby."

"So she was like family?"

"I wouldn't go that far. Her and her mama moved across the street when the girls were little. Like kindergarten little. Not as smart as my Courtney, but mannerly, considering."

"Considering?"

"Her mother was a drunk and fraud and thank the good Lord she's spending the rest of her life behind bars where she belongs."

"Actually, Mrs. Cattanach—"

"Now, you call me Shirl."

"Okay, Shirl. Truby Falls isn't in prison anymore. I just—"

"What the Sam Hill are you talking about?"

"I just came from the courthouse. She got out a month ago on early release, with time served."

She stood straight up, marched to a tv tray in the corner, and grabbed a pack of cigarettes. "That woman killed old Mrs. Cho and she got out in eleven years? For *murder*? What is our world comin' to when a person gets a lousy eleven years for murder?"

"It was arson," I said unhelpfully.

"She killed that woman plain as day. And now she's out doing whatever she wants, free as a bird?"

"Do you know where she'd go? I'd really like to talk to her."

"I know a whole block that'd like to talk to her." She lit a cigarette with a shaky hand. "But no, I don't know where she'd go. No one round here would talk to her, not after what she did."

"I heard she burned down her duplex on purpose," I said. "Kind of risky with Lexie around."

She blew a stream of smoke, then waved at it to clear it away. "Lexie spent more time here than she ever did in that pigsty. Booze bottles and fast food cartons. A shame. Truby always thought she was better than everyone else. Hardly."

"Oh? I hadn't heard that."

"You better believe it. She was all fancy pants in Beaufort until her husband lost his job. He drank himself into the bottle and Miss Designer Jeans followed. He sobered up and left her, and she moved here."

"Maybe she went back to him after she was released."

"He'd never take that skank back," she said. "Pardon my language, but it's true. Anyways, he died before she burned down her house. Liver failure. Lexie was lucky as a duck those folks took her in. She didn't have a stitch of family left."

"This was ten years ago?"

"Longer than that. Let's see...the girls were eight when the fire...nineteen now...about eleven years. Lexie went right into foster care after the arrest. Her mother signed off parental rights when she went to prison. Those people adopted her right away."

"I know the Allens well," I said and took a fake sip of tea. "Big supporters of the Ballantyne Foundation."

"They're a decent couple, even if they spoiled that girl. Private dance lessons, though she'd never match my Courtney. She dances like an angel."

I remembered what the other moms said about Courtney not letting her mother attend performances. "Do you go to all of Courtney's shows?"

"Oh no, not anymore," she said and stubbed out her cigarette in a metal ashtray with a bean bag bottom. "My baby doesn't need me to hold her hand. She knows what she's doing. I'll go to dress rehearsals, opening night, closing night, that kind of thing."

"I didn't see you at the dress rehearsal last Tuesday afternoon," I said, leaving out the part where I didn't see her because I wasn't there.

"I was there," she said. "I remember Tuesday quite well. The rehearsal was delayed and Inga was red hot."

"What happened?"

"Berg showed up an hour late and made everyone wait. Can't do anything without the Mouse King, goes on in the first act. Like we've got nothing better to do."

"He was late?"

"Yep, and Inga chewed him up like a butter biscuit at brunch. Nearly cut him from the whole performance. He tried to blame my Courtney, said she told him it started at five thirty. Bunch of malarkey. Everyone had a copy of the schedule."

I thanked her for her time and hoped she didn't notice my mostly untouched glass of sweet tea on the coffee table. Since it mingled with nine dozen other things, I wasn't too worried.

I put my hipster on top of the forms in the car and noticed the scratch paper the clerk handed me. Truby's attorney, Hal English. The clerk had scribbled a phone number and address, along with the name Baker and Tuckett, a law firm in Beaufort.

The clock on the Mini read 3:04 p.m. I thought about what Shirl said: Berg had been late for rehearsal last Tuesday. The same day Mamacita thought the ground near the belladonna plants had been trampled. Coincidence? Hardly provable.

Another glance at the clock: 3:05 p.m. The drive back to the island would take forty-five minutes, thirty-seven if I pushed. Plenty of time (eighteen minutes) for a quick stop.

The offices of Baker and Tuckett were right on Main Street in downtown Beaufort, at the far end, away from the water and quaint public parking lot.

I found a spot a block away and fed a quarter into the meter, then jogged over to the glass door with the firm name etched out in gold.

"Can I help you?" A girl greeted me wearing a USC sweatshirt. "It's casual Friday. We're having our holiday party. But we're not actually open officially, though we're here."

"I'm sorry to interrupt," I said, once I could interrupt. "I'm looking for Hal English. He worked on an arson case about eleven years ago."

"No one here by that name. But hang on a sec." She hollered down the hall as she walked, asking someone if they had heard of Hal. Two minutes later she returned.

"He retired like five years ago," she said. "But we have two other attorneys who could help. They're really good. They'll be back soon. For the party. But not sure they can take your case before the holiday. Unless it's an emergency."

Another woman appeared. She, too, wore casual Friday attire. A plaid reindeer sweatshirt and green cords. "What can we do for you?"

"I'd love to talk to Hal English about an old case. See if he'd let me take a look at his files." I pulled out my barely official-looking PI credentials. "It's really important."

"Hal's in Sugarloaf Key, Florida. Or one of those keys. If you leave your number, I'll ask him to call."

"That would be great." I jotted a note on one of my business cards. "It's about the Truby Falls arson case, eleven years ago."

"I'll tell him," she said. "You know, we sent all those files to Truby about a year ago. Hal may've kept a copy, though I don't know. Closed case and all."

"You sent her the files? Is that standard?"

"Not necessarily standard, but not unusual. Sometimes clients want them in prison. Even at the end of their sentence." She shrugged. "It's their case."

I thanked her and jogged back to the Mini. The reindeer lady seemed responsible enough to call Hall right away, but I couldn't be sure. I'd try and track him down myself. I'd have to call on the fly. Right now I needed to use my turbo power to get to the Big House before the Ballantynes arrived. They were due at four and I couldn't be late.

EIGHTEEN

(Day #8 – Thursday Morning)

I called information in Sugarloaf Key and there was an H. English listed. He didn't answer, so I left a voicemail. Which was probably my tenth message for the day between him and Rory and Jane. I was beginning to think no one would call me back when my phone rang.

"Elli, hi, I'm glad I caught you. It's Kyra," a pleasantly sweet voice said when I answered. Kyra Gannon, Matty's sister-in-law.

"Kyra, nice to hear from you. How are the kids?" I asked as I sped over the Palmetto Bridge and onto Sea Pine Island.

"A handful! Can you believe I have three of them? I can't. And under five. Making dinner is an all-day event." Two little girls sang in the background as pots clattered with pans. "Anyhow, El, I know you're busy, but we'd love to have you for Christmas Eve dinner."

"Oh, that sounds lovely, but—"

"But nothing," she said. A baby started to cry and Kyra's voice faded in and out. "You give that back. She had it first." A pot or pan or some other metal clangy object banged into another. "It's Christmas Eve and you need to eat," she said to me.

"The Ballantynes come home today," I said and turned into the Oyster Cove gate. "Or should I say are home today."

An enormous white Rolls pulled up to the Big House steps just as I pulled in behind it. The driver's door to the vintage Corniche slowly swung open.

"Think about it at least," Kyra said above the cacophony of three children under five in the kitchen playing. "Matty's looking forward to it."

"I promise, I will," I said and hung up.

"Elliott! Hello!" Mr. Ballantyne said. He held his arms wide and wrapped me up snug. "Merry Christmas!"

I hugged back, then ran to the other side to open the door for Vivi. She was seventy-two years of petite energy. As frail as a baby bird, but strong as an eagle.

"My dear Elli," she said. "How we missed you so! I can't wait to tell you all about the trains." We walked up the steps arm in arm.

Tod greeted us in the entry holding two cups of peppermint cocoa with whipped topping on a tray. "Merry Christmas," he said. "And welcome home."

"Tod, you're an angel," Vivi said and took a sip. "This cocoa is straight from heaven. Oh, the tree, Elli. It's magical!"

"Indeed, my dear," Mr. Ballantyne said. He bent down and touched a Candyland box. The first one he gave me. "Our best Christmas." He stood and put his arm around me. "Though since then, they've all been our best."

"That was my favorite Christmas," I said. "The year you gave me that Candyland game. You wrapped red ribbons around the trees on the back lawn to create the Candy Cane Forest."

"And Vivi wore a tin foil crown!" Mr. Ballantyne said. "Queen Frostine, if I remember correctly. In her Candy Castle."

"You remember," I said.

"Of course we do," Vivi said. "I still have that crown. Probably a bit misshapen. But I think I shall don it Christmas morning. In honor of you, sweet Elli, and your magical tree."

"It's good to be home," Mr. Ballantyne said and kissed the top of my head.

"My darlings, I'm a bit tired from the trip," Vivi said.

"I'll get your bags and take them to the residence," Tod said.

The Ballantynes' residence took up the entire third floor and boasted an enormous master suite, two guest suites, a game room (my favorite), and a balcony that spanned the entire back of the Big House.

"Shall we retire for the evening, Vivi?" Mr. Ballantyne said.

"Carla can send up dinner whenever you're ready," I said. "You rest, and tell me all about Guatemala tomorrow."

"Deal," Vivi said and kissed my cheek.

"And the case, Elli? Progress?" Mr. Ballantyne said.

I smiled confidently. "Absolutely. I'm just about to wrap it up."

"What I like to hear," he said with a slight nod. A nod that told me he almost believed me, but he had faith in me. "Goodnight, my dear, until tomorrow!" He took Vivi's arm and together they walked up the center staircase. I watched them as they paused on the landing and hoped they were too tired to peek into the ballroom. Which was empty as an abandoned warehouse. One with gorgeous wood inlaid parquet floors and antique crystal chandeliers. But no tables, chairs, linens, flowers, Christmas greenery, or silver finery befitting a Ballantyne ball.

This is what happens when you push everything until the last day: nothing is done. I arrived at the Big House at a sprightly eight a.m. decked out in khaki shorty pants and a faded orange tee. Dozens of workers scurried to and fro, cleaning and polishing and setting up décor and seating. Luckily, the Ballantynes loved hustle and bustle. Especially during the holidays. Unluckily, my investigation, the one I confidently boasted was about to wrap up, had to wait. I didn't have any more time left to push. The Palm & Fig Ball was in ten hours and we had twenty hours' worth of work.

Carla served lunch for the entire crew on the back patio which mostly spilled over onto the lawn. I don't know how she managed to prepare homemade cashew chicken salad sandwiches on brioche with sides of apple slaw in the midst of the madness, but I ate two plates full to show my support.

Tod rushed out as I was gathering up the paper dishes and tossing them in the rubber bin. His normally perfectly-combed coif was mussed and he had a mayo smudge on his cheek. "Jane and Carmichael are having a smackdown in the foyer," he said.

"Seriously? Right now?"

"Obviously right now."

"Where are the Ballantynes?"

"Out for a drive. They left an hour ago, but they could return any minute."

I wiped my hands on my pants and jogged through the solarium and down the hall to the front of the Big House.

"It's already up," Chef Carmichael said, standing in the middle of the foyer. "You can't stop it."

"Don't tell me what I can and cannot stop," Jane said. "It's crass and it's coming down." Jane pointed to Tod. "Get it down. Now."

"Touch it and I walk," Carmichael said.

"Then walk," Jane said.

"What are you touching? What's crass?" I asked as Tod ran up the center staircase.

"Carmichael put a Wharf sign in the ballroom," Jane said. "Like a banner at a moose lodge."

"It's not a banner," Carmichael said. "It's a tasteful plaque next to the bar."

"A plaque or a banner, it's not staying," Jane said.

"Definitely not," I said. "You're not a sponsor, Chef. Besides, most of the guests know you and your restaurant. It's unnecessary."

"It's not for them, it's for the tv crew," Carmichael said.

"What tv crew?" I said.

Tod and two workers carried a carved wood sign that said Wharf in a fancy script. "Where do you want this?" Tod asked Carmichael.

"Right where I had it," he said.

"The Wharf delivery van is parked near the side entrance," Jane said. "Stick it in there."

"I'll tell you where to stick it, Jane," Chef Carmichael said.

"What tv crew?" I asked again.

"The Stream Kitchen," Carmichael said. He followed Tod out the door and down the front steps. "They're filming Rory tonight at the ball."

"Oh no they're not," I hollered and rushed after him. "No way!"

He stopped and spun around. "They film or I walk."

"You can't keep threatening to walk. The ball is in four hours!"

"I'll concede the restaurant sign, but that crew will film tonight." He stood with his hands on his hips and a scowl on his face.

Jane said from the doorway, "Okay, Peter and the Wolf. You get your film crew. But that tacky sign goes."

He marched away without commenting and I marched toward Jane. "Are you crazy? You gave in too quickly. We can't have a film crew at the Palm & Fig."

"I signed the consent waivers two hours ago," she said. "It'll be good for the Foundation. We had one chef drop out and another accused of murder. We need to show support for Rory, and also show that we didn't need that hack cook."

I watched her walk away in her spotless silk suit and barely worn heels, barking orders at workers and creating more chaos. My phone buzzed in my pocket and I happily grabbed at the distraction.

"Elliott? It's Mimi Ransom. How are you?"

"Mimi," I said and dramatically chastised myself for not checking caller ID, waving my arms and making faces into the crisp December air. "How nice to hear from you."

"I'll make this quick. I know you're probably enjoying some downtime before the ball tonight."

Two men shouted behind me and I heard a small crash. I sat down on the bottom step near the drive. "Not yet. Working on the finishing touches."

"I wanted to invite you to Christmas Eve dinner," she said.

"You may have plans, but I do hope you'll consider. I sent an invitation two weeks ago, though with the rush of holiday cards, I'm sure the mail is behind."

"I'm so sorry, I didn't get it." I thought of the cards, letters, and bills stacked on my desk at home. I probably should go through them one of these days. "It's so kind of you to think of me."

"Of course. Nick adores you and insisted I call to personally invite you again. Not that I needed much persuading. You'd be greatly missed if you didn't join us."

"Thank you," I said. "I usually spend the evening with the Ballantynes, though I'm not sure what we have planned this year."

"It would be a delight for them to join us, too," she said. "Their invitation went unanswered as well."

I felt myself flush and rested my head in my open hand. She must think me a hillbilly. "They've been in Guatemala. Just flew home last night. I'm sure they'll attend to their mail today. And I'll absolutely speak with them and get back to you."

"Take your time, dear," Mimi Ransom said. "I'll have plenty of food, no worries on that front. Enjoy the ball and please give my best to Vivi and Edward."

I said I would and clicked off.

That made two invitations for Christmas Eve dinner. One with Matty and his family, one with Ransom and his family. And Christmas was in less than a week.

"Hey El, you want the poinsettias stacked by the bandstand in even rows or a pyramid?" a worker asked from the open door.

"I'll come up," I said.

I brushed off my pants and went back inside. Before I decided where I'd spend Christmas Eve dinner, I needed to get through the Palm & Fig. Which wouldn't be any less stressful. Both Nick Ransom and Matty Gannon would be in attendance. Along with Rory the murder suspect and an entire film crew. I took a deep breath. Nothing I couldn't handle.

NINETEEN

(Day #8 – Thursday Evening)

The ballroom dazzled in frosty white and delicate pink from the sparkling lights to the bubbly champagne. A twenty-seven piece orchestra played lively Christmas tunes while men in smooth tuxedos twirled ladies in shiny gowns.

"You clean up nice," Tod said. We stood together in the corner near the dumbwaiter and staff entrance on the far side of the ballroom. Tod wore a sharp black tux with a white orchid pinned to his lapel.

"Oh, this?" My pale pink strapless dress was silk with a skirt adorned in pink feathers. It floated when I walked and the pointy toes of my strappy kitten heels barely peeked out from the hem.

He ignored me.

The Ballantynes greeted each guest personally, visiting tables to chat and hug and spread more holiday cheer than Mr. and Mrs. Claus. And they might as well have been the Clauses. At each place setting sat a gift wrapped in pink paper to hide the beautiful Tiffany blue box inside.

"Mrs. Kramer was singing earlier," Tod said. "But I stopped her before Edward noticed."

"Why stop her?"

"She was sitting on the piano with a poinsettia on her head using her soup spoon as a microphone."

"Good call," I said. "And I got Mr. Colbert a cab. He was trying to drive his Jaguar home from the passenger side. Told his wife to buckle up, they were headed for Big Ben."

The camera crew wasn't as intrusive as I had feared. Turned out even the highest of society enjoyed the spotlight. Even if it was for an internet streaming website.

Perhaps they didn't know that part.

The troupe from *The Nutcracker* mingled with the Ballantyne Board members as donors danced and dined. Matty had arrived with Zibby and Deidre, and the entire room was filled with laughter and chatter and clinking crystal glasses.

"Final course just went out," Carla said as she joined us. "Then dessert. Pink strawberry cake with sweet buttercream frosting and a chocolate ganache."

I hugged her. "It was wonderful. As usual. I even tried your crispy lobster dumplings."

"No, you didn't," she said.

"Okay, I didn't, but they looked amazing," I said. "How's Carmichael?"

"Arrogant and bossy," she said. "But I admit, he made a decent consommé. Paired beautifully with my dumplings."

A cameraman and grip strolled by and filmed two servers carrying plates to the corner table.

"And Rory?" Tod asked. "She sneak out the back before the coppers got her?"

I smacked him. "Shush. No coppers, Bugsy. And those camera microphone things pick up the faintest sounds, so keep it down."

"Rory's been a dream," Carla said. "And I'm not saying that for the cameras. She's a talent, for sure. I may need to steal her away from Carmichael."

I spotted Rory at Zibby's table near the band. She sat on the edge of the chair next to Zibby's and speared an asparagus stalk from Zibby's plate.

"I'm going to say hello real quick," I said.

With a hug to Zibby's shoulders, I knelt between her and Rory. "The food is wonderful," I said to Rory. "I hear you're quite the talent in the kitchen."

She smiled, probably the first one I'd seen since I met her. Her blue hair shone under the chandelier lights and her cheeks practically glowed. "It's been amazing. Working with Chef Carla and Chef Carmichael for an event this prestigious is a dream come true." She waved at the camera crew filming the dance floor. "And The Stream Kitchen is here. I can't believe it."

"You deserve it," Zibby said. She spread her butternut puree onto a piece of roll. "You're going to win that show, I know it."

"Mind if I interrupt?" Matty said.

I stood and he gently kissed my cheek.

He looked incredible. His soft wavy hair around his tan face, his fitted tuxedo on his toned body. His warm hand reaching for mine. "Let's dance."

We swayed close to one another while the orchestra played a romantic wintery tune.

"How's Rory doing? Must be better if she's here working," Matty said.

"Actually, it's about the same. The police aren't storming in to arrest her or anything, but she's still their main suspect. Or maybe their only suspect."

"Really? She's such a good kid," he said.

"That's what you said about Vigo Ortiz."

The music rolled into another slow song and we continued to sway.

"He's a good kid, too," he said. "I've know most of Inga's dancers for years. They're all good kids."

I smiled and pulled back, looking up into his face. "You're the nicest headmaster on the island. You think all the kids are good kids."

He twirled me, then pulled me close. "I feel bad for them. I was talking to Berg. He really loved Lexie. He would've done anything for her. They'd been best friends for years. He's heartbroken he never got his chance with her. He should've told her how he felt, and now it's too late."

But I knew timing had nothing to do with it. Lexie knew how

he felt, but didn't want him to cross over from friend to boyfriend. Berg may have been better off regretting a move he never made rather than suffer the hurt of unrequited love.

A slow heat crept up my neck to my cheeks, and I swallowed hard as a realization hit me. Matty was my Berg. He was my friend, my good friend. Not my boyfriend. No matter how I tried, I couldn't seem to cross over from friend to boyfriend.

"Kyra mentioned she spoke with you about dinner next week," he said. "I'd love for you to come."

I nodded and started to sweat.

"School's on break now for two weeks. Maybe we can get away for a couple days after Christmas. New Year's in Maine? Get a cabin, just the two of us?"

Matty had the most beautiful brown eyes. Warm and deep and happy. He'd do anything for me. And I missed him so much. We could talk and drink and laugh all night. Any night. Except lately.

"El, you okay?" he asked.

The last notes of the song faded and the dancers applauded the band.

"I need some air," I choked out. It was just so damn hot in there. And my fitted feather dress wasn't helping.

He grabbed my hand and led me across the dance floor and down the grand staircase of the Big House. The cool night air drifted over us once he opened the foyer door. With the moon barely a sliver, a million stars sparkled against the midnight blue sky.

Matty stood behind me and rubbed my bare shoulders. I placed my hands on his and held them tight.

"Matty, I love you," I said. "With my heart and my head and my soul."

"Elli, you are—"

"Wait, Matty. Please let me finish. You bring me happy, and I can't imagine my life without you. I never want to live my life without you." Tears filled my eyes and slid down my cheeks. I squeezed his hands. "You're my best friend, Matty. And I miss you.

I want my friend back."

"I'm right here."

"We're not the same. We haven't been since you kissed me last May."

He dropped his hands from my shoulders. "You mean when Nick Ransom moved back to the island."

"This isn't about Ransom. This is about us. Or the us that we were."

"What are you saying?"

I wiped my cheeks and turned to face him. "I'm sorry, Matty. I'm so so sorry. I just want us to go back to the way it was."

"Tell me what you really mean. Just say it."

I stared at him. The hurt on his face and his rigid posture. He stood a foot away from me, but it might as well have been a hundred feet. A thousand. My heart ached. It was hard to breathe.

"Matty..."

"Finish it, Elliott. I need to hear it."

Another tear fell down my cheek. I felt it rush down and imagined it splashing onto my dress. I imagined a million more would fall before the night was over.

"Please, Matty, I don't want to lose you. You mean everything to me," I said. "But I don't think we should date anymore. You want kids and I don't. I know we're not there yet, but we will be. So many things don't fit, Matty. We're all awkward and strained and I hate it."

Ransom's slick racer roared up the drive with two squad cars behind him.

Matty glanced at me, then trotted down the steps before Ransom got out of his car. Matty disappeared into the night, around the side of the lot to the valet.

I didn't wait to talk to Nick or watch Matty drive out of my life. I hurried into the Big House and into the powder room off the foyer. I quickly dabbed my eyes and blew my nose and took three very deep breaths. My heartbreak meltdown was going to have to wait.

I returned to the foyer as Ransom, Parker, and two uniforms started up the grand staircase.

"Whoa, wait," I called and rushed up to block Ransom, who led the team.

"I'm sorry, Red," he said. "But I have orders."

"You absolutely do not have orders," I said. "There is no way the captain wants the police storming the Ballantyne's Palm & Fig Ball."

"Not the captain, the county prosecutor. He just got elected, going to make a name for himself, and he's on his way."

"I don't care." I frantically waved the team down the stairs. "In the library, now," I said. "Please," I added. "Ransom, please."

He turned to the officers behind him and nodded. Parker led them to the library and closed the doors. Ransom and I followed, remaining in the foyer outside the library doors.

"You cannot arrest Rory. Not here and not tonight."

"I came myself to make this as unobtrusive as possible."

I wildly waved at the library. "Yes, two Sea Pine police officers, Corporal Parker, and you, the Lieutenant, speeding up the drive. Totally unobtrusive."

"It's my job, Red."

"Oh with you and your job. What about other suspects? You had to have known about Lexie's mother. She's a convicted killer and she could be anywhere. Anywhere! You had access to all her records and a ton of databases. The second you heard about her, you probably ran a check within the hour. And you didn't share with me."

"Because I don't need to share with you. You," he said and pointed at my chest for emphasis, "share with me."

I smacked his hand away. "Do you understand the word share? It implies a two-way street. You know that Lexie's birth mother is a suspect."

"Perhaps," he said.

"Oh my God, you talked to her already?"

"Not exactly. We're still tracking her down."

"She's a murderer!"

"Arsonist. Released due to good behavior. She was in the Operation Behind Bars program. An advanced horticulture student."

"Do you hear yourself? We're dealing with a plant poison. You know, a *horticulture* poison."

"Collards and snow peas aren't exactly poisonous."

I stomped my foot in frustration and he held his hands up. "Calm down," he said. "We're looking for her. But she was a model inmate. Sweet, kind, and no motive to kill her only child."

"Don't tell me to calm down," I said. A couple danced on the landing near the top steps of the staircase and I lowered my voice. "There's something to this, Ransom. Truby Falls goes to prison for killing someone. She gets out and her daughter is murdered. What about the victim's family? Maybe they wanted revenge against Truby."

"Mrs. Cho had no family."

"Who has no family? That's ridiculous."

"How much family do you have?"

It felt like a slap and I took a step back. But he was right. I had no family. None. Perhaps a random cousin twice removed, but no one who would take out revenge on my behalf. "There's still something to this."

"I can't ignore the evidence, and it points to Rory Throckmorton. Don't tell me how to do my job, Elliott."

"Don't tell me how to do mine!" I whisper shouted. Another couple joined the first on the landing and I checked my watch. A quarter after ten. Carla was probably serving dessert. Or maybe it was already served. I couldn't think straight. "You owe me, and for once, you're going to help me."

"I'm going to arrest her. I don't have a choice."

"Both the Ballantynes will have to be carted to the hospital on matching stretchers if you arrest Vivi's cousin's niece in the middle of the Palm & Fig Ball, where she happens to be working as one of the prestigious guest chefs. And she's being filmed for a tv show." I ran my hands through my hair. "Jesus, I'll need my own stretcher."

Ransom checked his own watch and relented. "Fine, we'll wait until the ball is over. I'll ask Parker to wait outside with the patrol officers."

"And have them move their cars to the side of the house. Opposite the valet. Way, way out of sight."

"Not a word to Rory," he said. "Or anyone."

"Not a word," I said and started to walk away.

"Hey, Red," he said. "For what it's worth, I wouldn't have done it this way."

I nodded and plastered a smile on my shocked, saddened, worried face. I entered the ballroom where the dessert plates were being cleared. I spotted an untouched one and ate that sucker in three bites. I watched the Ballantynes swirl and sway on the dance floor. Zibby danced on a chair. Guests thanked me and Tod and hugged and air-kissed and hollered festive wishes.

"Hard to believe you pulled it off," Tod said. "But it looks like the Palm & Fig was a huge success."

"Well, it ain't over yet."

TWENTY

(Day #9 – Friday Morning)

I ached and I cried and I wanted to erase all my memories from the night before. I broke Matty's heart. My sweet, wonderful Matty. I broke my own heart. I loved him and needed him and missed him already. Fear and panic came over me in waves, some small, some large, thinking he'd never speak to me again. He'd never smile at me or confide in me or laugh with me. It left a hole in my heart.

I wanted my life back. Simple, easy, happy. My cottage, my friends, my Ballantyne. Boys messed it all up for me. I wasn't a diary person, but in that early morning moment, as I hurt and ached and cried, I understood the need. The urgent need to release the emotions. The catharsis of writing them down.

Slowly, and with every cell of energy I had, I rolled over and glanced at the clock: 9:37. I'd been awake for five hours. I went to grab another tissue from the box, but it was empty. Crumpled and tattered tissues littered my nightstand, bed, and floor. I shoved them all into the empty cardboard box and trudged to the bathroom to get another.

The act of moving helped. I was on a roll, so I brushed my teeth, then took the tissues back to bed. For the one hundred fifty dozenth time, I thought about the Palm & Fig. But this time, I allowed myself to get past watching Matty as he left me and the Big House and never looked back. Ransom left shortly after our argument, though he only left the premises. He remained parked on the street waiting for the ball to end.

While things didn't get better after that, at least they didn't get worse. Parker and her two cohorts sat at a bistro table near the side door to the mudroom. A server spotted them when she and two other servers took a break after all the plates had been cleared from the ballroom. Word got to Carla which spread to Rory and Zibby. Rather than panic and flee, Rory fixed dinner plates for the three of Sea Pine's finest, including dessert, and thanked them for waiting. Zibby kept them company until Rory finished cleaning up with the rest of the crew somewhere around one thirty a.m. Luckily, the Ballantynes had retired upstairs before Rory left in handcuffs. Southern hospitality aside, that was not something any of us wanted to deal with in the middle of the night.

The morning boasted a crisp blue sky and overly bright sun, just like the fifteen mornings before it. So unfair. I'd write that in my diary, too. I didn't want a happy day. I wanted the whole of the universe to match my blue mood with murky skies and no sunshine. After thirty minutes of cursing the weather and the sun and the diary I didn't have, I got sick of myself. I grabbed Lexie's iPad and decided to read her diary instead, randomly choosing reviews.

Product: Beige carpet cat scratching post (2 stars)
Title: Cat Fight
OMG the cats in the house are getting vicious. Scratching is the half of it. A whole litter of snapping felines vying for one stupid tom cat. I'm so over it. They can take it out on this and I can get some sleep.

Product: Calculator with adding tape (2 stars)
Title: Doesn't 1 + 1 = 2?
I don't remember the original figures. I didn't pay attention to math when I was a kid. I'll need more info to balance it out.

Five diary reviews later, I noticed something coincidental. Another reviewer's name kept recurring. SeasTheDay57. I clicked on the name to view the profile. Over five hundred fifty reviews. All random products, just like Lexie's. I scrolled through three pages. Just. Like. Lexie's. In some instances, their reviews were back-to-back. I read one, then the other.

This wasn't a diary, this was a conversation. Like serial killers talking to one another through personal ads in the newspaper. I flipped back to the cat scratching post review and found a review from SeasTheDay57 time-stamped five hours later:

Reviewer: SeasTheDay57
Product: Beige carpet cat scratching post (4 stars)
Title: Cat Scratch Fever
Cats need something to take out their aggression, this will do the trick. Another thing that will do the trick: ignore the cats. And if they aren't yours and you're moving soon, just hang in there. Like those cute cat posters say. Remember their aggression isn't aimed at you!

I sorted by date and went back to the first entry. I opened a new window and did the same thing for SeasTheDay57. The same week, they both left a review for name tags. Lexie's was first.

Reviewer: LXinthekitchen
Product: Sticker name badges with Hello printed on them (3 stars)
Title: Breaking the ice
It's awkward introducing yourself to someone you've never met or reintroducing to someone you haven't seen in a long time. These stickers make it easier. Put on your name and walk up to anyone. Gives you courage to go first: Hi, I'm a classically trained dancer and I live in an apartment with three roommates near my college.

Reviewer: SeasTheDay57

Product: Sticker name badges with Hello printed on them (5 stars)

Title: Make new friends

I've never been so happy to see Hello My Name Is badges! I was very relieved to see them when I went to a work event. I could just say, it's nice to meet you. I love the outdoors and hope to soon move closer to the ocean.

The first hundred or so reviews were pleasant conversation. Nothing too personal, nothing overly familiar. Getting to know one another. Like a date. Was this some kind of new way to date online?

Halfway into the second hundred, things slowly got more personal. Lexie wrote:

Reviewer: LXinthekitchen

Product: Wooden Christmas nutcracker ornament (5 stars)

Title: An annual tradition

I bought these as gifts for my entire troupe who will be performing The Nutcracker *the week before Christmas. It's a must see! I'm lucky to have an extra ticket for any night so someone special can join me.*

The single tickets! It's always the tiniest oddball piece that puts the puzzle together. Even though I hadn't yet put the puzzle together, I knew this was key. Lexie bought tickets for SeasTheDay57 and they were going to meet for the first time at *The Nutcracker*. My guess: Lexie wasn't sure which night, so she got one for each night, just in case.

Questions flew into my mind like baseballs from an automatic pitching machine. And they came faster and faster. Did SeasTheDay57 show up early? Was SeasTheDay57 stalking Lexie? Did SeasTheDay57 kill Lexie? Did SeasTheDay57 kill other people? Was he a pedophile? A serial killer? Who was SeasTheDay57? Did

Lexie know SeasTheDay57? Did I know SeasTheDay57?

I threw off the covers and ran downstairs. I was starving and foggy and needed to get it together. I downed an ice cold Pepsi, which is not as pleasant as it sounds. Those bubbles burn after seven swallows. I dumped cereal into a bowl, splashed milk on top, and shovel ate it over the sink.

Humming and vibrating on adrenaline, caffeine, and sugar, I raced upstairs and snatched up the iPad and my notebook and flew downstairs to my desk. My desktop took roughly five hours to boot up, so I pushed the monitor out of the way, nearly toppling my tiny tree, and worked on the iPad.

I pulled out details from review entries going back to the beginning, which was six months earlier. The get to know you entries lasted about three months. Then they slowly became less reserved, less formal. More off the cuff and real emotions broke through.

> *Reviewer: LXinthekitchen*
> *Product: Winnie the Pooh Book (5 stars)*
> *Title: Back to Pooh Corner*
> *I loved Winnie Piglet!! I remember carrying them both everywhere I went (as if they were one: Winnie Piglet). I think I got them the second I was born and I still have them. They sleep on my pillow when I'm away, keeping my room warm and each other company so they don't get lonely without me.*

> *Reviewer: SeasTheDay57*
> *Product: Winnie the Pooh Book (5 stars)*
> *Title: A Hundred Acre Wood*
> *Oh how my daughter loved them! I read this book to her as a baby, every night. The stuffed animals were actually a first birthday present and they were inseparable, all three. It makes me so happy to see this!!*

SeasTheDay57 wasn't a serial killer or a stalker or an online dater. She was Lexie's mother.

And then I got to the October ninth entry. SeasTheDay57 posted a loving review for a pair of opal earrings, citing it was her favorite birthday month. Delicate ones with tiny diamonds. They weren't ordinary stud earrings, but rather a tiny cluster shaped into a daisy of opals. Opal, the October birthstone (which I discovered after a quick Google search). The exact pair I saw Johnnie Mae wearing at the theatre the night Lexie died.

Johnnie Mae, who was overwhelmed with emotion that night. Who shook with grief when talking about losing her only child years ago. Eleven years ago, give or take. Like when the authorities arrested her for arson and put her daughter into foster care.

Could Johnnie Mae Tidwell really be Truby Falls, Lexie's birth mother?

There were no profile pictures for SeasTheDay57. I went back to the Google tab and found two old photos of Truby from the newspaper. One was a candid the reporter probably got from a neighbor, the other was taken at the courthouse during the trial. The resemblance between Truby and Johnnie Mae was definitely there, but only if you were looking.

Truby Falls weighed a solid fifty pounds more. In the candid shot, her curly hair was bleached to near straw texture and her skin was tanned like saddle leather. She held a drink in one hand and was laughing at something off-camera.

Johnnie Mae was thin, almost too thin, with pale skin and gray hair pulled into a bun. Her eyes were plain brown, but they were the same. Her smile was probably the same, too, but I'd never seen Johnnie Mae smile. I wasn't sure anyone had. Prison changed her appearance to the point of unrecognizability. And she used it to hide in plain sight.

I continued reading the entries, but with a new perspective. And with that perspective came clarity. And urgency. During the last month, the entries stacked up multiple items in the same day. The conversation ping-ponged from product to product. Lexie and

Johnnie Mae knew what they were talking about, but I struggled to follow along. I took frantic notes, scribbling and reading, then scribbling more. Johnnie Mae wrote about the evidence against her, or at least I thought so.

> *Reviewer: SeasTheDay57*
> *Product: Calculator with adding tape (2 stars)*
> *Title: Audit Season*
> *It never added up to me. I didn't believe I'd make such a mistake, and after I cleared my head and focused on things, I started keeping better records. It was too late to change the outcome, it had already been filed, but I had to double check and find the correct result.*

Which brought me to the entry from Lexie I read earlier:

> *Reviewer: LXinthekitchen*
> *Product: Calculator with adding tape (2 stars)*
> *Title: Doesn't 1 + 1 = 2?*
> *I don't remember the original figures. I didn't pay attention to math when I was a kid. I'll need more info to balance it out.*

Johnnie Mae began to spell it out:

> *Reviewer: SeasTheDay57*
> *Product: Clear nail polish (1 star)*
> *Title: Choosing the perfect color*
> *Like in photo #1, I loved clear. And a particular clear. My favorite color, at least then, was clear. So clear it looked like a tempting drink. Never went for the neutrals like amber or butterscotch. And I mean never! Not even if I chipped something or was desperate. I stuck with clear. Spent every night with that bottle and I never strayed. You like what you like. And the clear doesn't smell like the other*

colors. To see a pic of my table with amber polish is definitely wrong.

> *Reviewer: LXinthekitchen*
> *Product: Clear nail polish (1 star)*
> *Title: I see it but not sure I believe it*
> *A nice bottle of clear isn't a good argument to stick with clear. Everyone tries something different. Where's the fun and where's the proof?*

Johnnie Mae mentioned a photo, and Lexie replied she'd seen it. I made a note about crime scene photos. If her attorney, Hal English, sent the photos to Johnnie Mae, maybe she sent them on to Lexie. Talking booze? Vodka is clear, or gin. Saw "amber" on the table, out of place. A "tempting drink" that "doesn't smell." Definitely not talking about nail polish. It fit. Truby got drunk the night of the fire. A picture of the booze bottle would be evidence in the trial.

> *Reviewer: SeasTheDay57*
> *Product: Wicker chaise set (2 stars)*
> *Title: Passing the time*
> *For smokers like me who can't smoke in the house, this is perfect for nights outside. I cannot light up inside. Ever. I lounge on my chaise with an ashtray and a pack on the side table. Check out photo #2 for a close look at what I mean. It's called a habit for a reason and if you're like me and love your nighttime naps you'll need an outdoor chaise because you can't smoke cigs on the living room sofa.*

> *Reviewer: LXinthekitchen*
> *Product: Wicker chaise set (2 stars)*
> *Title: Night under the stars*
> *I remember nights outside like it was yesterday! This fits for me and the situation. Anything else wouldn't work.*

Reviewer: SeasTheDay57
Product: Glass footed dessert dishes (3 stars)
Title: Proof is in the pudding
Proper glassware choice is essential for entertaining.
Photo #3 demonstrates how obviously awkward when you
get it wrong. NEVER use glass outside. Plastic is the only
choice. I understand making 1 mistake, but not 3.

Reviewer: LXinthekitchen
Product: Glass footed dessert dishes (3 stars)
Title: Got them!
I'm a believer! Why can't everyone see the truth in
proper glassware?! I'm definitely going to tell my
associates. We cannot let others think this is right!

Reviewer: LXinthekitchen
Product: Digital camera with stabilized zoom (5 stars)
Title: Clear as day!
The photos are clear and sharp and I see every detail
even a hair out of place. Out of the 5 photos I have, the 5th
really brings it together. If I were a professional with this
amazing equipment, I would be able to change the world or
at least my world. I've scene the evidence of detail and I'll
get Hal to reopen the box. You know people do wonders
these days with evidence. Fingerprints, DNA. Imagine what
I could do with a camera! Back in a flash!

Lexie must have called Hal, or at least intended to. She was
barely coding her message for the last review. And it was her last
review. Posted the day she died.

My brain was buzzing while my fingers scratched out notes.

Johnnie Mae wanted a relationship with her daughter.
Somehow, she reached out from prison and Lexie was receptive.
They set up the Amazon review communication channel so no one
would know. Smart. According to Shirl, everyone hated Truby.

Drunk of a mother who recklessly killed an innocent neighbor for an insurance payout.

Johnnie Mae served her time. She sobered up, slimmed down, and became a model prisoner. She also studied her own case and the evidence against her. Realized it was a setup. She didn't set the fire or kill her neighbor. She explained it to her daughter, who did her own research.

Something about clear nail polish (vodka?), chaise lounges (smoking outside vs. inside), pudding dishes (glass vs. plastic), and then a camera (a detail in photo #5 that Lexie identified, but didn't say what). Did Johnnie Mae know what it was? Or who set the fire?

I bet Lexie knew who started it. And it got her killed.

I wasn't jubilant or excited or pumped with adrenaline. I was frustrated. I'd had this stupid iPad the entire week and it was all right there. Would Ransom have figured it out if the police had the iPad? And why couldn't anyone just spit this shit out in the beginning? Why didn't Johnnie Mae say something to the police or her attorney or anyone when Lexie was killed?

The clock on the iPad said 12:37. Today was the Friday before Christmas and the last day of performances. Plural. Not just the evening performance, but also a morning performance for the school kids. Maybe no one knew where Truby Falls the ex-con was, but I had a pretty good idea where Johnnie Mae the volunteer was. At least until the curtain fell and all the little dancers plié-ed their way home.

It didn't take long to get ready and out the door. I thought the morning performance started at eleven. With intermission and ovations and the re-hanging of glittery wardrobes, the backstage should still be lively.

It was not.

There were only three cars and two trucks parked in random spots across the tree-lined lot. I parked cattywampus and rushed inside. Two crew members were talking on their way out.

"Excuse me," I said. "Where is everyone?"

"Show ended an hour ago," one of the men said. "Lunch break

and then the place will fill up again around three."

I thanked him and watched them go.

The theatre was dim and quiet. I peeked into the dressing rooms. The lighted vanities stations were empty, except for hundreds of accessories: clips, bands, pins, brushes, and pots upon tubes upon palettes of makeup.

Without people to create the cacophony of theatre buzz, the building felt eerie, abandoned. I walked toward the stage and heard a noise. A scrape on the wood surface. I climbed the steps and entered the opening scene of *The Nutcracker*. A mansion living room painted on heavy canvas served as a backdrop. An enormous Christmas tree stood at the far side of the stage. Its long branches were decorated with shiny bulb ornaments and had so many lights, it illuminated the entire stage. Colorful packages were arranged in clusters around a large nutcracker toy. Two tufted chairs fronted an imaginary fireplace with prop tools, including a brass grill.

I was about to walk away when I noticed a pair of legs sticking out from beneath one of the chairs. They were frail and stickly and they moved.

"Johnnie Mae?" I asked.

She bumped her head as she scooted out. "Elliott! You startled me. I think everyone has gone."

"I actually came to see you."

"Me?" She stood about ten feet away. She looked tired and sad, her hair bun frayed and her skirt dusty.

"I want to talk about Lexie," I said gently. "I know you're her mother. Her birth mother."

She put her hand to her throat. "I—I don't know what you're talking about."

"Yes, you do." I gestured to the two chairs by the fireplace. "But I don't understand why you didn't say something after Lexie died."

Johnnie Mae eased into the chair and sat at the very edge. She looked both ready to run and ready to collapse. "How did you find out?"

"The Amazon reviews. At first I thought Lexie used them as a diary, then I realized she used them for communication. Very clever. It took me a week to figure it out."

She smiled the faintest of smiles. "Lexie's idea. She said no one would know. She actually did use it as a diary at school. That's where she got the idea. She was so smart. But what led you to me?"

"Your opal earrings. I saw them on a review and remembered you wore an identical pair."

Johnnie Mae touched one of them briefly, softly brushing over the stones. "Opals are her birthstone. I bought them so she'd know it was me. You know, recognize them from the review and know who I was. But she never got to see them. I waited too long."

"Why didn't you say something after she died? To me, the police, anyone? I know you two were trying to figure out who set you up for arson."

Johnnie Mae sat up straight. "You read all that?"

"I didn't read all the messages, but I did read the final ones. The ones that talked about photographs, presumably evidence from your trial."

"Those damn photographs! I got my girl killed."

"You didn't kill Lexie, Johnnie Mae."

"Yes, I did. I was a horrible mama to her. I should've protected her. I should've been there. And I never should've sent her those photos."

"Tell me about the photos. What did they prove? Who set you up?"

"I don't know what or who. Lexie said she found something in one of them."

"Photo #5."

"Yes, but I don't know what because I have looked at that damn thing until I'd memorized every last grain of film. And I'll tell you as sure as I'm sitting here, nothing jumped out at me. *Nothing.* But it jumped out at her, and hours later, she was gone forever."

"Maybe Lexie confided in someone. Courtney, Vigo, Berg?"

"Never. She swore she wouldn't tell a soul until we went to my attorney with the proof. It was imperative we maintained secrecy."

"Was this all through Amazon?"

"Mostly. When I mailed the photos I was still in prison. Understandably, she didn't want to give out her address. A friend helped me out. And no, the friend isn't involved."

"Let me help. Maybe I'll see what she saw."

"I don't have them and I don't know where they are. I've looked everywhere. Her apartment, the dance studio, even the Wharf. Everywhere except her parents' house and the Stream Kitchen set. Even here." She waved her arms around the theatre. "And I'm still looking. This place is huge, and they have to be here."

"Lexie hid them?"

"She must have."

"Unless someone took them."

Tears filled her eyes and she gripped my arm. "Please don't even think that. If someone took them, then we'll never know, and she'll have died for nothing."

I held her hand on my arm. "She didn't die for nothing. We'll figure it out. Tell me what the other photos meant. Something about vodka and plastic drinking cups?"

"Yes!" She wiped her face. "The photos are of the living room, what was left of it. In one photo you can see a bottle of scotch, which I never drank. Never. It was a gift bottle that had been in a cupboard forever. Definitely not something I would've had open. In another photo, my ashtray and cigarettes, burned and smashed, but still you could make them out, were on the carpet by the charred coffee table. I never smoked inside the house. Couldn't, the landlord forbade it. That may have been a crappy, cheap house, but it was all I could afford. I couldn't afford to lose it." She got up and walked over to the tree.

"And the pudding dishes?"

"I used a plastic cup for drinking. I'm not proud of who I was," she said with her back to me. "I'm ashamed and horrified and I have to live with it. But I know what I did and didn't do and how I acted. I drank at night, on the porch, vodka in a plastic cup. Not a drinking glass, like was found. Not scotch, and not inside." She picked up a fallen ornament and hung it back on the tree.

I joined her. "All very circumstantial."

"I know. Proves nothing. But Lexie saw it and knew in her heart I didn't burn down our house for money. I didn't kill our neighbor. I didn't abandon her. Someone else started that fire and wanted it to look like it was me."

"But who? You have no idea?"

"I have an idea, I just don't have proof," Johnnie Mae said. "Oh my God, what will I do?"

The ornament she was holding fell and rolled across the stage, behind one of the chairs. I walked over to grab it when every light in the theatre went out. Two loud clunks. Darkness fell in an instant. It consumed me. As if the air itself were black.

"Hello?" Johnnie Mae said.

I started to rise. Running footsteps pounded across the stage. Johnnie Mae screamed a half scream. Then a muffled thump.

Silence.

I froze. A statue of fear. Swallowing panic.

A soft footstep. A creak.

I gently eased to the floor on all fours. I crawled to my left, toward the fireplace and the side stage. Someone knocked out the lights and struck Johnnie Mae. They had to know I was near the chairs. I crawled faster.

Something swung in front of my face, maybe three inches away. Air whished by accompanied by a soft grunt.

I flew back and smacked into the fake wall behind me with a thump.

The weapon slammed above my head. It missed me, but kept crashing toward me. Faster and faster. Frantically trying to find me in the pitch black.

I covered my head with my hands. Swung my legs out in a sweeping motion. They rammed into someone. A thud and a grunt. And a roll.

Scrambling forward, I searched for a weapon. Anything. I

grabbed onto something heavy, wooden, just as a hand grabbed mine. I yanked the wood object, kicking and screaming. I hit someone. Hard.

"You bitch!" A familiar voice. Female, outraged. She clawed at me. Kicked me in the shoulder. "Give that back."

I swung with everything I had and missed. But kept swinging. I hit her leg, maybe a thigh. She cried out and came at me.

Her arm wrapped around my neck and she squeezed. It was so dark. I couldn't see or breathe or get any bearings. I tried to scream, but no sound choked out. She squeezed tighter. We stumbled forward, then back. I elbowed her in the stomach. Once. Twice. Finally I twisted free. With one huge push, I rammed my hands into her shoulders and she screamed.

Metal music stands and chairs clanged and rattled as she fell into them. I grabbed my cell from my pocket and turned on the flashlight.

My foot was an inch from the stage edge. Courtney Cattanach lay crumpled on the floor of the orchestra pit. She still moved. Slightly.

I dialed 9-1-1 with shaking hands and climbed down into the pit, scaling the stage wall with one hand while I held the phone with the other.

I told dispatch, in broken sentences, to get to the Sea Pine Community Theatre with an ambulance. I searched for something to tie Courtney's hands and feet. I found a necktie and a hair ribbon. I tied as fast as I could, then stayed close. I waited for the police. I kept my flashlight on and noticed the wooden weapon she'd used to attack Johnnie Mae and me. The oversized nutcracker. It lay broken by her feet. A folded envelope stuck out from the cracked head. I quickly pulled it free.

Inside were five crime scene photos of a burned out living room.

EPILOGUE

(Day #10 – Saturday Morning)

A brisk breeze blew across the Carolina blue sky as I sat on the patio next to the Big House pool. I wore a sweater over my linen tunic and sipped hot cider from a ceramic mug.

"Quiet day back?" Carla asked, sipping next to me.

"I love January," I said. "Cold, but calm. Hibernation time for most of the residents."

After the arrest of Courtney Cattanach for the murder of Lexie Allen, Mr. Ballantyne encouraged me to take some time off. Truth is, I didn't need much encouragement. We spent Christmas together, then I caught a flight (or scheduled one, since the Ballantynes let me take their jet) to Carmel-By-The-Sea, California. I spent ten days at the Cypress Inn, Doris Day's hotel. Madison Night, a friend I met after a luggage snafu, recommended it, and it was exactly what I needed.

"How's Johnnie Mae?" I asked and leaned back with my feet tucked under me.

"Gone," Tod said as he walked up with a box in his hand. "Came by to thank you after you'd left. Said she'd leave you a review when she settled in someplace, but it might be awhile."

"That poor woman," Carla said. "I doubt she'll ever settle in anywhere. At least until the trial is over."

I nodded and sipped. "Even then. Courtney Cattanach

destroyed her life, and then took her daughter's. Kind of impossible to recover from that."

"That wicked child had nothing but dumb luck," Carla said.

"And it would've continued if she would've just let it be," I said. "Courtney never intended to kill Johnnie Mae or her neighbor or set up a fake insurance claim with that fire. She was eight. She only wanted Lexie to be taken away from her mother so she could live with them."

A girl who wanted what she wanted. She pieced together an eight-year-old's plan and went for it. Sneaky, clever, out of control. She must have been furious when Lexie didn't end up living with them. With her mother in prison, Lexie got a new life. A better life. Better than her old one, better than Courtney's.

But Courtney held on to their friendship, taking charge, keeping it together. Until it started to fall apart. Lexie went to a different school, then a different career. In the end, it was every man/woman/dancer for herself.

"That's one bad, bad little girl. What gave her the idea to start a fire?" Tod asked. He put the box on the table and poured a cup of cider.

"Courtney's mother," I said. "She used to harp on Johnnie Mae's drinking, and how one day she'd pass out drunk while smoking and burn the house down. Child services would take Lexie from her, and how wonderful life would be without Johnnie Mae in the neighborhood. In Courtney's mind, that meant Lexie could live with them."

"The logic of an eight-year-old girl," Carla said, shaking her head.

"Seriously," I said. "Courtney hated Johnnie Mae because she didn't like Lexie spending so much time across the alley at Courtney's. Felt she was a bad influence."

"Even a drunk mother's instincts are spot on," Tod said.

"Tod!" I said.

"What? She admitted she was a drunk," Tod said. "Had she spent less time with her vodka and more time with her daughter, none of this would've happened."

"I don't think anyone could've predicted a second grader would be so devious," Carla said.

Dumb luck it went down the way it did," I said. "She didn't set up Johnnie Mae for arson, it just looked that way."

"Why didn't Johnnie Mae say something at trial?"

"Humiliation and doubt," I said. "She was still trying to sober up. She knew it wasn't arson, but she wasn't sure if she caused it accidentally. Later, after years of therapy and sobriety, she reviewed her own case. That's when she saw the inconsistencies."

Carla poured more hot cider from a steel carafe on the table. "Why not speak up then?"

I wrapped my hands around the cup and blew across the top, steam floating through the air. "I don't know. But the shame of it all? That fifth photo Lexie was killed over? The one Johnnie Mae and I were attacked over? It showed a barrette. A kid's barrette."

"*Courtney's* barrette," Tod said. "That's something."

"Not really," I said. "It proved to Lexie and Johnnie Mae that Courtney likely set the fire, but it would never hold up in court. A little girl who didn't like to share her barrettes, and never once went over to Lexie's house, is hardly evidence. Johnnie Mae and Lexie would've never gotten the case reopened. And fingerprints and DNA were long gone."

"Not to play armchair detective," Carla said. "But Lexie figured out the significance of the picture the day she died. More dumb luck Courtney found poison berries and somehow get Lexie to bake them into killer cupcakes and then eat them? All within the span of like an hour?"

"Not exactly," I said. "Courtney knew Lexie was communicating with her mother as soon as they moved into the condo. She also knew they were looking at evidence from the fire. Courtney panicked a week before they found anything incriminating. To her, it would all come out and ruin her. She has major auditions right after the holidays."

"*Had* major auditions," Tod said.

"Indeed," I said. "She may have had dumb luck, but she wasn't dumb. She came close to getting away with murder. Used Lexie's passion for cooking, and their friendship, against her. Grabbed a handful of Mamacita's berries, swapped them in the kitchen, and encouraged her to bake something special for opening night. Luckily, no one else ate them."

"Did you hear about Inga?" Carla asked. "She's still in a coma."

"Courtney attacked her, too, and for nothing," Tod said.

"Yeah," I said. "Courtney thought Lexie confided in Inga, gave her the pictures to hide on opening night."

"That girl acted on the wrong impulse every time," Carla said. "Such a shame, chicken."

"Berg probably would've been next, if she hadn't found the pictures at the theatre," I said.

"He's running Inga's studio while she's in the hospital," Carla said. "And focused on lighter-themed choreography. At least for next season."

Tod handed me the box. "This came for you."

A belated Christmas present I gave myself. I opened the cardboard flaps to reveal a beautiful white box inside. A new iPad of my own. I don't know how I lived without one of those things.

We talked for another half hour, but moved onto more pleasant topics. Like the Ballantynes embarking on a thirteen-state tour of the nation's most impoverished neighborhoods with a team of educators and philanthropists. Their mission: to reimagine the education system in conjunction with affordable housing. I admired my Ballantyne family, and it comforted me to keep their home, and foundation, running while they went off to save the world.

I left Carla and Tod on the patio and grabbed my hipster from my desk drawer. I clicked off the lamp, tidied my desk, and left the Big House.

Matty was waiting for me next to the Mini. He leaned against the driver door, one foot casually crossed over the other.

"Hey," I said.

"Hey," he said back.

"The first board meeting of the year isn't until tomorrow," I said and mentally slapped my forehead. I did not know how to talk to him. My stomach started to knot.

"Yeah, I'm here to meet with Jane. We're putting together a proposal for the Sea Pine Prep senior class project."

"Cool," I said. I refrained from shuffling my feet.

"I'm sorry for the way we left things. You were right to say what you did. How you felt. I miss you, too. As friends. I don't want to lose it, either."

"Really, Matty?" I asked and the knot in my stomach started to unravel.

"Really," he said. "It may take me a while to work it out in my head, but I'll get there." He walked toward the entry steps and turned back. "I'm glad you're okay, El."

I smiled and waved and climbed into the Mini. I drove the two miles to my cottage at the beach. I switched my linen workday clothes for a sweatshirt and cotton pants (yes, they were sweatpants) and flip flops, then went out to the back deck.

The temperature grew chillier as the sun disappeared and the sky darkened. I stepped down to the sand and walked the twenty feet to Ransom's deck next door.

He was grilling my favorite chicken kabobs. The smoky barbecue scents escaped when he lifted the lid. A bottle of Riesling with two wine glasses sat on a table near the railing, with a panoramic view of the Atlantic.

"Right on time," Ransom said. He closed the lid on the grill and put his hands on my face. He kissed me as if he hadn't seen me in years. It was delicious. "Good to have you home," he said when he pulled away.

"Agreed," I said and poured a glass of wine. "And happy to be back at work."

"Yeah? Lots going on in the world of charity balls and ladies lunches?"

"As a matter of fact, yes," I said. "Zibby Archibald called. Her neighbor's parrot is missing and she wants me on the case."

He laughed, then looked at me with a straight face. "Sounds simple," he said slowly.

"Don't they all?"

I had just logged over a thousand hours toward my PI license and I couldn't wait to log the other four thousand and change.

Kendel Lynn

Kendel Lynn is a Southern California native who now parks her flip-flops in Dallas, Texas. She read her first Alfred Hitchcock and the Three Investigators at the age of seven and has loved mysteries ever since. Her debut novel, *Board Stiff*, the first Elliott Lisbon mystery, was an Agatha Award nominee for Best First Novel. Along with writing and reading, Kendel spends her time editing, designing, and figuring out ways to avoid the gym but still eat cupcakes for dinner. Catch up with her at www.kendellynn.com.

In Case You Missed the 1st Book in the Series

BOARD STIFF
Kendel Lynn

An Elliott Lisbon Mystery (#1)

As director of the Ballantyne Foundation on Sea Pine Island, SC, Elliott Lisbon scratches her detective itch by performing discreet inquiries for Foundation donors. Usually nothing more serious than retrieving a pilfered Pomeranian. Until Jane Hatting, Ballantyne board chair, is accused of murder. The Ballantyne's reputation tanks, Jane's headed to a jail cell, and Elliott's sexy ex is the new lieutenant in town.

Armed with moxie and her Mini Coop, Elliott uncovers a trail of blackmail schemes, gambling debts, illicit affairs, and investment scams. But the deeper she digs to clear Jane's name, the guiltier Jane looks. The closer she gets to the truth, the more treacherous her investigation becomes. With victims piling up faster than shells at a clambake, Elliott realizes she's next on the killer's list.

Available at booksellers nationwide and online

Visit www.henerypress.com for details

Don't Miss the 2nd Book in the Series

WHACK JOB

Kendel Lynn

An Elliott Lisbon Mystery (#2)

Elliott Lisbon blends her directorship of the Ballantyne Foundation with her PI-in-Training status by planning parties and performing discreet inquiries for charitable patrons. But when the annual Wonderland Tea Party makes everyone go mad as a hatter, Elli gets pulled into a shooting, a swindle, and the hunt for a Fabergé egg.

From seedy pawn parlors to creepy antique shops, Sea Pine Island's other half prove to be as wacky as the wealthy. Elli falls farther down the rabbit hole and finds a scheming salesman, a possessive paramour, a dead donor—everything but a bottle labeled "Drink Me." As events evolve from curious to crazy, Elli gets lost in the maze and finds herself trapped in a house of cards with a killer.

Available at booksellers nationwide and online

Visit www.henerypress.com for details

Don't Miss Elliott's prequel novella
SWITCH BACK featured in

OTHER PEOPLE'S BAGGAGE

Kendel Lynn, Gigi Pandian, Diane Vallere

Baggage claim can be terminal. These are the stories of what happened after three women with a knack for solving mysteries each grabbed the wrong bag.

MIDNIGHT ICE by Diane Vallere: When interior decorator Madison Night crosses the country to distance herself from a recent breakup, she learns it's harder to escape her past than she thought, and diamonds are rarely a girl's best friend.

SWITCH BACK by Kendel Lynn: Ballantyne Foundation director Elliott Lisbon travels to Texas after inheriting an entire town, but when she learns the benefactor was murdered, she must unlock the small town's big secrets or she'll never get out alive.

FOOL'S GOLD by Gigi Pandian: When a world-famous chess set is stolen from a locked room during the Edinburgh Fringe Festival, historian Jaya Jones and her magician best friend must outwit actresses and alchemists to solve the baffling crime.

Available at booksellers nationwide and online

Visit www.henerypress.com for details

Henery Press Mystery Books

And finally, before you go...
Here are a few other mysteries
you might enjoy:

PILLOW STALK

Diane Vallere

A Mad for Mod Mystery (#1)

Interior Decorator Madison Night has modeled her life after a character in a Doris Day movie, but when a killer targets women dressed like the bubbly actress, Madison's signature sixties style places her in the middle of a homicide investigation.

The local detective connects the new crimes to a twenty-year-old cold case, and Madison's long-trusted contractor emerges as the leading suspect. As the body count piles up like a stack of plush pillows, Madison uncovers a Soviet spy, a campaign to destroy all Doris Day movies, and six minutes of film that will change her life forever.

Available at booksellers nationwide and online

Visit www.henerypress.com for details

DOUBLE WHAMMY

Gretchen Archer

A Davis Way Crime Caper (#1)

Davis Way thinks she's hit the jackpot when she lands a job as the fifth wheel on an elite security team at the fabulous Bellissimo Resort and Casino in Biloxi, Mississippi. But once there, she runs straight into her ex-ex husband, a rigged slot machine, her evil twin, and a trail of dead bodies. Davis learns the truth and it does not set her free—in fact, it lands her in the pokey.

Buried under a mistaken identity, unable to seek help from her family, her hot streak runs cold until her landlord Bradley Cole steps in. Make that her landlord, lawyer, and love interest. With his help, Davis must win this high stakes game before her luck runs out.

Available at booksellers nationwide and online

Visit www.henerypress.com for details

THE DEEP END
Julie Mulhern

A Country Club Murders Mystery

Swimming into the lifeless body of her husband's mistress tends to ruin a woman's day, but becoming a murder suspect can ruin her whole life.

It's 1974 and Ellison Russell's life revolves around her daughter and her art. She's long since stopped caring about her cheating husband, Henry, and the women with whom he entertains himself. That is, until she becomes a suspect in Madeline Harper's death. The murder forces Ellison to confront her husband's proclivities and his crimes—kinky sex, petty cruelties and blackmail.

As the body count approaches par on the seventh hole, Ellison knows she has to catch a killer. But with an interfering mother, an adoring father, a teenage daughter, and a cadre of well-meaning friends demanding her attention, can Ellison find the killer before he finds her?

Available at booksellers nationwide and online

Visit www.henerypress.com for details

FINDING SKY

Susan O'Brien

A Nicki Valentine Mystery

Suburban widow and P.I. in training Nicki Valentine can barely keep track of her two kids, never mind anyone else. But when her best friend's adoption plan is jeopardized by the young birth mother's disappearance, Nicki is persuaded to help. Nearly everyone else believes the teenager ran away, but Nicki trusts her BFF's judgment, and the feeling is mutual.

The case leads where few moms go (teen parties, gang shootings) and places they can't avoid (preschool parties, OB-GYNs' offices). Nicki has everything to lose and much to gain — including the attention of her unnervingly hot P.I. instructor. Thankfully, Nicki is armed with her pesky conscience, occasional babysitters, a fully stocked minivan, and nature's best defense system: women's intuition.

Available at booksellers nationwide and online

Visit www.henerypress.com for details

LOWCOUNTRY BOIL

Susan M. Boyer

A Liz Talbot Mystery (#1)

Private Investigator Liz Talbot is a modern Southern belle: she blesses hearts and takes names. She carries her Sig 9 in her Kate Spade handbag, and her golden retriever, Rhett, rides shotgun in her hybrid Escape. When her grandmother is murdered, Liz high-tails it back to her South Carolina island home to find the killer.

She's fit to be tied when her police-chief brother shuts her out of the investigation, so she opens her own. Then her long-dead best friend pops in and things really get complicated. When more folks start turning up dead in this small seaside town, Liz must use more than just her wits and charm to keep her family safe, chase down clues from the hereafter, and catch a psychopath before he catches her.

Available at booksellers nationwide and online

Visit www.henerypress.com for details

DINERS, DIVES & DEAD ENDS
Terri L. Austin

A Rose Strickland Mystery (#1)

As a struggling waitress and part-time college student, Rose Strickland's life is stalled in the slow lane. But when her close friend, Axton, disappears, Rose suddenly finds herself serving up more than hot coffee and flapjacks. Now she's hashing it out with sexy bad guys and scrambling to find clues in a race to save Axton before his time runs out.

With her anime-loving bestie, her septuagenarian boss, and a pair of IT wise men along for the ride, Rose discovers political corruption, illegal gambling, and shady corporations. She's gone from zero to sixty and quickly learns when you're speeding down the fast lane, it's easy to crash and burn.

Available at booksellers nationwide and online

Visit www.henerypress.com for details

BET YOUR BOTTOM DOLLAR

Karin Gillespie

The Bottom Dollar Series (#1)

(from the Henery Press Chick Lit Collection)

Welcome to the Bottom Dollar Emporium in Cayboo Creek, South Carolina, where everything from coconut mallow cookies to Clabber Girl Baking Powder costs a dollar but the coffee and gossip are free. For the Bottom Dollar gals, work time is sisterhood time.

When news gets out that a corporate dollar store is coming to town, the women are thrown into a tizzy, hoping to save their beloved store as well their friendships. Meanwhile the manager is canoodling with the town's wealthiest bachelor and their romance unearths some startling family secrets.

The first in a series, *Bet Your Bottom Dollar* serves up a heaping portion of small town Southern life and introduces readers to a cast of eccentric characters. Pull up a wicker chair, set out a tall glass of Cheer Wine, and immerse yourself in the adventures of a group of women whom the *Atlanta Journal Constitution* calls, "... the kind of steel magnolias who would make Scarlett O'Hara envious."

Available at booksellers nationwide and online

Visit www.henerypress.com for details

CPSIA information can be obtained
at www.ICGtesting.com
Printed in the USA
LVOW10s1202160418
573642LV00004B/752/P